STEPHANIE
TROMLY

TROUBLE
MAKES A
COMEBACK

Kathy Dawson Books

KATHY DAWSON BOOKS
An imprint of Penguin Random House LLC
375 Hudson Street
New York, New York 10014

Copyright © 2016 by Stephanie Tromly

Library of Congress Cataloging-in-Publication Data

Names: Tromly, Stephanie, author.
Title: Trouble makes a comeback / Stephanie Tromly.
Description: New York, NY : Kathy Dawson Books, [2016] | Sequel to:
Trouble is a friend of mine | Summary: After Zoe Webster's friend Philip Digby—
the weird, manic and brilliant teen sleuth Digby—left town, Zoe experimented with being a
"normal" high schooler—but now Digby is back needing help, and not just to find his sister.
Identifiers: LCCN 2015046145 | ISBN 9780525428411 (hardback)
Subjects: | CYAC: Missing children—Fiction. | High schools—Fiction. | Schools—Fiction.
| Friendship—Fiction. | Mystery and detective stories. | BISAC: JUVENILE FICTION /
Mysteries & Detective Stories. | JUVENILE FICTION / Social Issues / Friendship.
| JUVENILE FICTION / Humorous Stories.
Classification: LCC PZ7.1.T76 Ts 2016 | DDC [Fic]—dc23 LC record available
at https://lccn.loc.gov/2015046145

Printed in the United States of America
1 3 5 7 9 10 8 6 4 2

Designed by Nancy R. Leo-Kelly
Text set in Calisto MT

TROUBLE
MAKES A
COMEBACK

. . .

I don't believe in Happily Ever After. Nobody over the age of thirteen with an Internet connection has any business believing in that noise. But the kind of junior year I'm having is seriously challenging the life-saving cynicism I've cultivated for years.

Actually, to be precise, I'm having an epic second semester. My first semester was a series of fiascos, all courtesy of my friendship with Philip Digby. Though, honestly, I'm not even sure Digby ever considered me his friend. Accomplice, sure. But then he kissed me, which made us what? More than friends? Something other than friends? I hate semantics.

Normally, I wouldn't have fallen for Digby's stray-puppy-in-the-rain act in the first place. But I was new in town, I had no friends, and I was still reeling from my parents' brutal divorce. And then I found out that Digby's four-year-old sister, Sally, was abducted from her bed in the middle of the night when he was only seven years old and, to add to the tragedy of losing Sally, the authorities thought either his parents or Digby himself was guilty. Even worse, all of River Heights was convinced they'd done it and had turned against Digby and his parents. The pressure tore that family apart. The stray puppy, it turned out, was also the underdog. I was powerless to resist.

By Thanksgiving, he'd gotten me arrested, then kidnapped, and then blown up in an explosion. On the upside, we'd also dismantled a meth operation and found a missing girl. We didn't find Digby's sister, though, so he left town to keep looking for her.

But not before he scrambled my brains with that kiss. And then—nothing. Not a peep from the jerk for the last five months.

Meanwhile, everyone had heard I'd been hanging out with him and that we'd somehow busted up a major drug operation. People in school were curious and I had to act fast if I wanted to convert my infamy into friendships beyond whatever weird crisis-based camaraderie I'd experienced while I was capering around with Digby. I knew I was the flavor of a very short month, so I forced myself past the Digby-sized hole in my soul and Made an Effort.

My first attempts at getting to know new people were disasters. But then I realized that I was boring people with details, and once I basically stopped talking so much and mostly asked leading questions instead, things improved. And then, finally, after a locker room conversation—about the injustice of school going all the way until December 23—with Allie and Charlotte, two of the nicer girls from my PE class, I was in. An invitation to lunch turned into eyeliner tutorials in the good bathrooms and weekends trawling the mall with them. Eventually, I realized that I was enjoying more than just the fact that I was finally feeling included. I was actually having a good time with Charlotte and Allie. They'd been friends since grade school, but I could tell they were trying their best not to make me feel left out. And it worked. Things were looking up.

My luck kept right on improving, in fact, until after winter break, when I got my first official boyfriend: Austin Shaeffer. It happened at the mall. I was with Allie and Charlotte when I saw some guy hauling ass out of the Foot Locker. I didn't have the time—or maybe I didn't take the time—to think. Before I knew it, I'd kicked a wheeled HOLIDAY SALE sign into the guy's path.

The guy hit the sign with a (surprisingly) satisfying *splat*. Digby would've loved watching the Foot Locker employees swarm the thief and pull all the fitness trackers still in boxes from his pockets. For the first time in a while, I let myself feel how much I missed life with Digby. I was so distracted, I didn't notice that a Foot Locker employee had started talking to me.

"Sorry, what?" I said. That's when I realized it was Austin Shaeffer. I didn't have classes with him, but I'd noticed him around school. It was hard not to notice Austin. He was handsome and athletic and one of the few guys who could be funny without being mean. He reminded me a little of Digby's friend Henry, although that might be because Austin was Henry's QB backup on our football team.

"You pushed the sign, right?" Austin said.

By this time, people were clapping. Charlotte pointed at me, yelling, "She's our friend. Our friend did that." Allie stooped for a selfie with the injured thief.

"How'd you know he shoplifted?" Austin said.

I almost said something about the weird bulge in the guy's coat and how his run's head-down urgency seemed more than a late-for-my-movie hustle, but I looked into Austin's big

7

blue eyes and checked myself. *Be normal, Zoe.* Austin Shaeffer doesn't care what you know about body language.

"Actually . . ." I said. "The truth?"

Austin leaned in, forcing me to notice his aftershave. "Yeah?"

"I tripped. The sign kinda . . . rolled?" I tried not to judge myself for the giggle I burped out to sell my lie.

"Zoe Webster, right?" Austin said.

"Yeah . . . and you're Austin—" Then suddenly Austin Shaeffer was holding my right hand. I'd forgotten about my latte and in the course of affecting coolness, I'd let my hand relax so much that coffee was pouring out the spout.

"Careful," Austin said. "So, Zoe Webster, you saved my ass. They would've fired me if my section got jacked again." He pointed at my cup. "You've probably had enough coffee today, but how about this weekend?"

Allie and Charlotte cackled while Austin entered my number in his phone.

"So cute . . . Austin Schaeffer's blushing," Allie said.

"Watch out, Zoe, Austin is trouble," Charlotte said.

"I'm not trouble . . . don't listen to them," Austin said.

After Austin left, Allie, Charlotte, and I talked about him for hours. They liked him, I liked them, I wanted them to like me, Austin Shaeffer apparently liked me, and by the end of the afternoon, I liked him *a lot.* After Austin and I had our first coffee date, Allie, Charlotte, and I parsed every moment I'd spent with him. Being inside that giddy echo chamber was at least as much fun as the date itself.

So now I have a boyfriend and I have friends. I got flowers

on Valentine's Day, I'm invited to sleepovers, and I'm doing decently on social media. Sure, there are moments when I feel alien in my own life but mostly, it feels good to fit in. Finally, finally, I'm a normal.

But that's all falling apart. Digby sauntered back into River Heights nine days ago, and now my happy ending is toast. Right this second, I'm about to make my entrance at the biggest party of the year. My boyfriend's waiting inside. He'll likely be the starting quarterback this fall, which means I'm dating the official Prince Charming of River Heights High. I'm wearing clothes way above my pay grade and riding in a fancy car with Sloane Bloom, my former nemesis who's somehow turned into my perverse version of a fairy godmother. But here, at the brink of my Cinderella moment, all that matters to me is whether Digby will be at the party. See what I mean? Happy Ending ruined.

But as usual, I'm getting ahead of the story. I need to tell you about the last nine days.

ONE

"April is the cruelest month," Mom said. "Just say it, Zoe. You told me so."

Because my mother worked from home on Friday afternoons, I'd thought I'd save time and get her to drive me to my job at the mall. Mistake.

Mom stood on the gas pedal, but our car was officially beached. The left-side wheels were on the asphalt, but our right-side wheels were up in the air because of the huge snow boulder Mom had driven over and gotten stuck under the car. I felt queasy from sitting tilted as the engine ground away uselessly beneath me. Plus, the car stank of the cigarettes Mom didn't think anyone knew she smoked during her solo commute to the community college where she taught English lit.

"Zoe told me not to park on this snowbank," Mom said to Austin, who was sitting in the backseat. "But it didn't seem so big last night."

11

"I'll go get your shovel," Austin said.

"Zoe, put those ridiculous things away," Mom said. She took a handful of my vocabulary cards and snorted. "What does this have to do with being a competent reader or writer?"

"Yeah, yeah, Mom. I know. Nothing. But it has everything to do with my doing well on the SATs next weekend," I said. "I am extremely stressed about it . . ."

Austin came back with our shovel and said, "I'm going to start digging, okay, Miss Finn?"

Austin was still in the "Miss Finn" stage with Mom. In turn, Mom still got shy and combed her hair before Austin came over. Actually, even *I* still did. Sitting in Mom's car, watching Austin, all muscles and sheer will, digging us out of the snow, I reflected on how it was probably a *good* thing that I still got nervous before Austin came over.

Austin flung a shovelful of snow over his shoulder, yelled *WHOA,* fell, and disappeared under the hood of the car. Mom and I jumped out.

It was a total movie shot: Austin on his back, his pretty face inches from the spinning tire. We pulled him out, so horrified we didn't even remember we'd shut the car doors until we heard the auto locks engage. There was our car, hiked up on a snowbank, doors locked, keys in the ignition, stuck in drive with the wheels spinning.

"No!" Mom belatedly threw herself on the car's hood. The car rocked under her weight.

"Careful, Miss Finn," Austin said.

"Get away from the front of the car, Mom." To Austin, I

said, "Quick, put the snow back. But not under the tire!"

"I think there are spare keys in the house," Mom said.

"*Go*. But if you don't find them fast, call 911," I said. "Or a tow truck."

"Oh, God, my life's a farce!" Mom ran into the house.

Austin resumed shoveling in the opposite direction while I kicked snow back under the car. Then a tall figure in black flitted across the field of my peripheral vision and disappeared behind an SUV. Something about his syncopated gait reminded me of something that made me super-happy, and then angry, and then confused.

Suddenly, there he was. Digby. Standing beside me. He seemed taller and broader than when he'd left, but that could've been because of his thick parka. He looked road-weary and his jaw was stubbled. He dropped his backpack in the snow. Clearly, it was the end of a long journey.

"Hey, Princeton," Digby said. "Need help?"

Digby held a screwdriver and a long antenna he'd removed from the SUV he'd passed. He pried a gap along the rubber seam between our passenger's-side door and the roof, fed the antenna through, and pushed the driver's-side DOORS OPEN button. He climbed in and killed the engine.

I got in too, realizing only when we were alone in the car that in the five months since he'd disappeared, I'd collected a ton of confrontational things to say without actually deciding on which to say first.

"Are you back?" I said.

Digby made a ta-da gesture. "Guess where I've been. Wait,

don't bother. You'll never guess. Federal prison." He laughed when my eyebrows shot up. "I went to Fort Dix to talk to Ezekiel."

Ezekiel. Just hearing that drug dealer's name made me relive the horror of his stuffing Digby and me in the trunk of his car and our almost getting blown up in his failed attempt to double-cross his boss.

Digby leaned in. "We've been looking at this all wrong, Princeton. Sally wasn't taken by some pervert . . . it's a whole other thing. When I finally got Ezekiel to put me on his visitors list, he told me about his friend—let's call him Joe—who ran a crack squat downtown. Apparently, some guys rented Joe's whole place for a week—exactly when Sally disappeared. Joe saw them carry in a little girl in the middle of the night. But when they left . . . there was a whole lot of stuff like *boys'* clothes and video games in the place." Digby paused dramatically. "Remember Ezekiel said they were supposed to take me?"

"Who's 'they'?" I said.

"Exactly," he said.

"Exactly what?" I said. "Who's 'they'?"

"Well, *that* I haven't figured out yet," Digby said.

"Did Ezekiel tell you anything real? Like, what these guys looked like? Or where the crack house *is*?" I said.

"His friend Joe said the guys were in nice suits and drove brand-new black SUVs. Ezekiel never got the address. Nice suits and black cars sounds like government types, and you know what that probably means . . . my dad," Digby said. "I

14

bet it had something to do with his old job at Perses Analytics."

"Where Felix's dad works?" I said. "I thought you said your dad's an alcoholic."

"Being an alcoholic was more Joel Digby's hobby. Alcoholics have to cover their nut too, Princeton."

"He was a scientist?"

"Propulsion engineer," Digby said. "I wonder what he was working on."

"But maybe you're just being paranoid. Or maybe your father gambled, and his bookie took Sally to collect on a gambling debt? Or maybe Ezekiel's evil and he's screwing with your head because you put him in prison?" I said.

"But those are such boring explanations," Digby said. "And, you know, Ezekiel and I got to talking and he's not such a bad guy—"

"He sold meth to kids and pretended to be in a weird cult to do it," I said.

Digby slapped the wheel. "Ah . . . the ol' Princeton reality check. I forgot how much fun it is."

"You forgot? Is that why I haven't heard jack from you in five months?" I said.

Digby looked genuinely surprised. "I was busy . . ." He pointed out the windshield at Austin, who was still shoveling. "You've been busy too. I assume he's . . . ?"

"Yeah. We're dating . . . we're together . . . he's my boyfriend—"

"Got it," Digby said. "Austin Shaeffer, huh? You teach him the difference between left and right yet?"

Months ago, he'd caught Austin writing an *R* on his right hand and an *L* on his left hand before scrimmage.

"That's a good luck thing he started doing in peewee football," I said.

"Well, I hate to call him stupid, but he's still shoveling and the car's been off . . . what? Two minutes?" Digby tooted the horn, threw up his hands, and yelled, "What's up, buddy? Yeah. Engine's off."

Austin got in the backseat. "Hey . . . you're Digby, right?"

"Hey, Austin." Digby pointed at Austin's gym bag and football helmet on the backseat. "Got a game later or something?"

"That's my workout stuff," Austin said. "Uh . . . we don't play football in the spring, dude."

I cringed at Austin's patronizing tone.

"Way I hear it, you don't play football in the fall either, *dude*. Still riding the bench praying Henry gets injured?" Digby said.

"Okay, Digby," I said, "that's—"

"I'm the backup QB. I play plenty. You'd know that if you knew anything about football," Austin said.

"Got me there, sporto," Digby said. "I'm up nights worrying about everything I don't know about football."

"Should I get the hose?" I said. "Digby, can we talk later? Austin and I were about to go to the mall."

"Afternoon mall date?" Digby said.

"No, we're going to work," I said. "I'm going to Spring Fling afterward."

"Spring Fling? Is that on today? Wait—work?" Digby said. "You mean that stuffed shirt of a father really did cut you off?"

16

"Dad's a man of his word," I said.

"You didn't use the secret I told you about him?" Digby said. "That information's good."

"You mean that stuff you got on him hiding money from Mom? No," I said. "I'm not a natural-born extortionist like you. I can't suddenly start blackmailing people."

"It's light blackmail," Digby said.

"I'd rather just work," I said.

"What's wrong with working?" Austin said.

"Wait a minute . . . this isn't your mom's car." Digby hooked his fingers on the gunlock bolted onto the dashboard. He found a removable police siren under his seat. "Is this . . . Officer Cooper's take-home car?" He worked it out. "They're still together? Your mom and the cop who arrested you are in a serious relationship? Princeton, your life is *interesting*."

"He moved in three months ago," I said.

"Wow . . . monotone. That happy, huh? Liza works fast." Digby dove across me and fished around under my seat.

"Hey, man. Not a fan of your face in my girlfriend's lap," Austin said.

There was a loud rip of Velcro and Digby's hand came up holding a mag of ammunition Cooper had stashed under the seat. "Whoa, I wonder if the gun's in here somewhere too."

"Maybe you should put that back," I said.

"Babe, I'm going to be late," Austin said. "We should take the bus."

"Come to think of it, I have mall stuff to do myself," Digby said. "I'll come with."

17

"Good," Austin said.

"Good," Digby said.

"Great," Austin said.

"Great," Digby said. He had that lethal bored expression I wished Austin knew to fear as much as I did.

"Wonderful," I said. "I better tell Mom we're not waiting for the tow truck with her."

TWO

Longest bus ride of my life. Austin is an old-timey *Lady and the Tramp* sweet kind of guy and he was being his usual affectionate self, sharing headphones with me and holding my hand. I'd seen Digby actively lash out at this kind of sentimental display before, but this time Digby just smirked at me. I was amazed we made it to the mall without incident.

"See you later, Austin. I'll walk Zoe to work." Digby's tone reminded me of the obnoxious message shirt a friend of ours used to wear: YOUR GIRLFRIEND IS IN GOOD HANDS.

Austin flinched but said, "That's cool, dude. I know how it is."

"Oh?" Digby said.

"Sure," Austin said. "Zoe told me everything."

"Really? What did she tell you?" Digby said. "Just so we're on the same page."

I'd been dreading this moment. Austin had gotten into the car before I'd had a chance to tell Digby there were things I hadn't told Austin. Our kiss, for example.

"About what happened last year with the explosion . . . I know you guys were tight," Austin said. "Like the brother she never had."

What a great thing to say to a guy with a missing sister.

"That's right. Brother she never had . . . that's me," Digby said. "Exact same page."

Austin gave me an extra-assertive kiss and left for work.

"Maybe if I hug you later, he won't have any choice but to whip it out and mark you with his pee," Digby said. "Better spend some time reassuring him tonight . . . *sis*."

"I didn't know what to tell him. You were gone—"

"Of course. What's to tell?" But his tone was all accusation.

"It's so annoying that you make me feel like somehow *I've* done something wrong." I walked away. He let me get pretty far before running after me.

"Hey, wait up," he said. "Where are you going?"

"I told you. Work."

I stopped for coffee. When he added two cookies to my tab, I said, "You still eat like a wolverine?"

Digby gave me his lazy sad-eyed smile. I wondered if, as he'd done before, he was planning on sleeping in his mom's garage, living on soup crackers and to-go packets of ketchup again.

"Work, huh?" Digby looked me up and down.

"What? You're freaking me out," I said.

"Give me a sec, I'm a little rusty. Okay, no makeup, so not any kind of cosmetics gig. Vintage dress, frumpy, dowdy housewife-y flavor . . ."

The barista helping me frowned at Digby. "Excuse *you*. Rude or anything?" she said.

". . . so not any kind of trendy retail. The food court's out. The face you pull whenever I eat . . . you don't have a future in food service," Digby said. "Those heels are surprisingly high for you, so you're not walking across a big department store . . ."

"Come on, let's speed this up," I said.

"Okay, fine. I'll go with either intern at the bank or the Hallmark store," he said.

Watching him flounder was comical.

"The florist? The crystals place? Not the Lotto shack?" he said.

"Uh-oh, you're more than rusty, my friend," I said.

We walked into The Last Bookstand, the used books place where I worked.

"Wait, this is new. It wasn't here when I left," Digby said.

"Excuses, excuses. Old Digby would've memorized the new mall map at the entrance," I said.

"Dammit," he said. "Old Digby *would* have memorized the map."

The store was empty, but I heard my manager working in the back. "Fisher! I'm here . . . sorry I'm late. Car trouble."

Digby sniffed. "Is that patchouli? Incense?"

"Patchouli incense," I said. "Listen, my manager, Fisher, had a hemp farm in Vermont. When you meet him, you're going to want to make fun, but you're not allowed. He's the nicest man I've ever met and he's had a tough year."

"Okay. No jokes. Hippie jokes are too easy anyway," Digby said. "Hey, uh . . . Princeton? I think I missed a birthday somewhere. I got you something."

The box's shade of blue was guaranteed to generate excitement from twenty feet away.

"Tiffany?" I said.

"Well, Tiffany dot com," he said. "Open it."

"You got me a locket?" I was surprised enough when I saw that he'd cut out and mounted photos in the little oval frames, but when I saw he'd chosen decent selfies of us at the winter ball, I was speechless.

"But maybe don't shower with it on . . ." he said.

"Right. The silver will tarnish . . ." I said.

"Also I hid two micro SD cards in there," he said.

"Of course you did," I said, passing the box back to him. "What's on them?"

"When I got home to Texas, I backed up my dad's computer onto those SD cards," he said.

"Backed up? You mean stole his files."

Digby popped out the pictures and showed me the SD cards walled in behind a clear coating.

"I potted them in resin so they wouldn't rattle around," he said.

"So, in sum, you stole top secret government information from Perses Analytics that you think people are kidnapping children to get, you put it in this necklace, and you now want me to hang it around my neck," I said.

"It's my backup . . . in case they find the copy I'm working on," Digby said.

"Why can't we bury it or something? Or put it behind an air-conditioning vent?" I said.

"You mean with my clove cigarettes and Victoria's Secret catalogs? Don't be ridiculous, Princeton," he said. "This is serious."

"No."

"Come on . . . the answer to who took my sister could be in one of those things," Digby said, pushing the box back across the counter.

"Then *you* wear it," I said.

"Are you kidding? They'll search me first thing," he said.

"And they'll search me second. I'm always with you," I said.

"Always with me?" Digby raised his eyebrows. "And how will Austin like that?"

Austin. Right.

"Hey, Zoe . . ." Fisher walked out of the back holding a vase of hydrangeas Austin had given me a week ago. "Check it out, these are still looking good . . . even though I absolutely loathe hydrangeas." I slid the box off the counter and into my jacket pocket. I just didn't feel like Fisher needed to see Digby giving me something in a Tiffany box.

"*You're* the hippie hemp-head from Vermont?" Digby said.

"I guess so," Fisher said. "Are you a friend of Zoe's?"

Kudos to Fisher for not flinching when Digby leaned into him and took a deep sniff.

"I'm so sorry, Fisher," I said.

"You must be Digby," Fisher said. "Recognize you from Zoe's stories, man. I like the suit."

Digby paced around Fisher. "And you're Fisher. Allegedly."

"Allegedly? Yeah, I am. No 'allegedly,'" Fisher said.

"I'm so sorry, Fisher, he's . . ."

"Your beard's new and still itches . . . I smell the alcohol in the anti-itch stuff you put on. Half your hair's glued-on hairpieces . . . like you had to grow it really fast . . . looks like six months' worth. Right when you showed up in town, I bet," Digby said.

"Digby. Hair? Really?" I said.

"But what's really interesting is the layout of this place." Digby was excited now. "See how the aisles are arranged so customers have to pass by the front desk to get in or out of the store? It looks like a crazy hippie hoarder maze but really, it's an Army Ranger ambush . . . the thieves are canalized past this choke point. How d'you know how to do that?"

"How do *you* know how to do that?" Fisher asked Digby. "*Canalized?* Wow . . . *that's* some word."

"So sorry, Fisher. Although, now that I'm thinking about the shelves . . . is this a fire hazard?" I said.

"Fire hazard. Wait." Digby ran out of the store and came back holding a fire extinguisher. "Princeton, did you have to rearrange the shelves? Around . . . December 20?"

"Uh, actually, yeah . . . we put in a rack of fancy booklights before Christmas—"

"But then he had you put the shelves back into this maze shape a couple of days later?" Digby said.

"Well, yeah, the booklights weren't selling," I said.

Digby showed me the fire extinguisher's tag. "The fire

24

inspector checked this mall on the twenty-first of December."
Digby pointed at Fisher. "You made her move the shelves on
the twentieth for the fire marshal's visit and then after you
passed inspection, you had her rebuild the ambush." Digby
pumped his fist. "Old Digby. What are you? Cop? Military?"
Digby said. "Or . . . worse?"

Fisher looked mostly sad for Digby. "The smell of alcohol's
probably from the mouthwash I used after my breakfast bur-
rito. The store's laid out like this because the collectibles are in
the back and this ain't my first time at the rodeo," Fisher said.
"And I put in hairpieces because my hair grew out patchy after
my chemo last year. Lion needs his mane, man."

Digby kept going. "Chemo, huh?"

"Digby, if you're ever going to draw a line . . . ever? Cancer's
got to be over that line," I said.

"Chemo. That's a good explanation. Solid." Digby walked
toward Fisher, not stopping even when he got so close that
Fisher had to start backing up. "But explain *this*."

Digby swatted my coffee cup off the counter. My scream
turned into a swallowed gurgle when Fisher caught the cup
without spilling a drop.

"Those are great reflexes," Digby said.

Keeping the rest of his body perfectly still, Fisher swept my
vase of hydrangeas off the desk. Digby similarly caught it.

"I could say the same thing about you," Fisher said.

"Would you two idiots have this stupid argument with
someone else's stuff?" I snatched the coffee and vase from them.
"Digby, stop picking fights. Are you tired or something? Hungry?"

"So hungry," he said.

"God, you're a toddler. Why don't you go eat something?"

"Yeah . . ." Digby said. "See you after you get out of work? We should talk."

The way he suddenly got intense when he said that made my heart thump. I didn't know if I was ready to *talk*.

Just when my awkward unresponsiveness started to get painful, Fisher said, "If you like, it's pretty slow right now . . . you could go hang out. I can text you if things pick up."

"That's the weirdest, most un-manager thing I've ever heard," Digby said.

"Happy workers work happily, man," Fisher said.

"More like employee turnover makes it hard to maintain a cover identity." Digby grabbed a book. "How much is this?"

"On the house, kid," Fisher said. "I'd *pay* money to get young people to read Pynchon."

"See what I mean? Weird." On his way out, Digby said, "Watch him."

"That's dark, man," Fisher said.

"That's nothing. He carries around a notebook where he keeps a list of suspects and motives so the police will have leads if he ever turns up murdered," I said.

• • •

Digby wasn't in the food court when I got off work. Or the video arcade by the movie theater. Or the game store either. I even checked with the ladies at the taco place where he used to score free food. They were excited to hear Digby was back, but no, they hadn't seen him. I gave up.

Mom was expecting me at Spring Fling, so I decided to head out. On my way to the bus stop, I called him to tell him so. As I walked by Ye Olde Tea and Crumpets Shoppe, I heard screaming followed by a huge crash. Then I heard it again. On closer listening, I realized it was in fact me screaming. My scream played over and over, my distress memorialized in what could only be Digby's ringtone.

Sure enough, there, laid out on a banquette in the teashop, was Digby. His head was propped up on his backpack, his parka was zipped up to his chin, and he had a cloth napkin draped over his face. The usual guy, Chad, was behind the counter.

"Is he with you? 'Cause homie can't sleep here," Chad said.

I tapped Digby's arm. "Digby. Hey." I kneed his ribs. Nothing. To Chad, I said, "Wow. He's *out*. I feel like I should be worried."

"Watch this." Chad came over and grabbed the plate on the table in front of Digby.

The plate got a half inch off the table when Digby muttered from under the napkin, "Not done with that."

"All day long," Chad said.

"Digby, come on, get up," I said.

"What time is it?" Digby said.

"It's Spring Fling time," I said. "I told you."

"Why are you going? Duck shoots and cotton candy? That isn't very NYC . . ." he said.

He was right. River Heights' famously hokey Spring Fling involved things like petting zoos and talent shows. This year promised to be even less entertaining because snow had been falling practically nonstop since February, and Spring Fling had been moved from its normal fairground site into the community center.

"Mom's running a literacy booth," I said. "I promised I'd help out. Plus, the SATs are a week from tomorrow. Spring Fling and the movie I'm seeing with Austin this weekend are the last fun things I'm allowed to do until then."

"Won't Austin mind if you and I went together?"

"He works until closing tonight," I said.

"So this is how it's going to be, Princeton? I get you after hours?"

We stared at each other and I wondered. How *would* it work out with Digby, Austin, and me?

"Whoa." Digby laughed. "Too much realness . . ." He picked up his backpack. "Duck shoot it is."

THREE

Spring Fling was never going to be any big whoop, but the relocation indoors eliminated whatever excitement there might've been. The rides stayed disassembled and only the smaller booths had been set up in the gym. But people were so thirsty for any hint of spring that the whole town came anyway. NYC Zoe would've hated the crowds, but River Heights Zoe actually found the packed community center festive.

Or maybe it had something to do with the sight that greeted us when we got there: my former tormentor-in-chief Sloane Bloom wearing an inflatable full-body sumo suit and a helmet shaped like a head of hair twisted into a top-knot with a chopstick through it. For five bucks I'd have the chance to smack her down at the Sayonara Smackshack that was being run by the Blooms' pet charity, the River Heights Children's Hospital. Her current opponent was a similarly outfitted preteen boy whose friends stood at the ring's edge, chanting, "Kill, kill, kill." I guess their guy wasn't getting it done, because after a while, they hopped the barriers and charged Sloane.

"One at a time, you animals," Sloane said. But they toppled her over and she rolled across the line, screaming, "No. No way. You're *not* getting a prize."

Sloane looked pathetic turtled on her back with her face streaked with melting makeup. I had to reach into my bag of memorable traumas I'd suffered at Sloane's hands to stop myself from feeling too sorry for her. I've never enjoyed watching the mighty fall.

From afar, I heard Digby say, "Get away from me. These aren't for sale."

Now, I was used to seeing chaos follow Digby around, but the sight of a mob of little kids trailing him, begging for one of the dozens of balloons he was somehow now holding, was arresting.

"Don't come near me with those," I said. But he did, and soon the kids were swarming around me too.

"Not. For. Sale." Digby swatted at one kid who was getting aggressive about snagging a balloon.

"Digby, stop," I said. "Hey, kids, the cotton candy stand's giving out samples." I immediately felt awful when I saw the cotton candy guy's horrified face as the pack ran toward his booth.

"Thanks for that, Princeton. I couldn't think with all those brats on me," he said.

"'Don't assault little kids' should be pretty much automatic, though," I said.

"You know, that's how they should teach health class. Stand us in a swarm of deranged kids and talk about abstinence," Digby said.

"What's the story with the balloons? Do I want to know or would I be an accessory if you told me?" I said.

"Nah, these balloons are Felix's."

He nodded in the direction of the Sayonara Smackshack and said, "Is that Sloane? Wow, Princeton, this is like the happy ending of a teen movie. You win."

"It doesn't feel like winning," I said.

Henry Petropoulos, our school's quarterback and the Ken doll to Sloane Bloom's Barbie, walked up to us holding a giant slushie and a towel. "Hey, man." He and Digby exchanged bro nods.

Sloane waddled over and without acknowledging either Digby or me, grabbed the slushie and took a long pull. She instantly bent over as far as her suit let her, and screeched, "I'm dying."

"It's just brain freeze, Sloane," Henry said.

"I know it's brain freeze, genius," Sloane said.

A Sayonara Smackshack employee called out, "Sloane, we need you back now."

"Coming." To Henry, she said, "I hate everything." Walking away, Sloane took another huge sip of slushie and predictably, screamed. The cup exploded when she threw it against the wall and slush spattered two little girls who hadn't run away fast enough.

"Everything okay? Why's she pissy at you?" Digby said.

"Who do you think helped her get into that suit?" Henry said.

"Shouldn't she be doing the makeover booth or something? Whatever the pretty girl gig is around here?" I said.

"Kissing booth." Henry pointed to it being manned by a girl with gold mermaid hair. "Lexi Ford's doing it this year."

"People paying money for physical contact. I don't understand how that's not prostitution," I said. "Why do they still have these anyway? It's so 1952."

"Kissing doesn't go out of style, Princeton," Digby said.

I heard the word *kiss* and suddenly, I was back at the bus station where he'd left me five months ago.

"You got five dollars?" Digby said.

"You're disgusting," I said.

But Digby didn't take the bill I held out to him. "Not me." He jerked his head toward Lexi. "Why don't you go make a feminist statement?"

"You need to learn what feminism is." To Henry, I said, "Is Sloane okay? I mean, with Lexi taking her spot as our queen bee?"

Before Henry could answer, he got a text. He read it, somber-faced. He passed his phone to Digby.

"What?" I said.

"Nothing," Henry said.

"There he is now." Digby cocked his chin in the direction of the barbecue stall where John Pappas, an enormous defensive tackle people called Papa John, was struggling to eat an overstuffed sub with his taped-up hand.

"John Pappas?" I said.

"What's up with his hand?" Digby said to Henry.

I felt bad when Henry shrugged. I'd been around the football team a lot lately, because of Austin, and heard the guys trash-talking Henry. He didn't know what was up with John's hand or anything else about the team, because they'd frozen him out. Even though they knew that it had been *Digby's* fault that their linebacker Dominic got arrested and expelled for having guns and drugs in school, it didn't matter. Henry's friendship with Digby had been enough to condemn him.

"He broke two fingers cleaning his garage," I said. Digby and Henry looked shocked. "What? Austin told me."

"Austin spends a lot of time with Papa John?" Digby said.

"Not really," I said. "Why?"

"Nothing," Henry said. "Coach Fogle wants me to help Papa John get back in shape."

"And speaking of athletic bodies . . . here comes Felix," Digby said. "Looking good, Felix."

"Feeling good, Digby." Felix jogged up wearing a River Heights Lioness Girls' Soccer uniform.

"Felix, tell me I don't have to explain why that shirt's not appropriate for you," I said.

Felix Fong was River Heights High's genius and was a glorious example of why you should never judge a book by its cover. Maybe it's because he was overcompensating for the fact that his parents had skipped him ahead three grades, but sweet and diminutive Felix Fong is fierce. If it weren't for Felix, Ezekiel and his accomplices would've gotten away. I mean, I watched Felix defibrillate a man *in the face*.

"Nope. It's the girls' team, I know. I'm their manager. Coach Bailey's going back to coaching just the boys. I do the schedule, budget, roster, the bus, that kind of thing. One of the moms does all the sporty parts," Felix said.

Then I realized. "Wait. Neither you nor Henry is surprised to see Digby. Why am I the only one who's surprised that he's back?"

"He texted me last week," Henry said. "We text all the time."

"We meet up online," Felix said. "We're working on some stuff together."

To Digby, I said, "So, this whole time, it was just me you weren't talking to?" To Felix and Henry, I said, "And where have you two been? Why didn't you tell me he was coming back?"

"Every time I saw you and Austin, you were always . . ." Henry said. ". . . having a private conversation?"

"Oh? They were mostly Frenching when I saw them . . ." Felix said. He pointed at the balloons in Digby's hand. "Thanks for holding that. I know the physics, but I can't unsee all the cartoons of kids getting carried away. I had nightmares for months after I saw *Up*."

"What's with the balloons anyway?" I said.

"They're for the team," Felix said. "Here they come."

The soccer team looked like gazelles on the Serengeti, all long legs and high ponytails swishing in sync.

"Whoa. There's, like, a hundred of them," Digby said.

"Twenty-four," Felix said.

"Wait. How many players on a soccer team?" Digby said.

"They're all on the team, but we dress seventeen for each game," Felix said. "Eleven start, six sub in."

"So not all of them get to play?" Digby said.

"Not every game," Felix said. "I mean, I'll try to get everyone in at least one game during the season, but . . ."

"Then what are you doing giving them balloons?" When Felix looked blank, Digby said, "You call yourself a genius and you can't figure out how twenty-four girls divided by seventeen spots equals you don't have to give anyone balloons?"

"Oh . . ." Felix said as the Lionesses flooded around him and washed him away.

"They're going to eat him alive," Digby said.

At the Smackshack, Sloane had been toppled again. She panted and grimaced as she tried and failed over and over to get up.

"Okay, I'd better go help her before she throws up," Henry said before running off.

"What are you going to do with the balloons? Maybe you could give them to those kids now," I said.

"What? Reward them for being brats? Nope," Digby said. "This is a teachable moment. I'm going to give them to those girls working the hot dog stand."

"Yes. That will definitely teach those brats."

"Why? Does that bother you?"

"What? Please," I said. "Go for it. A hot dog sugar mama sounds like your dream girl."

"Which reminds me . . ." He checked his phone. "Are you hungry? Or are you going to wait until Austin gets out of work?"

"No . . ." Then out of the corner of my eye, I saw Allie and Charlotte coming over to us.

I didn't want them to see me with Digby. I didn't want Digby to see me with them. But I had nowhere to go.

"Hey, Zoe. Who's *this*?" Allie said.

Charlotte elbowed Allie in the ribs, cocked her head at Digby, and said, "It's him."

Allie said, "Do you go to our school?"

Charlotte eyed Digby from the toe up. "Wow. You're exactly how I pictured. Nice suit." When Allie still looked confused, Charlotte said, "He's Zoe's true detective."

Allie remembered, finally. "Oh . . . that guy."

I knew Charlotte's and Allie's exaggerated California glamazon makeup and slack-jawed party girl drawls were offering up primo slapdown material, but thankfully, Digby swallowed down whatever mean thing he was going to say.

"Anyway, this place is lame without rides. Let's go to Allie's and make Rice Krispies treats and put in streaks," Charlotte said.

"I've got, like, five kinds of blond," Allie said.

"Coming?" Charlotte said.

"Can I catch up with you later? I have to stick around and help my mom," I said.

The way Charlotte looked at Digby and said "O . . . kay . . ." made me dread my next conversation with her.

When they left, he said, "Streaks? Those weren't cool the first time they were in."

"Ha-ha . . . don't be a hater. What do you care how people have fun?"

"Is that how *you* have fun?" When I shrugged, Digby said, "So . . . does the fact you're not going with them mean you're coming to eat with me?"

"No . . . it means I have to help my mom. Just like I said." I started walking away.

"Right now?" he said.

"Right now I'm going to the bathroom," I said.

• • •

I almost stroked out when I opened my bathroom stall's door and found Sloane standing in my face. "I need your help."

That was the last thing I would've ever expected to hear from top-out-of-sight rich and top-of-the-social-heap beautiful Sloane Bloom.

She pushed me back into the stall and locked the door. She still had on the bottom half of her inflatable sumo suit, so it was a tight squeeze for the two of us.

"What's the matter with you?" I said.

"I don't want to talk about it here. Come to lunch at my place tomorrow," Sloane said. "I'll tell you everything."

"Come to your place? You haven't said a word to me since last semester and now you want to have me over for lunch?" I said.

"What do you mean? I talked to you . . . um . . . ."

I let it hang a second. "Um-never. *Never* is the word you're looking for. You talked to me never." Sloane's outfit was practically pushing me into the toilet bowl. "And move back. Why are we jammed in here anyway?"

I got my answer when two girls walked into the bathroom laughing and bagging on some unnamed "she." Sloane put her hand across my mouth and silently shushed me.

". . . her inner fattie finally came out." I recognized the voice of one of Sloane's blond backup girls, Denise. "Wait. Is someone there?"

Sloane looked down at our feet and knitted her eyebrows: *Please.* Who the heck knows why I did it for her, but I climbed up onto the bowl so Sloane wouldn't be the weird girl caught with a rando in a bathroom stall.

"Sloane? Is that you?" When Sloane didn't answer, Denise said, "I can see the feet on your costume."

"Um . . . yeah, it's me," Sloane said.

"Are you okay?" Denise said.

"I'm fine," Sloane said.

The awkwardness that followed was painful. Denise and her friend used the stalls on either side of us in a silence they didn't break until after they'd washed their hands and left the bathroom. Before the door had fully shut behind them, they busted out laughing.

"What is happening to you?" I said.

Sloane unlocked the door and we stepped out.

"Just come to lunch, okay?" Sloane said.

Sloane Bloom wearing an inflatable suit, hiding in the bathroom, and being mocked? It was all very intriguing. "Yeah, okay."

"What's your number? I'll send you directions." I told her and she started typing it into her phone. "What's Digby's number?"

"Digby?"

"Yes, I need both you criminals on the case."

"Wait, what's going on? I just assumed your problems were . . ." I gestured vaguely at the door, meaning Denise.

"That? No. And even if I were having problems with my friends, how could *you* help me?" Sloane said.

Her messaged directions to her house came. "I've been to your house . . . this isn't the way to the Crescent."

"Season's started. We've opened up the summer house."

I didn't even realize I was giving her attitude until she said, "Oh, spare me this eat-the-rich crap. It's a miserable place and I'm miserable there. Boo-hoo. Does that make you feel better?" And then she left.

The rage that lit me up when I walked out of the bathroom and saw Digby talking to Bill surprised me. Bill (whose real name was Isabel but went by "Bill" because, well, it got her extra attention) was wearing a cowboy hat. It was probably a reference to something clever and relevant, but to me, it was just annoying. Of course, I knew my hostility wasn't real. It was just after-burn from Sloane. Or maybe it was from last semester when Bill had pretended to be my friend only to get close to Digby. But in that nanosecond, the word *MINE* flashed across my brain and I was bathed in hate. It didn't help that Digby and Bill looked guilty when they saw me seeing them. By the time

Bill said good-bye to Digby and scurried off, though, I'd gotten my feelings in check.

"I guess Bill's Internet famous now?" Digby said.

Since Bill and I last hung out, a post she'd written about her intentionally controversial lunchtime surveys and social climbing experiment had been republished by a bunch of snarky in-group blogs. After that, she'd become a commentator for a handful of them. This I knew from Bill's own blog, which I'd started off hate-reading but now legit-read to keep up with what was happening in school.

"Yeah." I didn't trust myself to expand on that.

I guess my curtness got to Digby, and he said, "She wanted to say hi—"

"I'm not asking you to apologize for having other friends, Digby."

"So, is it me or is everything upsydownsy around here?" Got to give it to him. The dude can turn on a dime and reset. "You're getting your hair did with the populars and Sloane's in a sumo outfit asking me to lunch. We *are* going, right?"

"Well, the idea of helping Sloane is . . ." I stuck out my tongue. "But on the other hand, the idea of Sloane having a problem . . . what would that even look like—" Then I remembered. "Damn. I can't. I'm seeing a movie with Austin tomorrow."

"How long do you think lunch is going to go?" Digby said. "What time's your movie? Seven?"

"The movie's at noon," I said. "*The Big Sleep* at the Cineforum."

Digby laughed. "Austin? *The Big Sleep*? You'll spend half the movie explaining what just happened."

"Okay, whatever. You'll have to go to lunch without me," I said.

"Wow, Princeton is double-booked. How do you like life in the fast lane?" Digby said. "Is it everything you thought it would be?"

Good question.

FOUR

The next morning, I'd just put away the contraband honey I used to sweeten my tea when Officer Cooper came in the door with an armload of files from work.

"Mike? Is that you?" I used "Mike" to his face to put him at ease, but really, he'd always be Officer Cooper: The guy who arrested me. Even after he started dating Mom and moved in with us, he was still Officer Cooper in my mind.

"Man, they need to plow those streets. Someone's going to wreck their oil pan on a snowbank," Cooper said. I guess Mom hadn't mentioned our little adventure in his car.

I pointed at the stack of files he was cradling. "Homework?"

"Budget cuts . . ." He stripped off his gear. "They won't pay for overtime and it's not like criminals suddenly decide to commit twenty-five percent fewer crimes when they hear the police department's shrunk by twenty-five percent. Know what we need? Interns. Hours of paperwork for no pay. Interested?" He laughed at his own joke.

I tried to stay cool when Cooper took a sip of my tea. I worried he'd taste the honey and I really didn't need to hear him preach about the enslavement of bees again. "Mmmm . . . your tea always tastes better than mine. What's your secret?"

"I, uh . . . put the Stevia in before the hot water. It's less bitter that way," I said.

"I've got to try that," he said.

My phone buzzed. Finally, a text. The movie was in half an hour and I still hadn't heard from Austin that morning. I grabbed my phone in a most uncool way.

"Is it that Austin kid?" Cooper wound up to pitch something profound my way. "Zoe . . . you know . . ."

"It's Digby. He's back," I said.

Cooper's big speech was under way.

". . . you learn to tell good ones from bad ones pretty quick doing my job." Cooper stared at me hard. "I'm not trying to act like I'm your father and I hope I'm not stepping over the line, but . . . that kid's not everything you think he is."

"He's bad news, I know," I said.

"You do?"

"Of course I do. He's inconsiderate, he's always got some scam going . . . It pisses me off the way he only calls when he needs something," I said.

"Then why are you still going out with him?" he said.

"What? I'm not going out with him."

"You broke up?"

"We were never dating . . . that was just the one kiss," I said.

43

"And it was months ago, anyway." I realized I'd never said that aloud before. I'd never even told Mom.

"One kiss?" he said.

"Wait, what?" I said. "Who are you talking about?"

"That kid Austin. Who are *you* talking about?" he said. "Wait. Did you say Philip Digby's back?"

He was as embarrassed as I was when we mentally rewound the conversation and realized our wires had crossed. Thankfully, another text came right then. This time, it was from Austin.

Sorry Zero cant make it lets go out tonite, it said.

I despised Austin's autocorrect always calling me Zero. But what upset me was that I'd already suspected he'd planned on bailing on me from the start. He'd muttered something ominous when I'd told him the movie was black-and-white. If I'd known he wasn't going to turn up, I could've done something else with my Saturday. For example, Sloane's weird lunch.

Then I realized it was only 11:40 and I could still make it if I wanted to. Which I really did because Austin would be upset I was hanging out with Digby and that would be exactly perfect. I texted Digby.

"Whoa. Your face like . . ." Cooper did jazz hands in front of his face. ". . . totally switched. What was that text? Digby?"

"Austin."

Then, suddenly, I heard myself scream from the porch. "I hate his ringtone," I said.

"Austin?" Cooper said.

"Digby."

Digby was standing at the door when I opened it.

"What are you doing here? I told you I had plans," I said.

"What are you talking about?" Digby held up his phone and recited the text I'd sent: "'Hey, too late for me to come to Sloane's? I'm home.'"

"Yeah, but I just now sent that," I said. "And you were already here."

"Should I have waited in the car to be polite?" he said.

"So you assumed my plans would be canceled?" I said.

"Relax, Princeton, I took a chance," he said. "Is that cake I smell?"

"In this house? Not likely," I said.

Digby pushed past me. "Officer Cooper."

"Call me Mike, Digby." He and Digby shook hands. "You all healed up?"

"My right arm clicks and it's maybe not as strong as it used to be, but I'm okay," Digby said. "So, I heard the city cut your budget."

"It's brutal. Half the office is empty desks and stacked-up chairs. Morale's in the toilet," Cooper said. "Hey . . . you ever think of maybe going into the academy after graduation? Play cops and robbers for a living?" Cooper turned to me because I was laughing so hard. "Why's that funny? He's a natural."

"A natural what? Cop?" I said. "More like robber, right?"

Digby looked at us watching him for a long second. "Do I have to decide right now or can I use the bathroom first?"

I pointed at the downstairs guest bathroom.

"Mind if I use the one upstairs? I'm a little shy." Digby ran up the stairs.

Once we were alone, I said, "Um . . . about that thing I said a while ago. Can we keep that between us?"

"Keep what between us?" Cooper said.

"The whole thing . . . with the kiss . . ." But he wasn't picking up what I was putting down. "And the confusion with the names . . . Austin, Digby, Digby, Austin . . ."

Cooper made a big show of getting it. "Oh . . . *that*. Yeah. Got it. Well, I mean, I'll try, but it's really hard for me because I can only keep one secret at a time. They never let me go undercover." He was messing with me. I dreaded finding out just exactly how. "So . . . I can either keep the secret about the confusion over the names or I can keep the secret about the honey you keep in your backpack."

Damn it.

"I taste the hot tears of exploited bees in every sip of your tea," Cooper said.

"Is it even technically a secret since you already knew?" I said.

"Well, if that's how your secrets work, then . . ." He pointed upstairs. "I guess it's okay to talk about your 'just one kiss' with Digby since *he* already knows...."

I gave him my bottle of honey when I heard Digby's footsteps coming down the stairs.

Cooper pointed at the box of Pop-Tarts Digby was eating from and said, "Where did you get that?"

Pop-Tarts weren't among the outlaw foods I was keeping in my secret stash of non-vegan food, so obviously, Mom was hoarding junk too.

"My pocket?" Digby said. I hated when he didn't care enough to bring his liar's A-game.

"It's mine. They're mine. Sorry," I said.

"Do you know what's in those? Gelatin," Cooper said. "You know how they make gelatin?"

"They boil cow feet. Yeah, you told me."

"Any more surprises hidden away?"

I didn't have it in me to lie again. "Sorry. There are."

"Maybe I haven't described the horror show that is the American processed food industry," Cooper said.

I dragged Digby away. As we were going out the door, I said, "Let's talk later, okay, Mike? Promise I'll read the pamphlets this time."

Once we were farther down the path, Digby said, "Vegan household, huh?"

"Yeah . . . a lot of changes since you left," I said.

"Like you suddenly becoming a good liar? These weren't your Pop-Tarts. They were under the bin liner in your mom's trash can. With her cigarettes, by the way. And I found your Oreos. How are Oreos not vegan?"

"Sugar's filtered through slaughterhouse waste, apparently," I said. "Hey, wait a minute. Those Oreos were in my underwear drawer. What were you doing there?"

"Following the smell of food, Princeton," he said. "I didn't see anything."

When we got to the curb, Digby unlocked an old windowless white panel van with OLYMPIO'S DINER stenciled on its side.

"It's a straight-up serial killer murder mobile," I said. "Do Henry's parents know you have their van?"

We climbed in. "Ha-ha," he said.

I strapped in and waited for him to start the engine. And I waited. And waited. "Is something wrong?"

Digby was staring out the window at two men sitting in the front seat of a black SUV parked in the driveway beside my house.

"Who lives next door to you now?" Digby said.

"Um . . . I don't know . . . They've been renovating since the place sold after Christmas. I haven't seen the new owners yet."

"Hunh. So, more new people . . ." Digby said. "Don't you think that's interesting?"

"Breaking news: People move into a house?" I said. "Anybody ever tell you you don't deal well with change?"

Digby climbed out of the van and leaned against the door, arms crossed and staring at the occupants of the SUV. I waited a minute or two and then got out to join him.

"What are you doing?" I said. The guys inside the SUV noticed us staring at them. "You're freaking them out."

"Actually, I'm not. And isn't that strange?" Digby said. "They're just sitting there."

I let him play his game another minute. "You're being weird."

"And look at their car . . . all the badges and logos are gone. Dealer plates . . . I'm pretty sure those windows are blocking more light than the legal limit . . ." Digby said.

"Really? Now you think my other neighbors are shady?" I said. "God, please don't tell me you're going to blow up yet another house on my street."

The SUV's doors opened and two men in dark suits got out and walked up the porch.

"Men in black suits," he said.

"*You're* a man in a black suit," I said.

The two men paused at the front door. One of them vaguely glanced in our direction. Maybe it was a little interesting how nondescript they were in their suits and sunglasses. I could barely make out any of their features.

"It's not their house . . ." Digby said.

"Maybe they're visiting," I said. "Or they need to find their keys."

"Or. They need to pick that lock," Digby said.

My front door opened and Cooper ran out with an empty baking tray. He crossed the lawn and handed the tray to the two men Digby and I had been watching. I called Cooper over.

"What was that?" I said. "Who were those guys?"

"Who? Dan and Dan? I borrowed their cookie sheet. They bought the place for a steal after . . . you know . . ." Cooper pointed at the now-empty lot across the street where the drug ring/cult's mansion once stood. "Apparently, it was still smoldering when they had the open house."

"Okay, are you happy now?" I said to Digby. "I know that you're determined to play this game, but I'm cold. And we're late for lunch."

• • •

Once we were on the road, I said, "Well? *Do* Henry's parents know you have their van? Or will we get stopped for driving around in a stolen vehicle?"

"What? Of course I asked, and by the way, did you really mean that back at the house? That if I had to choose between cops and robbers, you think I'd be a robber?" Digby said. "That hurts, Princeton."

"Oh, please," I said. "Actually, you've never told me what you want to be when you grow up."

"Ah . . . the hopes, dreams, and aspirations talk," Digby said. "What do *you* want to be?"

"My father calls that the three-hundred-thousand-dollar question," I said.

"Go to college for four years and then punt and go for three more in law school?" Digby said. "At the end of that, you'll be so deep in debt, the decision will have been made for you: lawyer."

I shrugged.

"Or maybe get out of college and work a finance gig in the city?" he said. "Car service and an expense account?"

I shrugged again. It had occurred to me.

"Who'd be the robber then, huh?" he said.

Digby turned onto the freeway and drove us across some shockingly beautiful upstate-y countryside. I realized from how taken aback I was that I hadn't spent much time outside city limits.

"Hey, let me ask you something, Princeton. How's Austin's money scenario?"

"What do you mean? His parents aren't super-rich or anything . . ."

"But, like, does he seem like he has a lot of stuff? Does he buy you nice gifts?"

"Nice gifts? I mean, he buys me things. Takes me out. He works." I looked over at him. "What are you asking me?"

"Just curious about the material realities of dating in high school today . . ."

"Yeah, right. What's going on?"

"You've been living with a cop too long, Princeton. You're starting to sound like one."

But I could guess what was behind his deflection.

"Are you doing research? Because Bill would be less flowers and fancy dinners than hot dogs and some danger zone make-out session she can post about on her feed," I said.

"Well, up to the part about posting stuff online, I would've said the same thing about you," he said. "Or are flowers and fancy dinners your thing now?"

I couldn't explain the mix of embarrassment and defensiveness I felt. I mean, since when did liking roses and chocolate lava cake make me a defective?

But Digby changed the subject before we could have that fight.

"You ever been to Bird's Hill?"

"No. What's up there?" I said.

"You are in for a treat. People like the Blooms only live down in River Heights with us plebes during the winter. Soon as spring rolls around, they all move up to their summer houses. It's a tradition from when this place was first settled and people in the valley dropped dead of malaria every summer," he said. "Bird's Hill is where the richest and oldest families have theirs."

"Summer houses? But there's still snow on the ground."

"People that rich, the stuff they own owns them right back. Calendar says it's time to go up the hill, so up they go," Digby said. "In our case, I hope the lunch cart's telling Sloane to roll out some shrimp cocktail and pastries."

"So this whole thing's just about food to you?"

"It's not *not* about food."

"I mean, you aren't more curious why Sloane would invite me—who she hates—to her house? What kind of problem could she have that makes her actually want to talk to *me*?"

"You people-pleasers. Seriously. You're so worried people don't like you, you can't even tell the difference between good hate and bad hate." Digby laughed. "She hates you for the same reason she's asking you for help. She respects you. She knows you're smart."

"Do you think that's why everyone hates you?"

"Nah . . . this town hates me because they think my family and I got away with killing my sister. And then I shoot my mouth off and they start to think maybe I enjoyed doing it too," Digby said. "Actually, the real question is, why are *you* here?"

I didn't know at first. Then the answer came to me and I was ashamed.

Digby smiled big. "It's okay, Princeton . . . it's okay that you want to see her beg."

FIVE

We got off the freeway and headed toward the base of a small mountain.

"Bird's *Hill?*" I said. "That's no hill."

"Right?" Digby said.

We turned onto the winding road and passed one elaborate gate after another, each increasing in ornateness as we went uphill. Digby said, "Screw the shrimp cocktail. I expect nothing less than an omelet bar and a chocolate fountain. White *and* milk chocolate."

The gatehouse security guards found our names on the list and let us in. On the long drive up to the main house, Digby said, "There's a half a million bucks of gravel on this road."

Sloane was waiting when we got to the front of the huge house and signaled us to drive around to the parking area in the back, where a fleet of catering, florist, and chair rental trucks were unloading.

"For real, Sloane, you shouldn't have . . . all we really needed was the catering truck . . ." Digby said.

"It's for my mother's young voters tea. Wait. I asked you here specifically because I didn't want it to get back to Henry that I was talking to you." She pointed at the Olympio's van. "Did you tell Henry you were coming here?"

"As every Cosmo girl knows, keeping secrets from each other is a Relationship Don't. The honesty you give is the honesty you get," Digby said. But Sloane looked genuinely worried, so he said, "Relax, I said I was taking Princeton to lunch. I didn't tell him where."

Sloane took us through the back door into the kitchen, where uniformed staff were putting together the tea party. We passed into the main part of the house and went along a wood-paneled hallway lined with enormous doors.

"What are in these rooms?" Digby said.

Sloane half-assed a tour. "Study . . . library . . . my mother's sitting room . . ."

Just as we passed, the sitting room door opened and Sloane's mother ran out. I assumed her no-makeup makeup, perfectly bobbed hair helmet, and floral garden party dress with a cardigan caped over her shoulders were a campaign costume. Who knows, though. These people might walk around looking like this all the time.

"Sloane? Where's Henry?" Mrs. Bloom said.

"Not here," Sloane said.

"I don't understand. Security said his parents' van is here," Mrs. Bloom said.

Elliot, the smooth-talking guy managing Sloane's father's campaign for Congress, burst out of the room reeking of stress and coffee. "Where's the QB? He's the entertainment. There are a lot of young jock voters coming." Elliot pointed at Sloane. "And why aren't you dressed? Who are these two?" Then he recognized Digby. "He's not staying, is he? Wait, why isn't the quarterback coming?"

"What's the big deal? I'm going to attend, Elliot. *I'm* the commodity," Sloane said.

"Now, how can you argue with that?" Elliot said. "But . . . there isn't going to be any blowback, is there? I mean, if you and the quarterback split?"

"What do you mean?" Sloane said.

Elliot just gawped.

"Oh, for God's sake, Elliot, Sloane is a big girl." To Sloane, Mrs. Bloom said, "He means, does Henry have anything compromising he might, say, put on the Internet if he were angry? If you broke up?"

"Excuse me?" Sloane said.

Mrs. Bloom and Sloane stared at each other. Sloane flinched first. "He doesn't have anything compromising, Mother. Not that Henry would ever do anything like that even if he did."

"But there are problems between you and Henry?" Elliot said.

"And now I'm done with this conversation," Sloane said. She took Digby and me upstairs.

• • •

My breath caught when Sloane opened her bedroom door. The room was a fairy princess dream of pink and gold filigree.

55

There was a canopy bed in the form of an open gilded lily. All the furniture was plush or velvet or brocaded. Look past the initial prettiness, though, and what you saw was . . .

"It's like the inside of a coffin," Digby said.

That.

"My great-grandfather had it built in 1940 for the daughter he never ended up having. My grandfather didn't have any girls either," Sloane said.

"This room's been waiting for you since 1940?" I said. "That's creepy."

"You have no idea. This is a replica of an actual doll's house in a museum in Chicago," Sloane said. "It's Sleeping Beauty's room."

"And you sleep in the bed she lay comatose in? No one between 1940 and now saw how symbolically messed up that is?" I said.

"I've never wanted to be a princess," Sloane said.

"Well, glory be, have you two actually found something to agree about?" Digby helped himself from an oversized tray of little sandwiches and mini tarts that had been set up for us. "So what's the problem, Sloane? Why are we here?"

Sloane sat down on her bed. "Henry's cheating on me."

"What? How do you know?" I said. "Wait, *do* you know so? Or do you just think so?"

"I *know* so," Sloane said. "He's been really distant and suddenly he has a second phone I don't have the number to. Plus, he's been working out like he's back on the market . . ."

"My father did the working out thing too when he was

cheating . . . but I think that's more like a midlife crisis . . ." I said. "Right, Digby?"

Digby kept right on eating.

"Digby," I said.

"Hmm? Oh, yeah," Digby said. "She's right, Sloane, Henry's working out for spring training." He polished off a sandwich and reached for another.

"He tells me he's at work, so I go to the diner but he isn't there. I ask him where he really was and he says he was with the football team. I ask him what they were doing and he says they were talking about plays . . ." Sloane said. "It sounds like BS."

"Austin says stuff like that too. I figured it out, though. It's because they aren't allowed to do any training during the off-season and their coach tells them to deny any team prep they do—"

"I found cash in his wallet last weekend. Lots of cash. I thought he was going to take me somewhere or buy me something, but he went out Saturday night and when I checked again on Sunday, the money was just gone," Sloane said.

"You looked in his wallet?" I said. Wow, she really *was* worried.

"He isn't cheating." Digby laughed at Sloane. "You should see your face. You look disappointed. What, did you want him to be cheating on you?"

"But I'm telling you . . ." Sloane said.

Digby cupped his hands around his mouth to amplify his voice. "He's. Not. Cheating."

"But he's up to something," Sloane said.

I pointed at Digby. "*You're* up to something. What is it?"

"Let it go, Sloane. Henry isn't cheating." Digby put a pile of cookies in his jacket pocket and walked out the door.

After he was gone, I said, "What did you want us to do, Sloane?"

"I don't know. I guess I was hoping Digby would say something . . . tell me I'm right or make me believe I'm wrong," Sloane said. "But he didn't do either, did he? I hate this bros before hos crap."

"I cannot stand that saying," I said. "But yes, that's definitely what's happening here."

"Meanwhile, my mother and Elliot are sitting around discussing how many points it'll cost Dad if my boobs end up on the Internet," Sloane said. "I feel like I'm going insane."

I thought I spotted the tiniest tears forming in the corners of her eyes. I realized I didn't really know what I'd do if she got upset. Maybe it was time for her regular crew to step in. "What do your friends say? Have they heard anything about Henry?"

"My friends?" Sloane said. "I can't talk to them about this."

"What? Why not?"

"Because it's fricking ridiculous and impossible."

"What do you mean? Cheating happens all the time."

"Maybe to people like *you*."

And with that sucker punch to the soul, I got up. "I should go. Digby's my ride."

. . .

Digby already had the engine running when I got in the van. "What was that?" I said.

"That was Sloane driving herself nuts." Digby pulled out onto the drive.

"Maybe she is, but you're being weird. Something's going on," I said. "You sure there isn't something going on with Henry?"

Digby laughed. "Ha. You just want to believe he's cheating on Sloane because then she'd be on your level."

"'On my level'? Meaning what?" I said. "Are you implying Austin is cheating on me? Because if that's what you want to say, then have the guts to actually say it."

"No, I'm not saying that—"

"That's what I thought," I said. We spent the rest of the ride in silence.

• • •

I saw Austin's car parked outside my house and became newly enraged that he'd bailed on me.

"Hey, Digby," I said. "Do you want to come in for some food? We can ask Cooper to make us ramen," I said. "The vegan ones are actually edible."

Predictably, Digby accepted and hopped out of the van with me. On the way to the porch, he said, "This sudden hospitality doesn't have anything to do with that blue Ford with the River Heights Buccaneers bumper sticker, does it?"

I shrugged.

"And I'm the cold dish of revenge you're serving up for dinner?" When I didn't answer, he pulled off the knit cap I'd been wearing. "Nice streaks, by the way."

"I know. They look crazy." I brushed the streaked bits back into my ponytail. "Allie left them in too long last night."

"I'm not asking you to apologize for having other friends, Princeton."

"Ha-ha."

"Now, should we practice our scene?" Digby threw his arm around my shoulders. "How's this?" He pulled me closer. "Too much?"

"Maybe a little . . ."

When my front door opened, Austin was standing in the threshold. "Babe, why aren't you answering my texts? Where were you?"

"Actually, where were *you*?" I wiggled out from under Digby's arm.

"I had to go do my conditioning," Austin said. "Football team stuff."

Digby cleared his throat and cocked his eyebrow at me.

"Henry's at work. Digby just picked up the van from him, Austin. How is there 'football team stuff' without the quarterback?"

"It wasn't anything official. Just a bunch of us doing some workouts Coach Fogle gave us."

"Then when you said 'football team stuff,' you weren't telling the exact truth." Digby stepped up to Austin.

"Can I help you, guy?" Austin took a step forward too, and bumped up against Digby's chest until they were nose-to-nose.

"Digby, can you give Austin and me a minute?" I peeled Digby away from Austin.

"Princeton, make sure he has the decency to work for it when he lies to you," Digby said.

"Seriously, bro, what are you doing here anyway?" Austin pushed me into the house so he could get between Digby and me.

"Actually, Austin, I invited Digby," I said. "Which is more than I can say for you since your invitation expired when you didn't bother turning up this morning." When Digby started laughing, I said to him, "You. Living room." I waited until Digby was gone before saying, "Austin, I don't know how you and past girlfriends used to do it, but you can't just not show up when you know I'm waiting for you."

"Sorry, Zoe, but I texted," Austin said.

"*After* you were supposed to be here," I said.

"This is crazy. I said I'm sorry. Can you hear yourself? You're acting like a little . . ."

"Like a little what?"

Austin just stared.

"That's what I thought." I grabbed his coat off the rack and shoved it into his chest as I pushed him out the door.

• • •

In the living room, Digby and Cooper were talking over a pile of Cooper's case files. Mom was drinking coffee and grading papers. Their chatter died down when I walked in trembling.

"Door slam. You okay?" Digby said.

"I don't want to talk about it."

"For what it's worth, Austin was in here for an hour telling us how sorry he was," Mom said.

Digby and Cooper both rolled their eyes.

61

"And on that note, I should go," Digby said.

"What about dinner? And, wait, where are you living?" I said. "Does your mom know you're back in town?"

"Not yet exactly . . ."

"I hope you're not a runaway again," Cooper said. "Your dad knows you left this time, right?"

"Yeah, he knows, Mike." Digby retrieved an envelope from his pocket. "Besides. I got my bona fides. State of Texas declared me my own man."

Cooper pulled out the paperwork and we started reading. It took me a while to digest that I was looking at a court order. Removal of Disabilities of Minority. Mom snatched it away, alarmed. "This says you have to provide for your own food, clothing, and shelter. Your parents aren't legally obligated to do anything for you."

"How much of that were they doing before?" Digby said.

"Can you do this?" Mom turned to me. "You think this is a good idea?"

"What? This is the first time I'm hearing about it, Mom," I said.

"I'm fine. I'll be at Henry's for now," Digby said.

"You're staying at Henry's?" I said.

"For now. His sister's not going to let me stay very long. I walked in on Athena doing morning yoga in her nightgown," Digby said. "It was as horrifying as it sounds. For both of us. But don't worry. I have options . . . maybe see what's going on at my mom's place."

I followed Digby to the front door. "About Sloane. She's really worried Henry's cheating."

Digby laughed. "It's nothing. Henry doesn't have it in him to cheat."

"Well, would you talk to him anyway?" I said.

"Wow. You really are a good girl. Love your enemies and everything," he said.

"Put her out of her misery already, okay?" I said.

"Sorry, Princeton, I don't do matrimonials." Digby opened the door, took two steps outside.

"Matrimonials? What does that mean?" I realized how late it had gotten. "Just stay for dinner and drive to Henry's afterward." When Digby hesitated, I said, "Eat here already. When did you ever say no to food?"

"You realize this would be the first time I'd be eating at the dinner table instead of hiding up in your room?" Digby came back in and took off his coat. "Wow. This is an occasion."

"Well, don't get too excited yet. Like I said, I'm going to ask Cooper to make ramen, but earlier, I heard him talking about a nut loaf," I said.

"What the hell is that?"

"Exactly. And you still won't know after you eat it either."

SIX

The next morning, I turned on my phone and it immediately chimed with the latest of many missed messages from Austin and Sloane. I had nothing new for Sloane, and I wasn't ready to slide back into my fight with Austin from last night, so I turned it off again. There'd be no avoiding Austin at the mall, though, because he'd scheduled to work too. After a while, just to give me a break from worrying about what I'd say to Austin, I instead contemplated what Digby had told me the night before about his plan to track down the stray crack dealer who may or may not have seen Sally after her abduction nine years ago. I wondered if the futility of all that was apparent only to me.

Eventually, overwhelmed by the massive problem salad my mind had thrown together, I got out of bed and got ready for work.

I made the mistake of lingering over my cereal in the kitchen and Mom walked in before I could make a non-rude escape. Her phone trilled right before she came into the room.

"Good morning," she said. "You look tired. How much sleep did you get last night?"

"Enough."

"What time did he leave?"

I shrugged.

"Do you think it's a coincidence that Digby comes to town and you and Austin immediately start having problems?" she said.

I knew I shouldn't engage, but it was too irritating to resist.

"Austin and I aren't having problems."

"Oh? So you've made up?"

I stared at her, but she wasn't shamed into going away. Her phone trilled again and I took advantage of her breaking eye contact as she read the message. I got up and put my bowl in the sink.

"I should go. I don't want to be late. It's going to be super-busy at the store today," I said.

"Wait, you're working? You don't work Sundays," Mom said.

"The college kids are all coming in to sell their books, so Fisher called me," I said.

"Do you need a ride?"

"So you can interrogate me some more? Wow, let me think. Hard pass."

Her phone trilled with yet another new message.

"And why is your phone ringing non-stop on a Sunday morning?"

Mom sighed. "I have crap going on. It's why I love your teen drama so much." She started typing a response. "My crap is just so . . . *middle-aged*."

• • •

By the time my lunch break rolled around, I was exhausted from explaining to entitled college kids why they were not going to make a profit selling us the books they'd spent all semester highlighting and using as coasters. I was in no mood for Digby's mind games when I bumped into him at the food court. "Not a great time, Digby. I'm going to talk to Austin."

He fell in step with me when I didn't stop. "Ooh . . . need some moral support?"

"Go away, gawker." I pushed him away. "Oh, so Sloane has been blowing up my phone." I paused so we could both absorb the weirdness of that statement. "She wants to know if you'll talk to Henry."

"Told you. I don't mess with other people's relationships," Digby said.

"Except mine," I said.

"Just don't let him off easy," Digby said.

"Great advice. Kthanksbye." When I pushed him away again, I felt a bump under the placket of his shirt. I tapped it. "Is that . . . ?" I reached under his collar and pulled out the locket he'd given me. "That was in my drawer with my . . ."

"Diary? Don't worry. I didn't read it . . ." Digby said. ". . . much."

I hit him. "You force me to keep it for you, then you steal it from my *locked* drawer?"

"I asked you to wear it, not leave it someplace obvious," Digby said.

"You don't get to tell people how to use your gift," I said.

"Give it back." He wouldn't. "You gave it to me. It's mine." I pulled it out from under his shirt and had just yanked it off his neck when I spotted Austin off to the side, watching us with a look of dismay that broke my heart. As angry as he'd made me the day before, he didn't deserve to feel as betrayed as his expression told me he felt.

Austin walked up to us and said, "So?"

"So . . ." I looked at Digby.

"I was just leaving. See you later, Austin." Behind Austin's back, Digby pointed at me and made begging motions.

When we were finally alone, Austin said, "What is it with you guys?"

"Nothing," I said. "We're just friends." I prayed Austin wouldn't notice when I slipped the locket into my purse.

"Don't tell me you can't see he's into you," Austin said.

"What?" I said. "That's crazy. And anyway, he's not what you and I are fighting about—"

"Look, like I told you, I was with some guys on the team. I'm sorry I didn't call you earlier and I'm sorry I made you miss the movie," he said.

"You still don't get it. That's not what's bothering me. What bothers me is that when I asked where you were, you said 'football' to, like, imply that it was a team thing I should just automatically be cool with," I said.

"It *was* a team thing. I was with guys from the team, talking about next season—"

"Seriously? You're really trying to sell me that same story again?" I said.

"Sorry."

"Because if you want to hang out with friends, you should just tell me. It's super-insulting when you lie," I said.

"It's just . . . I feel bad, you know, because you never . . . you don't really have friends . . . I mean, like, *friends* like mine," Austin said.

"Wait. So now you're saying you lied to protect my feelings? Because I'm some kind of . . . what? Anti-social loser?" I said.

"What's with you? Suddenly, everything I say to you is, like, a problem," Austin said.

Of course he was right. My own line of questioning was bumming *me* out. "Okay. Yeah . . . sorry. I guess I'm a little tired."

"Oh, yeah? Why's that? How late did Digby stay? Did he stay over?" Austin said.

"So it's your turn to make accusations now?" I said.

The truth was, Digby *had* stayed until really late the night before. He'd chatted innocuously with Mom and Cooper until they went up to bed. Then Digby and I had heated up a frozen pizza and he told me about his visits to Ezekiel in prison.

"First couple of times I went down to Fort Dix, Ezekiel wouldn't see me," Digby said. "The third time I was there, I watched him pick up cigarette butts in the yard and smoke them. So I started sending him cartons of cigarettes. Anonymously. A carton at a time. Then I sent a nice little care package with cookies added in with the cigarettes. This time, I signed it and wrote a note telling him to put me on his visitors list. And then I stopped sending him stuff cold turkey," Digby said. "I got this a week later." He handed me a piece of paper.

"'Visitor Information Form.' Ezekiel's real name is Nicholas Peavey?" I said. "He's like a Dickens character."

"Let's just keep calling him Ezekiel," Digby said. "Doesn't sound half as cool to say I almost got killed by little Nicky Peavey."

"'Question seven: Relationship to above-named inmate.' You wrote, 'I was his victim.' 'Question nine: Did you know this person prior to his current incarceration?' Your answer was, 'Yes. He once beat me up, kidnapped me, and then tried to kill me in an explosion,'" I said. "Are you kidding me?"

"It was my first draft. First drafts always suck," Digby said.

"How was he?" I said.

"Surprisingly normal. He's gained some weight. They put him in a cell with an embezzler and some low-level mob guy whose main job in life is to take the fall and go to prison," Digby said. "He asked about you, by the way."

"Ezekiel did?"

Digby leered at me.

"Ew," I said. "I don't need to worry about what happens to me when he gets out, do I?"

"It's not like he's planning on coming after you or anything. He wasn't even mad at *me* anymore after I pointed out that if I hadn't gotten him popped, the bosses would've probably killed him by now for stealing all that money from them," Digby said. "So, really, I did him a favor."

"Yes . . . I'm familiar with these favors of yours," I said.

"Anyway, I think I have a line on Ezekiel's friend Joe. He goes by the name 'Bullet Time.'"

"The guy who ran the crack house? Who saw Sally nine years ago?" I said. "What I don't understand is if this Bullet Time guy had information, why didn't he go to the police nine years ago when he could've collected the reward for helping find Sally?"

"I don't know. I'll ask him when I see him."

"You know where he is?"

"Not yet . . . but I have people working on it," Digby said. "It helps to have friends in low places."

"And then you're just going to show up. At his crack house," I said. "And start asking questions?"

"Relax. I never go into a place without knowing how to get out," Digby said. "Besides . . . aren't you coming?"

"I'm not sure how useful I'd be if you took me," I said.

"You see stuff I miss all the time. Just like . . ." Digby stared at me. "I see stuff *you* miss too."

I groaned. "That's an Austin comment again, right?"

"I'm just saying, Princeton, the kid's a player. Girls for glory. The football team—that's how those guys are."

"Henry's on the football team," I said.

"Henry's not normal and you know it. In fact, that's who you should talk to. Go ask Henry about Austin," he said.

"Why do I need to ask Henry? I'm asking you," I said. "This hinting around is lame. Do you have any solid information?"

He hesitated, then said, "No, I don't. And you're right.

70

None of my business. Forget it. I'll go to Bullet Time's place on my own."

"Okay." But I could see it was killing him.

He said, "But you know—"

"And yet you are still talking," I said.

"Just promise you'll make him work, okay? Make him work to deserve you."

And so there I was, standing in the middle of the mall, crabby with sleep deprivation and interrogating my boyfriend, trying to prove to my inner Digby that I was making Austin work to deserve me. It felt mean and lowdown.

"Can we start over?" Austin said.

I willed my face to ignore my brain and smile. "Let's get coffee," I said.

"Okay, but first . . ." Austin kissed me.

I guess I was angrier than I thought, because our kiss felt weird. "We should hurry. My break's over soon."

"What? Fisher's cracking the whip?" Austin laughed.

"It's because he's so nice that I don't like coming back late, Austin," I said.

"Okay, fine." Austin put his arm around me and said, "But maybe after work . . . I could go to the market, get some food . . . you could come over, we could make pasta, watch something . . ." He rubbed my neck.

"Why don't you come over to my house? Mom and Cooper are going to the movies, so we'd have the place to ourselves for a while," I said.

"My parents are up in Maine with my sister looking at

schools. We'd have the place all night. Plus, I checked with Allie and she said she'd cover for you and say you're crashing at her place. She could even pick you up at your house so it'd all look legit," Austin said.

There it was. It only took me a second to decide. I wasn't ready. And it annoyed me that he'd schemed with Allie about *our* date.

"You and Allie really have this all planned out. Did she also decide on an outfit for me?" I said. "And when were you two sitting around talking about me?"

"Whoa. I bumped into her at the market after Spring Fling. Did I just get Allie in trouble? Don't be mad at *her*—she was just trying to help out," Austin said. "And why are you mad at all anyway? Don't you want us to spend time alone? That's all your friends and I are trying to make happen."

It was true. I didn't know why I was mad. "I don't feel comfortable lying to my mom."

"Oh, come on. It's the tiniest lie," Austin said. "Besides, are you telling me you didn't lie to your mom when you and Digby were running around town last year blowing up houses?"

"Look. I'll pick you up at seven and you can come over for pasta. That's it," he said. "Don't look so tense. It's just pasta."

"Right. Of course. Just pasta."

SEVEN

It was complicated getting ready for my dinner date with Austin later that night. I didn't want to send the wrong message, and every outfit I tried on read like a potential invitation. I finally decided on skinny jeans that I neutralized with a long hoodie and boots with knee-high laces that take forever to undo. It was a mixed message but it was the only one I was comfortable sending.

When I got downstairs, Mom was in a killer dress putting on lipstick and getting ready to go out. "It's fancy for dinner and a movie, but it's Mike's last night before shift change. I'm just waiting for him to get home," she said.

Ah, shift change. It was Cooper's last day on every cop's favorite shift, the eight a.m. to four p.m. He was about to start the dreaded graveyard shift: midnight to eight a.m.

"Oh, great. Graveyard Cooper," I said. Cops all got a month on each shift and in the three months since he moved in, I've known three versions of Mike Cooper, each different according to what shift he was working. Graveyard Cooper was grumpy and made dark, sad jokes.

Mom noticed my clothes. "I thought you were going to Austin's place."

"I am," I said.

"Really? You usually get a little more"—she made a weird shimmying gesture—"with your clothes."

Just then, the door opened and Cooper walked in. With Digby. And Digby had his huge backpack with him.

"Digby? What's going on?" I said.

"Guess what I found when we raided the Capri Motel on the south side this afternoon? Two assault rifles, seven handguns, eighty large in small bills, a suitcase of drugs . . ." Cooper said. "And this fricking guy."

"Was all that stuff his?" Mom said.

"Of course not, Mom." To Digby, I said, "It wasn't, was it, Digby?"

"Of course not," Digby said. "If I had eighty grand, I would've checked into the Holiday Inn."

"He was living in the motel. Living in it . . ." Cooper said. ". . . aloooooone."

"You said you were going to your mom's after you moved out of Henry's," I said.

Digby said, "I didn't say I'd go right away—"

"Don't try that with me," I said.

"Know what they say . . . you can't go home again," he said. "I just need some time to work up to it . . . and I had all that balloon money, so I thought . . ."

"'Balloon money'? What is that? Some heroin paraphernalia thing?" Cooper said.

"Whoa. Stand down, Officer Cooper. I literally sold some balloons." To me, Digby said, "Felix's balloons."

"I said he could stay here until he figures things out with his mom," Cooper said.

"You what?" Mom said. "Shouldn't we have talked about this first?"

"And let him live in God-knows-where?" Cooper said. "I couldn't leave him there."

"Mom, please, it won't be for long," I said.

Mom made a face at Cooper, who said, "I'm not happy about it either . . ." He made a helpless hands-up gesture. It was a change to see someone besides me in the classic Digby no-win situation.

The doorbell rang.

"That's Austin." I looked at Digby. "Please don't be an idiot."

The first thing I noticed when I opened the door was that Austin had dressed up.

"Austin. Hi . . . you look great," I said.

"Thanks . . . and *you,* you look . . ." God love him, Austin tried.

The collared shirt under the sweater and pea coat was a departure from his usual athletic gear. The second thing I noticed was that he'd put on cologne. Lots of it. Like, seemingly, every ounce he owned.

"Wow. Hello, J.Crew," Digby said.

"I cannot seem to get away from you, dude," Austin said.

"Big date tonight?" Digby said.

"Zoe and I were just going to make pasta at my house," Austin said.

A hush descended over the room. Like the needle skipped off the record.

In the silence, Cooper pointedly unsnapped his gun holster and put it on the dining room table with a solid thump. "And will your parents be at this pastavaganza?" he said.

"Well, my parents are gone for the weekend . . ." Austin said. "But I'm very responsible."

"You hear this?" Cooper said to Mom. "Unsupervised."

"Don't stay out too late, Zoe," Mom said.

"That's it?" Cooper said.

"Mike, I trust Zoe," Mom said.

"*She* isn't the problem," Cooper said.

"It'll be okay." Digby patted Cooper on the shoulder. "She put on her combat boots and look, she didn't even shower. Her hair still has the ponytail bump from earlier today. He's staying on the bench tonight."

"Maybe we should go, Mike? The movie's starting in half an hour," Mom said.

"We should probably get going too, babe . . . if you don't want to stay out too late," Austin said. I would've thought the disappointment in his voice was tragic if I weren't so relieved that I no longer had to worry about arguing with Austin about not spending the night.

To Digby, Mom said, "Food in the fridge, no pay-per-view, please, and the Wi-Fi password is—"

"Wait, he's staying here?" Austin said.

"Actually." Digby pointed at Austin. "I was going to ask if you could give me a ride."

"Where are you going?" Austin said.

"Where do you live?" Digby said.

"Mulberry and Eames," Austin said.

"Perfect," Digby said.

"A bunch of buses go there," Austin said.

"Sure, we can take you," I said.

"Where are you going, exactly?" Austin said.

"Just start driving and I'll tell you where," Digby said.

"I don't know . . . we still have to start cooking the dinner and it's getting late . . ." Austin said. "Sure you can't take the bus?"

"Austin. Come on. There's, like, one bus an hour after five o'clock." I stared Austin down until he finally nodded.

"Shotgun," Digby said. "Kidding."

• • •

We got in the car and Austin pulled away from my house, driving fast and jerkily. He turned up the music to kill any ideas of conversation, but we didn't make it a block before they started fighting.

"Oh, come on, J.Crew. Are you pouting? Upset you got all lathered and shiny for nothing?" Digby said.

"What is it with the Princeton J.Crew crap? Use our names," Austin said. "Your little nicknames aren't clever."

"Okay," Digby said. "So, *Zoe,* I noticed the guest bedroom's right next to your room. We'll practically be roommates." The extra bass he put into saying my name was perfectly calibrated to drive Austin crazy.

Austin slammed on the brakes. "What's your problem, guy? If you like her so much, why didn't you do something about it when you had the chance?"

"The way you're going, man, I think I still do," Digby said.

"Can you two not talk about me like I'm not here? Digby, I know what you're doing. Cut it out," I said. "And Austin? Can you not drive so fast? I'm nauseated."

"Why are you making me do this, Zoe?" Austin said.

"Come on, Austin. We're almost there." I turned to Digby. "Right? We're almost there, right?"

"Yeah, sure, just go two more blocks and then a right on Linden," Digby said. "And then six miles down the highway."

"That's downtown," I said. Was he going to find Bullet Time's place *now*?

"And the exact opposite of where my house is. Not to mention insanely dangerous." Austin pulled over and cut the engine. "This is ridiculous. Sorry, Zoe, I'm trying to be cool, but he's hijacking our date and he knows it." To Digby, he said, "Get out of the car."

"Austin," I said. I sensed the impending doom of one of Digby's schemes, but I didn't want to say anything in front of Austin. "Digby . . . stop being a jerk."

"Okay, look," Digby said. "I haven't seen Princeton in a while. I guess I got carried away. But I can walk from here."

He opened the car door but didn't get out. "I'll talk to you later, Princeton."

"Wait," I said. "Austin? Please?"

The three of us were deadlocked. Thankfully, Austin was the first one to give in.

"Fine," Austin said.

Digby shut the door. He and Austin stared at each other in the rearview mirror.

Austin started the car and we drove in silence except for the occasional "take a right" or "left here."

Finally, Digby said, "152 Irving Street. We're here."

"Here" was the middle of a still-ungentrified part of downtown. The street was made up of squat brick buildings in varying stages of disrepair. He was totally going to look for Bullet Time.

"I'm just going to be a minute, okay?" Digby said.

"You expect us to wait here for you, dude? Just sitting here in the open like this?" Austin said.

Sure, some of the windows were boarded up and yes, the mean old dog sprawled across one of the stoops was growling in a menacing way, but still, there was nothing to panic about.

"Relax, Austin, I don't think it'll be that big a deal if we wait." To Digby, I said, "You'll be quick, right?"

"Like I said, just a minute." Digby jumped out and jogged down an alley.

Once we were alone, Austin exhaled loudly and said, "Do we need to talk? You keep telling me not to worry, but he's always hanging around. You're sure *nothing* is going on?"

"There's nothing going on between Digby and me." I noted

that by answering in the same present tense Austin used, I hadn't been lying. Well, not *lying* lying.

"And he hasn't said anything to you like . . . how you should dump me or anything like that?" Austin said.

"What?" Technically, still not a lie.

"Because he doesn't like me, you know." Austin looked guilty. "Like . . . from before you moved here."

"You knew each other? I didn't know that." I was in for a rough ride if Digby really was nursing a grudge against Austin.

"We took the same bus in middle school . . . one time, I was . . . having fun. I took his coat, threw it out the window, and . . . it blew into the river before the driver could get it . . ." Austin said.

"No wonder he hates you," I said.

"So he *has* been talking smack about me."

"Well, I mean, do you blame him?"

"Should I apologize?" Austin said.

"No. There wouldn't be any point," I said. "You threw his coat out the window?"

"I was trying to get in with some older guys. One of them had cool parents who had barbecues and let us drink beer. You realize how clutch that is?" Austin said. "Maybe I should just say sorry. This is really hard on you, isn't it?" He stroked my hair.

"Look, I'm really sorry about tonight . . ." I said.

"Don't apologize," Austin said.

"I . . . I guess I'm just not ready—"

Austin kissed me. A nice no-pressure kiss. "I wouldn't want

you to do anything you didn't feel ready for. But you know . . .
when you're ready . . ." He kissed me again. This time, his kiss
had more of a message. "I'm right here, Zoe."

"Yes . . . I'm glad . . ." I said. "Look, I should go check on
Digby." I pulled up my hood and got out of the car.

EIGHT

I went down the alley leading to the back of a red brick warehouse, where I found Digby standing beside a row of overturned trash cans.

"Oh, Princeton, did I ruin pasta night?" he said.

"On the contrary, I'm here to speed this along so Austin and I can get back to our date," I said.

"Ah, it's working? The Old Spice is getting you in the mood?" he said.

"So he got dressed up. It's sweet when people make an effort to look nice." I pointed at Digby's rumpled suit and untucked shirt.

"This old thing? I woke up like this," he said.

"Rolled right out of bed in it, it looks like," I said.

"Well? Are you ready for the Austin Shaeffer experience?" Digby said. "Although . . . would you be rooting around in the trash with me if you were?"

"Can we just focus on whatever we're doing here?" I said. "What *are* we doing here?"

"This is Bullet Time's place," Digby said. "I found it."

"I knew you were railroading us into one of your missions. Wait. *This* is the crack house that the guys in suits supposedly rented out to stash Sally? It's weird." I looked around. "I'm not getting much of a danger vibe here . . ."

"Look at you," Digby said. "Nothing scares *you,* huh?"

"Unless . . . do you think I have some kind of post-traumatic thing? Where I'm like, numb to danger or something? Should I be worried?" I said.

"We're millennials, Princeton. We're *all* post-traumatic. Besides, you're right. It used to be a lot scarier here . . . drive-bys and turf wars. Much more impressive," he said. "But they've been cleaning up. I'm sure if we come back a year from now, it'll be all plaid shirts and fixed-gear bike hipsters."

"Are you going in to talk to Bullet Time?" I said.

"Can't. Turns out he's dead."

"Then why go through the trash?" I said.

"Recon. I want to see what kind of people live here now." Digby lifted a garbage can. "Here, help me empty this one out." When I groaned, Digby said, "Oh, come on, you know you've missed this."

A slice of garbage pizza plopped onto my shoe. "Oh sure. I mean, how could I not?" I said. I kicked around at the pile at my feet. "Can you tell me what we're looking for? Just so I don't accidentally mistake it for trash. Oh, wait. It's all trash."

"What are you talking about? This is an information jackpot." Digby pointed at the empty packages of cornmeal and sugar. "I mean, they're bakers. Bakers don't get violent during a break-in." Digby kicked the packages and thought again. "Of course, these are also ingredients for manufacturing explosives . . ."

"In which case, they'd be exactly the kind of people who get violent during a break-in." And then I heard myself. "Wait. Did I just say 'break-in'?"

"You know what? You were right the first time. What are we doing digging around in trash?" Digby said. "Let's just go see if anyone's home. We might not even need to break in."

I followed him out of the alley and around to the front. "What are you going to tell them when they come to the door?"

Digby rang the bell. "Actually, I don't know." No one answered. "But luckily, we don't have to find that out."

My heart dropped when I saw his lock-picking kit come out. "Oh, no . . ."

Once he had the door open, I peered in and saw that the warehouse was packed full of haphazardly piled stuff well on its way to being garbage. In the center of the floor space, though, was an island of order: an elaborate structure of copper tubes and glass jars. Digby said, "You coming?" and walked in.

"No." And I meant it too, until I heard a huge crash of glass breaking. That was followed by another. And then a series of smaller ones. I ran in and found him standing in the middle of a mess of broken glass and spilled liquid. "What is all this?" An acrid smell set me off on a coughing fit. "It smells like . . ."

"Farts and alcohol? Yeah . . ." he said. "I'm pretty sure this is moonshine."

"People drink this for fun?" I said. "It smells disgusting—"

And then we heard the voices of two people at the front door, one male and one female.

"Hey, Mary, you left the front door open again," Male Voice said.

"Why would you just assume that?" Female Voice—presumably Mary—said.

Digby and I didn't have too many options, so we shut ourselves into a coat closet by the front door just as the man and woman walked past us into the warehouse.

"You make an ass of yourself when you assume stuff," Mary said.

"You're not telling that joke right," Al said.

"Who's joking?" she said.

Then she gasped. "Al! Look! Someone's been in here."

"Not again," Al said.

"Footprints . . ." Mary said. "They're in the closet. Better get the bat."

The closet door opened to reveal that Al was an angry dude in disheveled nightclothes and house slippers that were filthy from being worn outside. Mary was an equally disheveled woman wearing an umbrella hat carrying a sack of groceries. The deranged goofiness of their outfits reminded me of murder clowns and killer dolls.

"We don't keep cash in the house and we don't own anything nice you could hock," Al said to us. He raised the bat he was holding so Digby and I could take note that it had nails sticking out of it.

Mary watched me cowering and said, "Oh, they're just kids, Al . . ." She offered me her hand and led me out of the closet. "This one can't have been using for that long . . . she isn't sick-skinny like her boyfriend here." She frowned at Digby. "Are you her pusher? I bet you are. You look like a pusher." She dug out a five-dollar bill and put it in my hand. "Here. Go get a sandwich."

"Oh, now, that's just going to make 'em keep on coming back," Al said.

"This is for a *sandwich*. Not drugs," Mary said.

"Yes, yes . . . sandwich. Not drugs." I grabbed Digby and backed out toward the door.

"Actually, I'm her sponsor and we're here making amends," Digby said.

"Oh?" Mary said.

"Nine years ago, she was living near here and she took something she wanted to replace," Digby said. "Were you the folks living here nine years ago?" When Mary and Al shook their heads, Digby said, "Do you know who was? Also, do you rent or own this place?"

"You know what? You sound like one of those real estate people who've been coming by trying to evict us. Is that what you're doing here?" Al started advancing toward us.

"No, no," Digby said. "But, really, how long have you been in this place?" Digby and I continued backing up and then, as Digby passed over the threshold, something in his pocket thunked against the jamb.

"What was that?" Al said. He reached into Digby's jacket pocket and pulled out a bottle of their moonshine.

Digby laughed, looking like he was going to talk his way out of it, when he suddenly snatched the moonshine back from Al and yelled, "Go!"

We took off running down the street and back around the corner, yelling for Austin to start the car, but he didn't hear us because he was bent over the screen of his phone. Digby dove into the backseat and I jumped into the front, screaming and incoherent, which was all right because at this point, we didn't need to do much explaining. Looking in the rearview mirror and seeing Al rushing toward the car with his spiked baseball bat pretty much said it all.

Al landed a hit on the trunk before Austin managed to peel out, swearing. "What was *that?*"

He was annoyed that Digby and I had already progressed to the hysterical-laughing-with-relief phase. "What's so funny? It's going to cost so much money to repair that dent."

Digby passed him the bottle of pilfered moonshine and said, "Here. Maybe it'll ease the blow."

"What is it?" Austin sniffed the closed bottle, winced, and then smiled. "Nice."

"I don't even understand why we ran. It's not like they had a gun."

"Whoa. Maybe you *do* have PTSD," Digby said. "Didn't you see that guy? He looked like an ogre."

"Why was he so mad?" Austin said.

Digby took out a stack of envelopes he'd stuffed in his pocket. "He probably thought we were in there to steal their booze." He ripped open one of the envelopes.

"When, really, you were there to steal their mail?" I said. "What is it?"

"They are behind on rent . . ." Digby said. "Well, I'm disappointed we didn't get to look around. Maybe next time—"

"Next time?" I said.

"The checks get sent to a P.O. box," Digby said.

"So, you figure out who gets these checks and you figure out who owns the building. And then what?" I said.

"And then we deal with whatever we find then, Princeton . . ." Digby said. "Meanwhile, Felix and I will work the other angle. We'll be in the computer lab at school tomorrow if you're interested . . ."

"This is what you do together? I don't get it. Why's this fun?" Austin said.

"It isn't fun," I said.

"So, what kind of pasta are we having?" Digby said. "I vote penne."

"Nice try," I said. "You're going home."

"Bummer. I was looking forward to that penne," Digby said.

"Austin, could we swing back to my house and drop Digby before we go to your place?" I said.

"Actually, babe, some guys are getting together and I was thinking . . . it's pretty late and I haven't even started cooking yet . . ." Austin said. "Maybe rain check? Tuesday?"

I couldn't blame him. The night was already ruined. But while it made sense, I think Digby accurately summarized my feelings about the moment when he silently mouthed to me, *BURN.*

We walked back to the house. Austin's car was barely around the corner when Digby started up.

"You're welcome," Digby said.

"Shut up. I don't want to hear it," I said.

"No, really, you weren't feeling it, I could tell," Digby said. "Remember . . . he's just a boy, standing in front of a girl, asking her to take her shirt off."

"You're an ass," I said.

"But seriously, I don't understand why you're, like, *offended* that Austin wants to break himself off a piece. That's the whole point of dating, isn't it? It's a mating ritual," Digby said.

"Excuse me? So you're saying that when I started dating him, I somehow got on a schedule that automatically ends with sex?" I said.

"Whoa whoa whoa. That's not even remotely close to what I'm saying. All I meant is that it makes sense that he wants to," Digby said.

Mom and Cooper had already left and even though Digby was being annoying, I was glad I didn't have to sit home alone that night. We went straight into the kitchen and without consultation, started preparing our dinner. I got the water boiling and he assembled the ingredients for a pasta dinner.

"You know what *doesn't* make sense is that your dad didn't notice you were gone for three months," I said. "I mean, he *knew*, right?"

Digby shook his head.

"There's no way. I bet he did," I said.

Digby shrugged. "All I know is, when I got home, he didn't say anything. When I showed him my emancipation papers, he didn't say anything. And when I told him I was coming back here, he didn't say anything then either," Digby said.

"You just lived in the same house? In silence?"

"Well, we talked about stuff like what's for dinner or chores or whatever. What I meant is that he and I don't talk about anything *real,* and when I skipped three months of talking about dinner or chores, he didn't care enough to notice." Digby saw I looked sad about that and said, "And I don't need him to care . . . I don't have parents like *you* have parents."

"Honestly? Both of my parents have been such pills lately, I could handle a little distance," I said.

"Meh. You've got another year and you'll be out of here," he said.

"What about you? What are you going to do after next year?" I said. "Actually, what are you even doing back here now? Aren't you technically done with your high school coursework?"

"Yeah . . . but I don't think I'm into the whole college thing yet."

"So, you're just going to . . . what? Hang out?" I said. "Isn't that a waste?"

He was quiet for a bit before he answered. "Look, you know how you think of leaving to go to college like it's going to reset your life and kick off something new? It's the same deal with me. I want to get on my college campus and worry about midterms and stay up all night writing papers . . .

maybe start wearing clothes with colors or even pledge a frat."

I cracked up. "Too far."

"Okay, maybe not the last thing, but you know what I mean."

"Sure. You want to be a normal person."

"And I can't be that until I figure out what happened to my sister."

"Are you kidding? You're saying you won't move on with your life until you solve a mystery that the police and the FBI haven't been able to make sense of for nine years?" I said. "You're like a kid holding his breath until he gets his way."

"I'm not saying I have to solve it or put the bastards in jail or anything. I just need to *know* . . . That'll be enough," he said.

I laughed at that. "Yeah, right. As if that would *ever* be enough. This might be one of those things where you have to learn to let it go."

"You mean, I don't need closure for me to start healing? You sound like my therapist. That was the one insight she bothered coming up with before she sent me to a psychopharmacologist . . . which reminds me. I have an appointment with her tomorrow."

"You're seeing someone here?" I said.

"Sure. Medicare. I figure I should get it while it's free," he said.

"Can't believe you found someone so fast," I said.

"Actually, I'm just going to my old doctor," he said.

Now I remembered that Henry had told me that it was this River Heights therapist who'd given the police information that she'd gotten in session with Digby that misdirected the investigation and, in Henry's words, tore the Digby family apart. But I also remembered that Henry hadn't wanted Digby to know this about his doctor.

Seeing the torn expression on my face, Digby said, "Yeah, she's not the best, but like they say . . . better the devil you know . . ."

"Um . . . but you know so many devils. Why not pick someone new . . ." I could feel myself coming off as shifty, but I couldn't stop.

Digby stared at me.

"It's okay, Princeton. I know," he said. "I know what she did. I know she told the police about my father's drinking. His gambling. My mother's psychotic episodes . . . I know she's why the police stopped looking for suspects and just built a case against us."

"You do? Then why are you going back to her?" I said.

"Because I just don't need to sit in therapy for another three months re-explaining how I didn't get to have a childhood because after a horrible tragedy happened to my family, our entire town turned against us and to this day, still think we murdered my sister," he said. His eyes had filled up with tears and when he blinked, a big fat one rolled down. "Understand?"

"Uh . . . I . . ." I didn't know what to do. I wanted to hug him, but I knew he hated being pitied. I felt myself start to cry when, inexplicably, Digby started to laugh at me.

"Oh, no, Princeton, I'm just kidding. You're not actually crying, are you?" He leaned down closer to the chopping board full of onions he was dicing for our pasta and said, "Oh sob, sob, my lost childhood . . ."

"You're such an ass."

"But, seriously, I think I would rather stick my hand in a meat grinder than go through having to tell some new person about Sally." He noticed the water had come to a boil and poured in the penne. "I need this to be over."

NINE

I woke up late the next day still exhausted and I'd zombied my way through my morning coffee and cereal when Cooper walked in through the front door.

"You're up already," he said.

"What do you mean? I'm late, in fact. But I'd rather take a tardy than rush. My head is killing me," I said.

"Did you forget? School's out today and tomorrow. All of them are," Cooper said.

I think Cooper misunderstood my stunned expression to mean I didn't believe him.

"I should know because there's always a mini-crime wave whenever there's one of these Chancellor's Conference Days," he said.

"Oh, right. Well, that's it. I'm going back to bed," I said.

But I was so excited about getting a bonus day that I had trouble getting back to sleep. I got up and started studying again. I was so focused, in fact, that I was late getting to my after-school shift at the bookstore.

Later that afternoon, I found myself alone in the store and decided to do an SAT practice logic question, but my exhausted brain was skipping around too much, so I gave up. For the second night in a row, Digby had kept me up talking. During our entire conversation, I was hyperaware we were still avoiding anything even peripheral to the topic of our kiss.

I wondered when it would come up. And then I wondered if I owed it to Austin to tell him. And then I realized that at some point, "not telling" Austin was going to turn into lying. "What am I supposed to do?" I said out loud.

"SAT logic problem set? Forget it."

I hadn't seen Bill come into the bookstore.

"The originality of the essay counts more for admissions committees these days. Of course, in your case . . . you're a legacy at Princeton, so you super don't have to worry. You're guaranteed to get in." She noted my frown and said, "I have nothing against that. Keep it in the family—I get it. In fact, tell your dad I'm available if he's looking to adopt . . . Anyone who pretends they wouldn't trade places with you is a dirty hater."

From somebody else, I maybe would've thought that kind of honest assessment of the seriously unfair college admissions system was interesting, but coming from Bill . . . I was just annoyed.

"Can I help you find something?" I said.

"Actually, I came to talk about Digby," she said. She handed me a cup of coffee that she'd bought for me. "I wanted to ask if you'd be cool with it if he and I went to a movie. Sometime."

"Why are you even asking me?" I said. "It's weird."

"I know, you and Austin Shaeffer are, like, four months strong now. Mazel tov, by the way. That looks rock solid. But you and Digby last semester . . . and now he's living with you—"

"He's not 'living with me,'" I said. "He's staying at my house. Huge difference."

"But still."

"Still what?" I was determined not to cooperate.

"Okay . . . let's do this." Bill took a big breath. "Zoe, sorry I stole Digby's number from your phone, and sorry you felt used, but honestly, I really did have a great time hanging out with you. You were my friend." She stuck out her hand for me to shake. "I still want to be friends now if you'll let me."

I didn't possess enough spite to leave her hanging. I shook her hand. The girl knew how to put on a scene.

"I've been wanting to talk to you for months. This was just the first non-psycho way I've found to do it," she said.

"Wow. All this to go on a date with Digby." And then it clicked into place. "You two already have plans, don't you?"

Bill laughed and shrugged.

"Then what are we talking about right now, exactly?" I said.

"Busted. I'm being sneaky to apologize for having been sneaky," she said. "But that was the absolute last sneaky thing."

"I'm sure," I said.

"Come on, Zoe, let's at least try," she said. "Since if everything goes well, I might be around a lot more."

"I don't respond well to threats, Bill."

"Ha-ha. Does the fact that you just cracked a joke mean you sorta forgive me?" she said. "Friends?"

Her visit started to make even more sense. She'd lost Darla, her usual social sidekick, to the drama department and the crew of theater kids Darla now ran around with. Bill was making nice because she was lonely and needed new friends.

I couldn't listen to her grovel anymore so I said, "Fine. Enjoy your movie."

• • •

I finished the last logic question in my book near the end of my shift and realized my other test prep book was in my locker at school. On the one hand, I'd probably have only an extra two hours of studying that night. On the other hand, there was no telling if they'd be *the* two hours I needed to be ready for the real thing on Saturday. I cursed a blue streak.

"Whoa. Does somebody need a hug?" Fisher said.

"Sorry, Fisher," I said.

"No problem. I'm not *that* old. I remember when," he said. "The whole boy meets girl thing is *heavy*."

"Huh? Oh, no . . . I finished my practice tests ahead of schedule and I'm trying to decide if I should sneak into school to get my book so I can study tonight," I said. "The SATs are this Saturday."

"That's a weird problem." Fisher sighed. "Maybe I *am* that old. I don't understand all this hurry-up-and-get-there ambition your generation has. Where are you all going?"

"Well, for now, my locker in school, it looks like," I said.

"Come on . . . you're seventeen. When is the happy?"

"After Saturday," I said. "Then I can stop studying on the clock . . . Sorry, Fisher. I feel like I took advantage of you today."

"No way. You saved me yesterday. Anyway, the store's been so packed lately, we haven't had time to talk in a while." Fisher hovered, emanating a shifty vibe. "That was Digby, huh?"

"Umhm . . ." I said. "Go ahead. I know you've been waiting all this time to ask me, so go ahead. Nose away."

"No, no . . ." Fisher demurred but, ultimately, he couldn't resist. "He's taller than I thought he'd be," Fisher said. "Is he back in town for good?"

"Nothing that guy ever does is for good," I said.

Fisher laughed. "But seriously. He's staying?"

"I dunno. I asked him the same thing," I said.

"What did he say?" Fisher said.

"I never got a straight answer," I said. "Huh. You're very interested in Digby."

"Oh, you know. I'm just looking out for my number one employee. You seem distracted since he got back," Fisher said. "What's going on there?" He wiggled his eyebrows.

"*Nothing* is what's going on there," I said. "In fact, his future girlfriend was just in here warning me that they're going to date."

"Warning you?" Fisher said. "Total power move. She obviously thinks you're a threat."

"Well, whatever," I said. "She's weird. He's weird. I say good luck to them both. They can have each other." I accidentally slammed my book bag when I put it on the table.

"Oh, yeah. Nothing going on there at all," Fisher said.

"Don't *you* start being weird," I said.

• • •

I tried the school's front door first, but it was locked. It was raining pretty hard, so I went to the cafeteria's loading dock gate and used the tin can shim (which Digby gave me last year as a memento) to open the padlock on the chain around the door's handles. I was dismayed by how thrilled I felt when the shackle clicked free.

Walking through the cafeteria's kitchen, I remembered I'd missed lunch. I grabbed a bag of hot dog buns that was sitting out. The empty chairs, the stale garbage and B.O. miasma, the lone electric fan spinning on low—it was all very Left Behind. I walked down the dark halls toward my locker, a little freaked by the apocalyptic ambiance, when I felt the presence of someone close by. I turned to find some dude looming right over me. I swung my bag of hot dog buns at him. He dropped an armload of stuff when his hands went up to defend his face. Then, before he could recover, I punched him hard in the gut and screamed.

"What do you want?" I said.

To which the dude on the ground said, "For you to stop hitting me, first of all."

Of course it was Digby. I'd completely forgotten he said he'd be here with Felix, working on that other angle to the Sally case in the computer lab.

"I see you still have that punch of yours, Princeton."

"The hell were you doing sneaking up on me?" I said.

He took a bun out of the bag. "I wasn't sneaking up on you."

"Then why are you in your socks?" I picked up his shoe from among the things he dropped when I'd hit him and handed it to him. I walked over and opened my locker.

"How'd you get in?" he asked.

"Used the shim you gave me on the padlock in the back," I said.

"Oooh . . ." he said. "Sexy."

I took my SAT book out of my locker.

"Aaand the thrill is gone," Digby said. "Are you seriously doing this?" He pulled my flash cards from my locker and grimaced.

"Doing what? Taking care of my future?" I said.

"Listen to you. 'Taking care of my future.' Why so serious?" Digby said.

"You mean the test my entire high school career's been counting down to?" I said.

"It's all a big corporate scam, you know," Digby said.

"And by 'all,' you mean life," I said. "So you're not taking it this Saturday?"

"Yeah, sure I am," he said.

I picked up the bag of buns and hit him again.

"Ow, what?" he said.

"It's a little hypocritical to make fun of the test when you're taking it too," I said.

"I'm not making fun of the test, I'm making fun of *you* for taking it so seriously." He pulled another bun out of the bag in my hand and stuffed the entire thing in his mouth.

"Gross. And as always: Thank you for the excellent pep talk," I said.

"Felix and I are working on something at the computer lab. You want to watch?" he said.

"Tempting, but I need to get some studying done tonight," I said.

"All work and no play . . . you know what they say," he said.

"Speaking of play . . . one of your new playmates came by the bookstore for a chat with me today," I said. "Bill asked me for permission to go to the movies with you."

Something went down the wrong pipe and Digby coughed a few times before he said, "She told me she would. I thought I'd talked her out of it."

"Well, you didn't," I said. "Are you—" I caught myself before I started begging for deets.

"Sorry, what?" he said.

"Nothing," I said. Now we were both awkward.

"Anyway, I'd invite you and Austin to double . . . but you probably have study plans."

"Wait. So when Bill said 'sometime,' she meant *tonight?*" Even when she was telling the truth, Bill couldn't help being a liar. All that fake permission-asking and sneaking around like I was some disapproving mom was annoying. "Okay. Have fun." I turned and walked away, not stopping when he called out.

"Don't wait up," he said. "I'll let myself in with the keys Mike gave me."

TEN

I got about three hallways away before I allowed myself to beat the living crap out of the bag of hot dog buns by smacking them against the wall until they were basically just a bag of crumbs. I felt incredibly relaxed afterward.

A voice behind me said, "Um . . . Zoe? Everything okay?"

"Henry. What's up?"

"What'd he do?" Henry said. "Only Digby can piss someone off this bad."

"It's okay . . ." I said. "Why are *you* here?"

"First string's getting their VO2s measured," Henry said.

"Excuse me?" I said.

"They're making sure we're fit to play," he said.

"Man, this school's like Hotel California. Check out anytime you like, but you can never leave," I said. "Felix and Digby are in the computer lab right now."

"Digby's here? I need to see him, actually," Henry said.

"He's—" Just when I pointed behind me, a figure scuttled across and disappeared around a corner.

"What was that?" Henry said.

"That looked like Felix," I said.

By the time we got to the hallway Felix had turned onto, he'd disappeared around another corner.

I called out, "Felix."

Henry grabbed my arm and said, "Careful. Coach will bust you if he catches you trespassing."

"You know, when people say this school runs on football, they don't mean that football literally runs the school," I said.

"Don't get mad at me. I just don't want you to get busted," he said. "The entire coaching staff's here today."

We set off again. We got close to Felix and I said, "Pssst . . . hey," but that just quickened his pace. "Why's he running away from us?"

Henry and I accelerated into a jog and followed Felix up some stairs. My bag was heavy with books and my laptop, and when I got to the third-floor landing, I was panting and Felix was gone. Henry and I were about to split and go room to room when I heard a faint wheeze coming from a locker. That's right. Felix had stuffed himself into a locker. Henry and I banged on the door.

I'd laughed when I read once that a giant anteater could kill a hunter. Now, though, in the long instant between Felix bursting out of the locker screeching and tackling Henry so they both fell backward, the moral of the anteater trag-edy crystallized. Doesn't matter how small or cute they are: Frighten something enough and it'll mess you up.

"Felix," I said. "It's us."

"Zoe?" Felix said.

"Yes, nutbag," I said. "Who'd you think it was?"

From down the hall, we heard, "You kids there." It was Coach Fogle, all thunder thighs and arm hair. "*Petropoulos.* What the H-E-double hockey sticks is happening here?" Fogle walked toward us, assessed the situation, and drew the most natural conclusion. "Son, you know this team—*heck,* all that is good and great about football in America—is under attack and here you are stuffing a nerd in a locker in plain sight like you're fourteen years old without a care in the world." He got in Henry's face and lowered his voice. "Are you ready to be a YouTube star? Because all these AV pinheads live for is whin-ing about their problems on the computer."

Below Coach Fogle's eye-line, Henry's hand made a slicing motion, which I took to mean Felix and I should split. Henry said, "But Coach—"

"I don't want to hear it. You need to keep your nose clean. It ain't like you're some running back. I got me a dozen of those. You're my QB, son." Coach grabbed Henry by the arm and when Henry winced, he said, "Is it your UCL again? Better ice that elbow and have one of the trainers give you a treatment—ask Chris."

With his back to us, Coach Fogle didn't see Felix and me sneak away down the hall. We were around the corner by the time Coach Fogle said, "Now say your sorries and come down for your VO2 assessment."

When we were farther away, I said, "Felix, why were you running from us?"

"I thought you were someone else," Felix said.

"Who?" I said.

"The girls on the team. Actually . . . since I have you here . . ." Felix said. "I wanted to tell you I'm sorry."

"For what?" I said.

"For last year . . . when I was so persistent . . . trying to convince you to go on a date with me," Felix said. "Anyway. I didn't mean to make you feel chased. Or like a thing . . . like you were a punch line to a joke . . ."

"Wow. Okay, Felix. I appreciate the apology—apparently, it's my day to be getting them. I just got one at the mall from Bill." Felix looked confused, so I said, "Never mind. But that was a lot of pretty specific detail. Is something going on?"

Felix hemmed and hawed. "It's my team."

"Team?" I said.

"The Lionesses," he said. "They're after me."

"For a spot on the team?" I said.

"At first, yeah. But then one day, I heard the goalkeeper tell the midfielders she wanted to *deflower* me. And then the rest of them got in on it and you know . . . those girls are *so* competitive," Felix said. "*Deflower* me? That sounds like it'd hurt."

"Oh, Felix, I'm sorry," I said.

"And those girls are on a hair trigger. The other day, I choked on some water and all of a sudden, they'd pinned me down, and they had my EpiPen out," he said. "I mean, at first, the attention was awesome, but now . . . I'm afraid."

We got to the computer lab and Felix opened the door. "Hey, Digby," he said.

Digby was hooking up terminals. "Hey, Felix." Then he spotted me. "Heeeey, Princeton. Can't get enough?"

"You're so annoying," I said.

Felix set up in front of a bank of terminals and retrieved an enormous bunch of flash drives dangling from an oversized key ring.

"I think we're finally ready. You want to do it?" Felix plugged in a pair of USB keys and started typing away when Digby nodded that he was. Instantly, engineering plans appeared, twinned on the two monitors Digby and Felix had linked.

And then Felix abruptly stopped typing and yanked out the USB sticks and froze.

"What?" Digby said.

Felix stayed frozen, hands raised off the keyboard.

We all watched the screens for a few seconds and when nothing happened, Felix smiled and said, "Okay . . . that was almost really bad. I put in the wrong drives. These "—Felix held up a pair of flash drives still on the oversized key ring— "have a custom decryption program I wrote for Digby to open his dad's files."

Felix held up the two flash drives he'd inserted and quickly removed and said, "*These,* though, have copies of a seriously malicious worm that would've basically nuked this terminal and eventually every computer networked to it."

"What?" I said.

"We're okay, though, because if it was going to happen, it would've already . . ." Felix said.

Felix was about to insert the uninfected drives when Digby stopped him and said, "Felix. Maybe I could take it from here." Digby took the USB drives from him. "You've already done so much . . . I don't want you to get in trouble."

Felix took the flash drives back and said, "Forget it, Digby. I want to be here. I owe you. Everything changed once people found out what you did to Dominic for me. You know how many people have forced me to write their homework essays? *Zero.* How many times my lunch has been stolen? *Zero.* How many lockers have I been stuffed into by anyone other than myself—"

"What?" Digby said.

"Zero," Felix said. "I want to do this."

Felix pulled up the engineering plans again.

"What's all that?" I said.

"What my dad was working on," Digby said.

I was quiet while they flipped through screen after screen. After a few minutes, Digby opened a bag of Doritos and ate as he scrolled. "I'm having a hard time believing anyone would kidnap my sister for this."

"I was thinking the same thing," Felix said.

"Why?" I said.

Digby tapped his screen. "These. Plans for retrofitting a wine cooler into a private plane." He clicked through some more. "This. A patch for a sat phone to receive network TV.

All these things were kinda cool ten years ago, but even then, nothing near kidnap cool." Digby pushed back his chair and opened his chocolate milk. "I mean, I'm questioning whether my dad was ever that good an engineer at all."

"Well, to be fair, this propulsion stuff's decent." Felix tapped the screen. "This one's a workaround for a satellite if the solar arrays don't deploy and the drive mechanism fails."

"Maybe . . ." Digby rolled his chair over to Felix.

I got on Digby's terminal and clicked back to the main page, where I found a folder named VAL. "What's this?"

Digby looked over. "Oh, my mom's stuff."

"What did she do?" I said.

"Admin. She was support staff. I remember she was on something she called the Fun Committee and they'd meet in our backyard," Digby said. "They planned office parties."

I opened it and found the FUN COMMITTEE file. "Can I open it?"

"Yeah, sure . . ." Digby went back to Felix's screen.

The photos were mostly just random shots of people goofing around in labs. Then I found a series of shots of a little girl I eventually realized was Sally. "Digby. Is this . . . ?"

His breath caught. "Yes. That's Sally." We went through the rest of the pictures in silence. The newspapers had run posed cute-baby pictures, but the ones on the monitor showed Sally at a backyard children's party. Unlike Digby's dark hair and eyes, Sally had long fair hair and bright green eyes. The eccentricity of her outfit—a pink tracksuit, a backpack, and a pair of plastic binoculars around her neck—struck me as being totally

Digby, though. "This is the day she disappeared. It was her birthday," Digby said.

I found a picture of seven-year-old Digby shielding his sister's face from their dad's confetti gun. Even before Sally had been abducted, Digby's sad brown eyes were knowing in a way most kids' aren't. "I don't understand how they could think you killed her. That *this* kid"—I tapped the screen—"killed anyone."

"I do," Digby said. "No one is impossible, Princeton. Anyone can do anything. The reasons only need to make sense to them."

But I couldn't shake the feeling that something was off about the image. "Hey, Digby, what's this?" I pointed at the pink bouncy castle behind Sally's head.

"Her Dora the Explorer obsession was in full force back then," Digby said.

"No, I mean, the lines are weird." I pointed at the parts of the bouncy castle showing on either side of Sally's head. "These don't match. Did your mom Photoshop your sister's face or something?"

Digby zoomed in. "Felix, could there be an image under this image?"

"Okay . . . let's look at what's under this graphic interface." Felix narrated what he was doing as he exited into Terminal mode and the usual Mac icons were replaced with lines of code.

"*No.* Don't go online," Digby said.

"But I need Droste Master at least to retrieve whatever's

hidden there," Felix said. "Unless, whoa, you want us to read every line of code?"

"Let's use something offline. In fact, wait." Digby pulled the USBs out of the terminals. "Let's wipe here. Keystrokes, everything." As Felix got busy, Digby said, "Princeton, lend us yours?"

Digby still looked shaken from having seen his sister's pictures and I felt bad hesitating. I gave them my laptop and they got to work on the picture. Felix eventually said, "Here it is. Your mom put it in your sister's hair."

Pixel by pixel, Felix rebuilt the images on my computer's screen: They were pages of run-on equations. Felix said, "Is that . . . ?"

Digby said, "It looks like . . ."

Then they were both silent.

"It's small," Felix said. "The units are in nanometers. I could ask my dad."

Digby scrolled down and pointed at a notation. "F.U.N. What does that mean? I always thought it was just office shenanigans."

"So, this file *is* your mom's? But you said she was admin," I said. "Is this stuff kidnap material?"

"Totally. Kidnapping, espionage . . ." Felix said. "But you know what's strange? This looks a lot like the stuff my father's working on at Perses . . . what I've seen of it, anyway." Felix clicked on the images. "I mean, I don't know exactly what he's doing. It's classified . . . the Department of Defense sent people to interview us and everything."

"Did they mention if there'd be a possibility *you'd* get kidnapped?" I said.

Felix looked worried. Suddenly, the green light above my screen flickered on and then off.

"Did you see that? I think my webcam turned on for like, a second," I said.

Felix went back into Terminal and dug through my operating system. "Guys. The Wi-Fi keeps turning itself back on. A bot must've installed itself when we opened those images."

"Turn it off," I said.

Felix's fingers never stopped typing even as he turned to give me a condescending stare. "I'm already blocking it, but it starts itself up every time I shut it down."

"Are you planning to keep blocking it until my battery runs down? Because that sucker's got a full charge," I said.

"It will eventually stay on long enough for the bot to find whatever it's trying to connect with," Felix said.

"Sorry, Princeton. Blame Steve Jobs for this internal battery nonsense," Digby said.

"What?" I said, even though I knew what was coming next.

Digby threw his chocolate milk all over my keyboard and my computer crackled, whirred, and died.

"I can retrieve your data for you," Felix said.

"I backed up last night." I sighed.

"I'll get you another one, Princeton," Digby said.

"You have another big payday coming up?" I said.

"Well, maybe give me a few months," Digby said.

"What was that, anyway?" I said.

Felix said, "Some bot that was written into the embedded images kept calling home."

"If we recovered that data, we could find out what it was trying to connect to," Digby said.

"Are we sure it *didn't* connect?" I said.

Digby and Felix were quiet.

"So . . ." I said. "Someone maybe knows we're in the school computer lab, trying to open these files?"

Digby grabbed the ruined computer off the ground and ushered Felix and me out the door. We double-timed it down the stairs and sprinted across the school. I led them out the cafeteria doors I'd opened and we stood, backs against the building, panting. After a few minutes of nothing happening, I felt goofy. Digby and Felix looked just as underwhelmed.

"Do you think it's bad I'm disappointed no one's turned up to murder us?" Felix said.

ELEVEN

At home later that night, I was just getting ready to quit studying and start winding down in front of the TV when the doorbell rang.

"Oh. My. Gah. I can't believe you're actually here," Charlotte said.

"What do you mean? Didn't you get my text telling you I'd be home studying tonight?" I said.

"Yeah, but I didn't know how studying would work now with your other friends." Charlotte snickered and rolled her eyes at Allie.

"My 'other friends'?" I said.

"We heard you were at Sloane's house," Allie said.

"So?" Charlotte said. "How was it?"

"Well . . ." I said. "Her house is huge—"

"What's her closet like?" Allie said.

"I didn't actually get to see—"

"Ooh, her makeup . . ." Allie said.

"We were only there for like, a minute—"

"We?" Charlotte said. "Who else went?"

"Uh . . . just Digby," I said.

"Digby," Charlotte said. "Austin didn't mention that."

"Austin told you I went?" I said. "When d'you talk?"

"Austin told Rob, Rob told Anna. Whatever," Charlotte said. "Why were you there with Digby?"

"She needed to ask us about some legal stuff . . ." I said.

"Legal stuff?" Charlotte wasn't buying it until she remembered, "Oh, because your dad's a lawyer? Is he helping her?"

I said, "I can't really say . . ." and allowed them to draw their own conclusions.

And that bought me peace for the rest of the evening.

• • •

Later that night, I'd just started to drift off to sleep when my door opened and Digby walked in.

"This vegan thing has seriously improved the food situation in this house," he said. "Remember when it was all grandma snacks in your nightstand?"

He was sandwiching a marshmallow between two Oreos.

"Where'd you get the marshmallows?" I said.

"Under your mom's desk," he said.

"It's bad enough you're invading my privacy. Please stay out of my mom's stuff," I said. "What are you doing here, anyway?"

Digby sat on my bed. "I couldn't sleep. Hey, how's your dad?"

"I don't know. Fine, probably," I said.

"Because I feel like you two haven't talked in a long time," Digby said.

"We haven't, I guess . . . but I'm seeing him next weekend—"

"That's too late," he said.

"Too late for what?" I said.

"I need legal real estate help. I checked the P.O. box address on the rent invoices from the former crack den and found the name of the company, but after I peeled back six layers of holding companies, all I got was a phone number in Hong Kong that went straight to voicemail," Digby said. "I need help getting to the next step."

"From my dad?" I said. "I don't think I can get my dad to do free legal work for me . . . he bills clients for shower ideas. One time he charged someone for a dream."

"Well, I mean, he could just ask a paralegal or something," Digby said.

Oh, God. That meant I'd have to deal with Barbara, my father's uptight paralegal. Barbara idolized my father, thought I was an entitled loser, and made it her ambition to replace me as the daughter my father never had.

"I guess, Digby, but—"

"Say it's a school thing," he said.

"Fine. I'll ask him the next time we talk," I said.

Digby picked up my phone from the nightstand and handed it to me.

"What? Now?" I said.

"I can't sleep," he said. "Come on, Princeton. This is *something*. I can feel it. This is about *Sally*."

I started dialing. "Okay. Eleven o'clock on a school night. He's going to know something's wrong—"

"Heeeey . . . how are you?" The warmth in my father's greeting surprised me.

"Um . . . Dad?" I said.

"Oh. Zoe?" It was his turn to be surprised. "Is everything all right?"

"Sure . . ." I said. "Sorry to call so late, but I need help with a project."

"You do?" he said.

I said, "Yeah—"

"Do you mean *yes*?"

I ignored how irritating that was. "Yes," I said. "Anyway, I'm having trouble with my research on a company in town. All I get is a voicemail in Hong Kong."

"And you want to see what? What they own? What they do?" he said.

"Yes, all that, please."

"All right. E-mail me the details and I will have Barbara deal with it tomorrow," he said.

"And how's the studying for the SATs going? Are you ready?"

"Oh . . . I'm super-sleepy. Thanks for the help, Dad. Good night." I couldn't hang up fast enough and when I did, my chest was tight and my pulse was thumping in my ears.

"He said yes?" Digby said. "Hey, are you okay?"

"I'm fine." But my breathy delivery was a giveaway.

"What's wrong?" he said.

"Nothing . . . he just asked . . . the SATs . . . this, uh . . ." I was horrified that I'd started crying, but I couldn't stop. "This . . . it's in five days . . ."

"Okay, you're having a panic attack and gulping down air is making it worse," he said.

I was too overcome to resist much when he peeled back my covers, flipped me over onto my belly, and climbed on so we were lying back-to-back on the bed.

"Just breathe, Princeton, and go to your happy place," he said. "Remember doing this for me? It works."

After a few minutes, the weight of him on top of me slowed my breathing enough so the buzzing in my head died down. It was incredibly comforting and even after the worst had passed, I didn't ask him to roll off. We lay like this for a while and I'd dozed off when Mom knocked on my door. Not fully conscious yet, I threw Digby off my back and onto the bed and buried him under the covers just as she walked in.

"Zoe? I thought I heard talking a minute ago?" Mom said.

"I was on the phone with Dad," I said. She looked concerned, so I said, "Nothing bad. I needed a favor and surprisingly . . . he said yes."

"He's your father," she said. "Why are you surprised he'd do something for you?"

"Yeah. Exactly. He's Dad. Why aren't *you* surprised he's doing me a favor?" I said.

And just as I'd feared she would, Mom sat down on the bed next to me. I didn't want to, but I shifted to make a little room for her, squishing Digby against the wall in the process.

"I know I've said unkind things about your father, and I regret that . . ." Mom said. "But it would make me really sad if what I said made you think you couldn't count on him anymore." The unmistakable sound of an upset stomach gurgled up from under the duvet.

"Sorry," I said. "Vegan ramen is . . ."

"I know. I actually came up to remind you that tomorrow's cheat night," she said. "Pizza? Burgers? Pizza with ground-up pig parts?"

"I guess I could go for burgers—" I almost screamed when under the covers, Digby poked me in the ribs. "On the other hand, pizza . . ." Another poke. "Is not what I want, so chicken it is."

"Is something wrong?" Mom said. "Problems with . . . ?" She cocked her head in the direction of the guest room.

"What? Digby? No," I said.

"Austin isn't threatened?" she said. "Because I was looking at Digby in the kitchen today and I have to say . . . he's really growing into his looks . . ."

"Good talk, Mom." I gave her a small starting push off the bed. "I've got to study tomorrow and I just really need to sleep now."

"Oh. Okay, honey." At the door, she said, "One last thing about your dad . . . I think you'd be happier if you didn't focus on the bad times and remembered the good times we had together instead. Maybe the secret to happiness is a little creative forgetfulness, you know?"

After she finally left, Digby popped up from under the covers. "Did your dad say yes?" I nodded and he said, "Do you think your mom will get enough chicken for me too?"

"Or make you watch us eat while you sit there smacking your lips? She's not a monster. Of course she will," I said.

"Wow. Maybe if my parents were this useful, I wouldn't have gotten emancipated," he said.

"'Useful'? That's messed up," I said. "Hey, why does it matter who owns that building downtown? It's not like they'd remember anything from nine years ago."

"I know, but I was thinking . . . Ezekiel said Bullet Time told him that some guys in suits driving SUVs gave him money to get lost so they could use his crack house," Digby said. "Why that particular downtown crack house?"

"You mean, why not just pick another place instead of paying him to go away?" I said.

"Right," Digby said.

I became suddenly self-conscious that he and I were both still horizontal and jammed close together under my covers.

"God . . . it's hot in here," I said.

"Still not wearing your retainer, I see." He wiped off the sweat from my top lip. "Hmm. This is very dangerous," Digby said.

I knew what he meant. Jammed in bed together and whispering in the dark like this . . . it was all starting to feel confusing.

"I can't guarantee the air quality, if you know what I mean," he said. His stomach gurgled again.

"Digby! Dammit," I said. "You really need to quit eating junk."

He got out of the bed. "I know . . ." He took my phone and started typing.

"What are you writing?" I said.

"I owe you one, Princeton." He showed me the e-mail he'd composed for me to send to my father's paralegal, and after I added a carefully worded greeting for Barbara, I sent the email.

"Wait until you read Barbara's response." I rolled my eyes. "You'll realize you owe me a lot more than one."

"She's mean?" he said.

"You'll see," I said. "I'm too tired to even explain it right now."

"Tired. Right. I should let you sleep. She's wrong, by the way. Your mom? Wrong. Forgetting about the bad times . . . that isn't happiness. That's amnesia."

He had his hand on the doorknob and he was about to walk out into the hallway.

"Hey," I said. "Are you crazy?" I pointed out the window, meaning I wanted him to walk around on the porch's roof to get back to his room.

"But my window's locked. Besides, it's more exciting this way," he said.

"I don't need any grief about you right now," I said.

"Why are we even sneaking around?" he said. "She already knows I'm in the house."

"Yeah, but I don't want her to think . . . you know . . . because we were in the bed . . ."

"We were back to back." He grinned. "Zoe, I know you're a good girl, but you know you can't"—he made a lurid motion with his fist—"when you're back to back, right? I wonder if that's why Austin is walking around looking so frustrated."

I threw my pillow at him. "Get out."

TWELVE

The next morning, the phone rang with fifteen minutes still left before my alarm was set to go off. I was super-peeved and answered the call with "What."

A sour voice I didn't recognize said, "Excuse me?"

"Who is this?" When all I heard was an exasperated sigh and a muttered curse, I checked my phone's screen and saw my father's office number. "Oh . . . Barbara. Hi."

"I found information on the holding company you asked about. I'll e-mail it," Barbara said. "I noticed something, though. I decided to call because you'd probably miss it on the page."

"Thanks, Barbara," I said.

"One of the company's directors is Jonathan Garfield Book. Book was a big lawyer here in the city, but he took early retirement ten years ago and became a non-executive chairman of the board of a huge multinational," Barbara said. "Which is why I thought it was strange he's on the rolls of your little local company. What does this company do?"

"Um . . . thank you so much for doing this so quickly, Barbara. I didn't mean for you to work on it so early in the morning," I said.

"That's fine. I like to get all the nonsense out of the way first thing," she said.

And on that delightful note, I got off the phone, forwarded Barbara's e-mail to Digby, and tried to fall back asleep. I couldn't, though, and got out of bed.

I found Digby on the landing, spying on Mom and Cooper fighting downstairs.

"Check your e-mail," I said. "What's going on here?"

"I think they're fighting about something she saw on the news," Digby said. "Are they always like this?"

"I guess maybe recently?" It sounded more like a tiff than a real fight to me, so the distress on Digby's face seemed outsized. "Couples fight . . . why is this worrying you? Don't tell me your parents didn't fight . . . they're *divorced*."

"My parents didn't fight like this. Theirs was frosty tension and our recycling bin filled up with empty bottles for months and then one day, my father tells me we're moving and I had two hours to pack," Digby said.

"Whoa," I said.

"Although, I should've known. He was boxing up his junk for a week before," he said. "I guess I counted on my mom getting custody."

"That's when you moved to Texas?" I said.

"We ended up in Texas, but we stopped all over the place, sometimes for weeks." He pointed to his coat. "I learned to pack light and eat whenever I got the chance because you never know when you'll stop next. Now, *that's* an education."

"No. That's child abuse," I said. The shouting downstairs got more intense. "We should go break it up."

They simmered down when Digby and I walked into the kitchen.

"Good morning," I said.

Mom kissed me and walked out.

"Everything okay, Mike?" I said.

"I've always known she has a problem with what I do for a living, but lately, I don't know . . . it seems like she's been looking for ways to be annoyed with me," Cooper said.

"What happened?" Digby said.

"I was telling her about this drug bust I almost made today and I guess she thought I was too excited," Cooper said. "But *shouldn't* I feel good that I was able to keep up in a foot chase with a kid twenty years younger than me? I chased him down near the high school."

"Drugs?" Digby said. "What kind?"

Cooper shrugged. "He threw out his stuff during the pursuit and I never found the drop bag when I went back over the flight path. I caught him but I had to cut him loose."

"I heard kids have been buying injectables," Digby said.

"Steroids, right?" Cooper said. "I heard that too. But, like I said, I didn't find his stuff. I was just amazed he didn't lose me. That kid was an ex-athlete . . . played football for the school once upon a time. Rob Silkstrom?"

"Silkstrom? No . . ." Digby had a blank look on his face,

which meant he was definitely up to something. "Before my time."

"Ugh, this macho crap still?" As Mom walked past Digby, she caught a scent of something, and then leaned in close to take a deeper sniff. "You smell like lavender. Zoe's perfume is lavender . . . "

I hated to leave Cooper alone, but Digby and I got out of there before Mom could interrogate us on how my perfume got on Digby.

• • •

Digby left and I went back up to study. It was Tuesday. The second Chancellor's Conference Day. The SATs were Saturday. It was time to get real. I put my head down and powered through the practice exams in my book. Hours later, while I was doing the last test, it clicked in my head that I was actually ready for the real thing.

I put down my pencil when I finished. I felt like my heart was going to blow out of my chest. But the celebrations didn't last very long because just a few minutes later, I slid right into worrying about the fact that Austin hadn't called. The last little while had been a mess of failed connections and weirdly awkward conversations, so I didn't know what was going on.

So, when the bell rang and I found Austin at my doorstep holding flowers, I was so relieved and remorseful that I straight up burst into tears.

"Are you okay? I called you so many times today," Austin said. "I wanted to talk to you about something—"

"Airplane mode! I'm so sorry, Austin, I forgot I turned it on when I was studying."

The way my entire being responded to his presence surprised even me. It all became very clear. What was I doing risking everything I had with Austin to play detective with Digby? Austin had every reason to be mad at me. I was a Bad Girlfriend, and yet here he was—with flowers no less.

I launched myself at him. I'd ripped off his jacket before we got the front door shut. By the time we got to the couch, I'd gotten his shirt off. Finally, I thought, this is The Moment. I wasn't sure how much of the rush I felt on seeing Austin was just the reflected excitement from my successful study session, but I felt ready. Ready to take the SATs and ready to be with Austin . . .

"Wait. You said you wanted to talk to me about something?" I said.

"What?" Austin said. "Oh, that? Nothing."

He kissed me again. This time, our kisses were slower and less frenzied.

And then there was a loud knock on the front door. Austin and I froze.

"Ignore it," I said.

"Okay," Austin said.

But then whoever was trying to get in began pounding on the door. I was about to tell Austin to ignore it again, when the doorbell started to ring over and over.

"I'm going to kill him," Austin said.

I got off the couch. "It's not Digby. He has keys."

I opened the door and found Sloane hopping around, agitated. "Wow," I said. "Even the way you ring the doorbell is entitled."

"I wouldn't be here if it weren't an emergency." Sloane stepped past me into the house.

"Please. Do come in," I said. I heard Austin scramble to get his shirt back on.

"How can I help you, Sloane?" I said.

"You have to come with me," she said.

"Excuse me? I'm in the middle of a date," I said.

Sloane vaguely waved toward Austin. "He'll wait." She passed me her phone, where, on the screen, a little blue dot was slowly tracking across a map.

"You—" It occurred to me she probably didn't want Austin to hear any of this. To her, I said, "Kitchen." To Austin, I said, "One sec. Girl problems."

In the kitchen, Sloane said, "You haven't told Austin about Henry?"

"No." I said, "And I haven't told anyone else, if that's what you're going to ask next."

Sloane stared. "Oh."

I took her phone. "I can only assume this means you've lost your whole mind and started stalking Henry?"

"*Again* he said he was going to work, but look . . . this is downtown," Sloane said. "Why is he downtown?"

"Well, technically, all you know is that his phone is downtown . . ." I said. She gave me a dirty look. "Fine. What do you want me to do about it?"

"Come with me," Sloane said.

"Take your driver," I said.

"I took a cab here," she said. "I didn't want to deal with Mom and Elliot."

"So take a cab downtown," I said.

"I tried," Sloane said. "The cabbie refused."

That's because according to the blue dot on the screen, Henry had gone into a particularly rough area called the Downtown Core. The businesses that made up the real Downtown Core had migrated a long time ago, and the neighborhood that kept the name was a bombed-out crime-ridden memory.

"Fine. Austin can drive us," I said.

Sloane grabbed my arm. "No."

"A second ago, you thought I'd already told him everything, so why do you care if we tell him now?" I said.

"I just . . . couldn't take it if everyone at school knew," she said.

Maybe it was the shock of seeing Sloane have a genuine emotion or maybe it was the fact that, even though he'd apologized, Austin had put my previous visit to Sloane's house in the gossip pipeline, but I said, "Fine. I won't tell Austin why I'm coming with you. But. When Henry gets mad, you better make sure he's clear that I told you this was a stupid idea. Got it?"

"Yes." Sloane composed herself and said, "Thank you for doing this, Zoe."

"Was that the first time you've ever thanked someone?" I said. "You looked like you were coughing up a hairball."

We walked back into the living room. "Austin . . . I have to go with Sloane real quick—"

"You're leaving?" Austin said.

"I'll be back in fifteen minutes," I said. "Twenty maximum."

Austin groaned and smacked a sofa cushion.

"Also, can I borrow your mom's car?" I said.

"I took the bus here," Austin said.

"Can't we take one of your cars?" Sloane said to me.

"Mom has it at work," I said.

"Your family has *one* car?" Sloane said.

"Well, I guess Cooper's car is here . . ." I said. "But it's a police vehicle—"

"He's *here*?" Austin said.

"Relax," I said. "He's asleep upstairs."

"Then let's ask to borrow his car," Sloane said.

I said, "You don't bother a sleeping cop on the graveyard shift—"

Sloane walked away to our foyer. By the time I caught up, she'd already dug through the bowl of keys and retrieved Cooper's.

"Sloane."

"You said so yourself. Twenty minutes tops." Sloane walked out the front door.

I wrestled on my boots and grabbed my coat. When I was halfway out, I heard Austin say, "Can't you just call a cab?"

THIRTEEN

Sloane hit the unlock button on the key fob until Cooper's car identified itself from its parking spot on the street. She already had the engine running by the time I got into the passenger seat.

"You know this is an unmarked police car you're stealing, right?" I said.

"Stealing?" Sloane put the car in gear and sped off. "Isn't this your step's car?"

"My step? No," I said. "My mom's boyfriend."

"Whatever. He won't tell on you," Sloane said. When I pshawed, she said, "Besides, it's unmarked."

"To civilians. Other cops *will* recognize a cop car being driven around by not-cops," I said.

"Maybe if we drive fast, they won't see our faces?" Sloane said.

"I'm not sure you understand how this works," I said.

Sloane handed me her phone. "Where is he now?"

It took me a moment to figure it out. It was the part of Downtown Core that people called The Jungle. Downtown

Core was bad enough, but The Jungle was, as its name implied, an altogether different ecosystem. Of course, Digby, Sloane, Felix, Henry, Bill, and I had all been down there before, when we'd skipped out of the winter ball to chase after Marina Miller, the missing girl who turned out to be a runaway. Between Bill being nearly assaulted, Felix getting trapped in a stolen ambulance, and Digby and me getting kidnapped and stuffed in the trunk of a car . . . let's just say the place brought back memories.

"Why's he in The Jungle?" I said.

"The Jungle?" Sloane said.

"Yeah, remember last year . . . that one night," I said.

Sloane looked worried. Clearly, she did remember.

"Maybe you *should* speed up," I said.

• • •

After a tense and mostly quiet drive, Sloane and I got to where the blue dot said we needed to be. "Northwest corner of Peco and Gray. That's here."

"Do you know how to read that thing?" Sloane said.

I yanked the phone away when she tried to snatch it. "Hey. Manners. I'm reading it right." I held up the screen for her to see.

We looked around. Two corners had the check cashing/payday loan/liquor store cluster of businesses. One corner was a weedy patch and a falling-down building. On the fourth corner, where Henry's blue dot was, stood a boarded-up convenience store beside a Laundromat.

"Should we go in?" Sloane said.

"Go in where?" I said. "It's abandoned—"

Just then, some kids walked out of the store.

"I guess it's open," I said. "Let's go."

We opened the car doors and were halfway out when I heard a thunk.

"What was that?" I looked at the floor under the dash. That's when I noticed her shoes. Specifically, how high the heels were. "Sloane, what the hell are those shoes?" In fact, Sloane's entire outfit was even fancier than usual. "What are you wearing? Are you going to a club later or something?"

Sloane hesitated before saying, "I left home thinking I was going to bitch-slap some guy-stealing slut. Clearly, I'm over-dressed for *this*."

"Okay . . . many objectionable words and concepts in what you just said, but we'll deal with that later," I said. "Just try not to break your ankle."

"So what just fell?"

I patted around the floor and picked up a long black rectangular tube. It was a gun's magazine, brimming with bullets. We both gasped and instinctively shut the car doors.

"Put it back," Sloane said.

"Put it back where? I don't even know where it fell from." I tried the glove box, but I didn't know the code to the combination lock.

"What do we do?" Sloane said.

"I guess I'll carry it?" I put the magazine in my pocket, opened the car door, and was about to step out. "Wait." I climbed back in and shut the door.

Sloane got back in too. "What?"

132

"Probably a bad idea to walk around with a bunch of bullets," I said. "The trunk?" Sloane's shrug wasn't much of an endorsement, but we got out of the car and opened the trunk. As I was stuffing the magazine into a corner of the trunk, though, I spotted some kids watching us from a nearby stoop. I suddenly didn't feel putting the bullets in the trunk was a great idea. "Cooper would kill me if these got stolen." I slammed the trunk shut and we got back in the car again.

We were looking around the interior of the car, stymied, when someone rapping on our window scared us half to death. It was Digby.

"Get out, crazy," Digby said. "Door open, door close, door open, door close . . . it's like first-day jitters at clown school."

I pocketed the magazine of bullets. Sloane and I followed him into the convenience store, which turned out to be cleaner and better lit than you'd think. Henry was there, sitting on a stool at a lunch counter against one wall.

"Sloane? What are you doing here?" Henry said.

"What are *you* doing here?" Sloane said.

I turned to Digby. "What are *you* doing here?"

"I'll tell you what we're *not* doing here is cheating on Sloane," Digby said.

"What's going on?" I said.

"Obviously, nothing," Digby said. "So go home now. Bye-bye."

"You thought I was cheating on you?" Henry said.

"Why did you lie about going to work?" Sloane said.

Henry looked like he was going to answer, balked, and then looked at Digby to bail him out.

"We came here to eat," Digby said. "This is one of those hipster speakeasy hamburger stands."

"Here?" I said. It looked like at least twenty years had passed since the place last served any food.

"Is he serious?" Sloane said. "I can't tell."

"Fine. Order something," I said.

"The truth is, we're here because . . ." Digby took a deep breath. "Because . . ."

Finally, Henry said, "Some guys on the team have been juicing."

"Steroids?" Sloane said.

"Yeah," Henry said.

"Have *you* been taking them?" Sloane said.

"Of course not. *Most* of us aren't. But these guys are going to ruin it for all of us."

"Henry, there are always going to be steroids. Guys need to bulk up," Sloane said. "Especially now. The college scouts are coming."

"No, I mean . . . some guys on the team are selling them," Henry said. "And we thought if we could just talk to their supplier—"

To Digby, I said, "'Talk to their supplier'? Really?" To Henry, I said, "Talk to them and say what, exactly?"

"Umm . . . stop?" Henry said.

To Digby, I said, "Are you kidding me? You can't be that naïve."

"Come on, Princeton, you know I don't roll that way. We're going to have a conversation with them, Felix is going to film the whole thing, and we'll give it to the police and they'll take it from there," Digby said.

"Wait. We only go to the police *if* they don't agree to stop selling to my teammates," Henry said. "If they promise to lay off, then we erase everything."

"That's nice." Digby patted Henry on the back. "Hang on to your hopes, my friend."

"Wait. Felix is *here*?" I said.

"In the Laundromat next door," Digby said. "He's in charge of calling 911 if things go south."

"Alone? You left Felix alone? Here?" I said.

Digby's phone rang. "Hello? . . . Okay." Digby hung up and said, "Felix said to tell you he's fine." He pointed at me. "But you two need to get in the car and get out of here."

"You're coming with me," Sloane said to Henry. "This is stupid dangerous. And how will next season go if you *get another* teammate arrested? Everyone will be out to get you, off the field and on."

"Sloane, I can't do nothing," Henry said.

Beside me, Digby groaned. "It's too late anyway. Here we go."

I put on my best poker face when Papa John, the defensive tackle who'd broken his fingers, walked into the store and greeted Digby and Henry.

"Hey, Zoe, what's up? Is Austin here?" Papa John said.

I didn't know if that was a casual kind of question or if that meant Austin knew about this steroids nonsense. I froze.

"Let's not tell Austin about this, okay? Zoe's the one with connections to sell to in New York," Digby said.

When Papa John looked dubious, Digby added, "She needs to cover some expenses she doesn't want Austin to know about." Digby's eyes flicked in the vague direction of my midsection and allowed Papa John to infer whatever he wanted to from that.

"And her?" Papa John pointed at Sloane. "Don't tell me she needs money."

Sloane stepped closer to Henry and said, "I go where he goes."

"Ride-or-die chick, huh?" Papa John laughed.

"Is it just you, John?" Henry said.

"No, my supplier's outside. The amount you need is more than I have . . ." Papa John said.

"But you're the only one on the team who's got stuff?" Henry said.

"What is this?" Papa John said.

"He's still trying to figure out if he can get it for cheaper from your competition," Sloane said. "Let it go, Henry."

"Yeah, let's do this," Digby said.

Papa John stared us down until finally, he said, "Fine. Outside."

As we followed Papa John out of the store, Sloane grabbed Henry's hand and gave him a look to say, Get it together.

• • •

Papa John's "supplier" was an extremely worked-out dude leaning against a muscle car chewing on a toothpick. It was such a cliché, I could've laughed.

If I hadn't been so freaking scared.

"Is that *you,* Silk?" Henry said. They slapped hands and bro-hugged. "I haven't seen you since . . ."

"The homecoming game," Silk said.

I don't know if Digby realized that this was the same Silkstrom guy with the bag of drugs Cooper chased down near school. If he did make the connection, he didn't show it.

Henry introduced Silk to us. "Guys, this is Rob Silkstrom. We won state twice when he was quarterback."

"It's great dealing with someone we know we can trust." Digby stuck out his hand to shake Silk's but abruptly pulled it back. "Whoa. Did anyone see that?"

We all just looked at Digby's wide-eyed crazy-man expression.

"Only me, then? Okay . . . anyway, I was saying it's great doing this with a friend of Henry's," Digby said. "By the way, who else on the team is down?"

"You're down with me and that's all you need," Silk said. "Henry, what's with your friend? Why's he so nervous?"

Digby was staring at his shaky hand but snapped out of it and said, "Sorry, man. Just a little blood sugar issue . . ."

I took a granola bar from my pocket, peeled it open, and handed it to him but he didn't take it. "He's fine, really. He just needs a little . . ." I held the granola bar up to Digby's mouth for him to take a bite. "Please, just go on . . ."

Silk looked uneasy when Digby slumped against the car behind him.

Henry said, "It's okay, Silk. We're here to buy. Let's do this."

Silk thought a little before opening his trunk and pulling out and unzipping a gym bag filled with big Ziploc bags of amber glass vials and pills.

Digby pointed to bottles labeled in a foreign script. "Is that Hindi?" he said.

"Thai," Silk said.

Digby Google translated it. "Nandrolone decanoate." But he looked skeptical.

"I've got American, but it'll cost more." Silk pulled up another bag and opened it. The labels said TESTOSTERONE. "This is legit Upjohn T." He pulled it away when Digby reached for it. "Double the price."

"Relax. We're good for it." Digby took a closer look, holding up the packages in a way I realized would allow Felix to zoom in on the labels.

"Wait a minute. I *know* you . . ." Silk pointed at Digby and then swiped at Papa John's head. "What are you doing bringing this guy? He's a narc."

Henry got between them. "It's okay, Silk. It's cool."

Digby, his so-called blood sugar issue clearly worsening, pulled out a rubber-banded roll of cash that ended up flying out of his hand. I caught it. "The cops got it wrong. I'm not a narc," Digby said.

Silk grabbed Digby and patted him down.

"It was a misunderstanding," Digby said.

"A misunderstanding? Because of you, one of the biggest East Coast operations got shut down," Silk said.

"We were there to make a deal. The expression was . . ." Digby made a vague gesture.

"You mean 'explosion,' right?" I said.

"What did I say?" Digby said.

Digby was pale and sweaty and his eyes couldn't focus as he swooned onto the car parked behind Silk's. I couldn't tell what it was, but it definitely wasn't his blood sugar.

Still, Digby and then Henry passed their pat-downs. And then my turn came around.

"Hey, what's this?" Silk was holding the magazine of ammo I'd tucked into my pocket. "Where's the gun?" Silk pulled out his own gun from his waistband, and let it hang by his side. "Where's. The. Gun."

A nearby car engine backfired and we all jumped. It was like a starter's pistol for the flurry of chaos that came next.

Silk, clearly in possession of his reflexes from his playing days, pistol-whipped Henry in the face and threw him in the backseat of his car. Papa John wrestled Digby for the gym bag of pills.

Then Silk turned the ignition. Papa John abandoned his struggle and barely had time to jump into the front seat before he and Silk drove off, the trunk of the car still open.

Sloane and I watched the car disappear around the corner, looked at each other, and screamed.

FOURTEEN

Felix ran out of the Laundromat and joined our panic-fest on the sidewalk. "What happened, you guys?" he said.

Digby tried to say "They took Henry," but at this point, he was slurring.

"Why do you sound drunk?" I said. "What is with you?"

"We have to call the police," Sloane said. "What are they going to do with Henry?"

"Oh, *wait*." I remembered Sloane's phone was still in my pocket. I turned it on and found the blue dot. "They're going up."

"Up?" Felix said.

"Give me that!" Sloane grabbed her phone and dialed 911.

Digby lurched toward me. "She means norff . . ."

"Digby, what's the matter with you?" I said.

Felix leaned against Digby to keep him from sliding to the ground. "Maybe we should get him to a doctor," Felix said.

Digby's head lolled around and his breathing was ragged.

He pulled a medication bottle from his jacket pocket. "How many orange bippies?"

"Orange bippies?" I shook out his pills and counted.

"Are there eight in there?" he said. "Although . . . I think I know what the answer will be."

"Seven," I said.

"They put me on hold," Sloane said. "Why does 911 even *have* hold buttons?"

"Think I'm having a reaction to my meds . . ." Digby said.

"You're not ODing, are you?" I said.

Digby shook his head and said, "Sorry, Princeton. I'll fix it." And then he leaned over the side of the car and threw up.

Suddenly Felix yelled, "They're hitting him. They're beating up Henry."

"What? How do you know that?" I said.

"I turned his phone into a hot mic." Felix unplugged his headphones from a small receiver he was carrying so we could hear. It was muffled but we could make out Henry getting pummeled and shouting in between hits, "I can get you your bag back! I can get you your bag back!"

"Bag?" Sloane said.

Digby held up the gym bag he'd taken from Papa John.

"Get in the car." Sloane hung up on 911 and ran back to Cooper's car with Digby, Felix, and me behind her.

Sloane got in the driver's seat and I took shotgun while Digby and Felix jumped in the back.

"Oh, man, this is awesome." Felix strapped himself in. "We are *back*."

"No, Felix," I said.

"Zoe, navigate." Sloane threw her phone at me and started the car.

"They got on the interstate." I showed Sloane the blue dot on the screen. "They're going north."

She peeled off so fast, I smacked my head on my window. "Sloane, maybe you should slow down . . ."

But she kept her foot on the gas and soon we were on the freeway on-ramp, picking up speed. A few miles out, Digby said, "We're heading to Niverton?"

"Niverton's the next exit," I said. "Why?"

Digby said, "Better cool it, Sloane . . ."

But it was too late. A black-and-white cruiser burst out of the tall bushes and lit us up.

"Now what?" I said.

Digby sat up and struggled with his seat belt. "Hit the gas, Sloane." Digby finally got his belt on with Felix's help. "Faster. Go way over the speed limit."

"What?" Sloane said.

"Do it," I said.

Sloane gripped the wheel tight and sped up.

In the mirror, we could see the squad car keeping pace.

"Faster," Digby said. "Fast as you can."

Sloane stepped on the accelerator again.

"Now hit the wig-wags," Digby said.

"The what?" I said.

Digby pointed at a switch on the command console mounted between Sloane and me.

It was a classic Planet Digby double down moment. Trying to get out of trouble for impersonating a police officer by impersonating a police officer *more*. I flipped the switch and the lights on our tail and grille flashed in alternation.

"Now speed up again," Digby said.

Sloane did and this time, the squad car didn't follow.

"How did you know they'd be there?" Felix said.

Digby's eyes were closed when he said, ". . . most famous speed trap on this interstate . . ." And then he was asleep.

"Silk just got off the interstate," I said. "Take this exit, Sloane. Then we turn . . . oh, wait a minute."

"What? Turn how?" Sloane pointed at the fork in the road ahead. "Left or right?"

"Wait."

If we turned right, we'd be following Silk's car down a windy road. But if we took the straighter road on the left, we could get in front of them and head them off. There was just the question of the patch between the two roads that I couldn't make out on the map . . .

Sloane took the phone out of my hand. "Right turn? I make a right turn, correct?"

"Wait. Take the shortcut," I said. "Go left."

"Shortcut? *What shortcut?*" Sloane was driving while swiping the screen one-handed. "I don't see a shortcut!"

I tried to convey the urgency. "We're missing it. *Sloane.* We're going to miss it!"

"Zoe, what shortcut?"

"Sloane! Just do it!"

143

Sloane and I were both screaming at that point. We were also about to miss the turn, so I made an executive decision. I yanked the wheel and made the turn myself, nearly running us off the road.

Sloane got the car back under control and said, "*God,* you almost killed us."

"Now what? The blue dot stopped." I worried we'd lost the signal from Henry's phone. "Felix, what's happening? Can you hear anything?"

"They're yelling at Henry to get out of the car," Felix said.

"Okay, Sloane, cross this field," I said. "Henry's pulled over on the road on the other side of this."

Sloane pointed at the area of greenery I was talking about and said, "That's not a field. That's a forest."

Sure, it was more overgrown than the phone led me to believe. "Not according to this . . ."

"Quit looking at that stupid phone and look at the *trees* in front of us," Sloane said.

"What, those saplings?" I said.

"Saplings? Those are *trees,*" Sloane said.

"Sloane, they're beating Henry up," Felix said.

I made a move to grab the wheel again.

"Don't. Even." Sloane turned off the road herself, but as we bumped along the uneven ground and wove through clumps of vegetation, I felt her hesitate and slow down, which frustrated me because I could see the road ahead.

So I smashed my hand down on her leg. The car shot forward.

As it turns out, reality was somewhere between our expectations. What the car punched through was a pretty dense not-a-sapling-not-yet-a-tree situation. It felt like we were all screaming forever, but just as the map promised, when we emerged on the other side, we were on the road, driving toward Silk's car way up ahead across a small bridge.

"That. Was. Fantastic," Felix said.

Sloane held on to the wheel with one hand and started hitting me with the other, keeping her eyes straight ahead. "You mess with my driving again and I'll kill you."

"This is *your* boyfriend we're rescuing, woman." I hit her back. "Quit it. Just keep driving."

"Uh, Zoe?" Felix pointed out the windshield, where we could just make out Silk standing over Henry, sprawled on the ground.

"Oh God," Sloane said, pressing harder on the accelerator.

"We need a plan." I looked to Digby, but he was a useless moaning lump in the backseat. "Okay. We drive over and stop. I tell them to let Henry go if they want the bag. I get Henry, *then* I give them the bag . . . you stay in the car with the engine running. Because the car is a weapon. Digby told me that," I said. "What do you think?"

"Good plan. Good plan. Except . . . Zoe?" Sloane's voice was high and tight. "It's jammed. The pedal's jammed."

"What? What are you talking about?" I said.

Sloane jiggled her right leg dramatically to show me.

"It's your stupid shoes," I said.

"It's because you jammed my foot down," Sloane said.

"Okay, stop panicking." I ducked under the steering wheel, where I saw Sloane's heel was wedged under the gas pedal. I pulled at her leg. "Well, it's really stuck." I sat back up. We were coming up on Silk beating on Henry.

"Oh, God, they're killing him," Sloane said. "They're killing him!"

It really did look like they were. "Okay, Plan B. Felix. When we get close enough, I want you to roll down the window and throw out that gym bag, okay? You get me?"

"I got you." Felix unbelted himself and last I saw before I got back under the dash to get Sloane's foot free, he was reaching for the bag. I was working on sliding out Sloane's heel when she leaned on the horn. I tried to get back up to see but Sloane's arm had me pinned. By the time I finally managed to sit up, Felix had already thrown the gym bag out the window. As I watched it arc away from the car, it struck me that there was something peculiar about it. And just as I saw the bag smack Papa John in the face and knock him down like he'd taken a bullet, I realized what the problem was.

"*Felix*. That was the wrong bag," I said.

"What?" Felix picked up Silk's gym bag from the car floor. "Whoa. They're exactly alike." Felix pointed out the window. "What was in *that* bag?"

"That was Austin's gym bag," I said. He must have left it in the car last Friday.

"We have to go back! I'm getting Henry!"

Before I could stop her, Sloane yanked the wheel to turn the car around. With her foot still jammed down on the gas, she sent us into a spin.

When Sloane wrestled the car back under control for the sec-

146

ond time, we were still going fifty miles an hour in the wrong direction. And Sloane was still screaming.

"Stop screaming, drive straight, and I'll get your foot out." I ducked back down. A few more fruitless tugs and I finally hit on unzipping her boot. Once her foot was free, the heel easily slid out from under the pedal. She slowed down and turned around.

By the time we got back within sight of Henry, the fight had taken a turn. Papa John was on the ground, unconscious. To the casual observer, Henry's bloodied face seemed like bad news but really, he had Silk on the defensive. This was not apparent to Sloane, though, and her scream was pure terror. Before I could stop her, she stomped her foot on the gas pedal, sped right toward Silk, and smashed her hand down on the horn. Silk and Henry broke apart and ran in opposite directions. By the time we'd come to a stop, Silk had jumped back into his car and driven off.

Sloane, Felix, and I ran out to Henry.

"Are you all right?" I said.

"Well, I tried to ask Silk to stop selling to the team. But he didn't see it my way," Henry said.

I bent down for a closer look at Papa John. "What happened to Papa John?" I said. "Did you knock him out?"

"He went down when the bag hit him." Henry pointed at Austin's gym gear strewn all around. "It was probably the ankle weights that did it."

"And in his defense, they hit Henry first. A lot," Felix said. "I heard the whole thing."

147

"We should go after Silk," Henry said.

"You should go to the *hospital,* Henry, and get checked out. Your eye is swollen shut." I looked to Sloane for support, but she was just staring at Henry, stony-faced. "Sloane?"

Sloane said, "We almost freaking died . . ." She ran up to Henry and smacked him on the chest.

"Okay, Sloane, you maybe should relax a bit," I said.

"Why couldn't you just mind your own business, Henry?" Sloane was shouting. "Why didn't you call the police if you cared so much? Tell Coach? How could you put yourself in this situation? Put *us* in this situation?"

"Because, babe, once I report it, I kick off a whole thing. The Athletics Association takes over. That process starts, it has to flow all the way through," Henry said. "I had to think of the guys." He approached Sloane and tried to hold her hand. "They'll lose their eligibility senior year—"

Sloane slapped Henry so hard, it made me gasp. She was about to go again, but I caught her hand and dragged her away. I hung on to her until she calmed down and stopped swearing.

Digby climbed out of the car and staggered to us. He looked at Papa John passed out on the ground, Henry's bleeding face, and me restraining Sloane in a bear hug. "So," Digby said. "What did I miss?"

FIFTEEN

Sloane and I left Digby and Henry at the ER and dropped Felix at his house. The ride back to my place was a tense odyssey. Austin was going to kill me. When I made the mistake of turning on the radio at one point, Sloane gave me a stare so mean, I felt physically afraid. I didn't even think to worry about what Cooper would say about our taking his car until we turned onto our street and found him standing in his empty parking spot, a steaming travel mug of coffee in hand and a bewildered look on his face.

"What the hell?" Cooper said when we got out of the car. "What did you do to my car?"

Only then did I notice that his car was covered in a network of angry scratches and gouges. "Oh . . . it must've been when we drove through those trees."

"Don't you mean 'saplings'?" Sloane said.

The tiniest snort escaped from me.

"It's not funny. You drove through trees in my car? This is

department property," Cooper said. "Zoe. Explain."

"It was me. I made her take the car," Sloane said. "There was an emergency."

Cooper looked at me. "Yes, there was . . ." I said.

"Digby had a reaction to his meds and we had to get him to the hospital," Sloane said.

"Is he okay?" Cooper said. "Where is he?"

"St. Luke's. He's okay but there's a mandatory psych evaluation." I muttered the last part.

"And it didn't occur to you brainiacs to call 911?" Cooper said.

I remember Digby told me once that people will believe anything you say if you make it sound enough like stuff they themselves have been saying. "They put us on hold. Budget cuts, I guess."

"Damn budget cuts. Someone's going to get killed by these budget cuts," Cooper said. "But still. Unauthorized use of a motor vehicle, impersonating a police officer . . ." He banged his fist on the car's roof. "Not to mention the multiple counts of conspiracy I'll commit when I help you morons cover this up because *of course* I can't arrest my girlfriend's daughter and the kid of our next congressman . . . yes, I know who you are." Cooper inspected the car and when he opened the back door, I could've given myself a high five for having had the presence of mind to leave the bag of steroids with Henry. But then Cooper said, "What the hell is this?"

My heart sank when I saw him holding up a bag of pills that, presumably, had fallen out of Silk's gym bag.

150

"These are steroids," Cooper said.

"Really? Are you sure . . ." I said.

"It's only my job to know, Zoe. Where did this come from?" Cooper pointed at Austin's gym bag, hastily repacked and now sitting in the backseat again. "Did it come from in there?"

"What? Of course not," I said. "Do you think it might've already been there? From one of your cases?"

Cooper looked at the bag of pills more closely. Thankfully, Mom pulled up and parked behind us just then.

"What's going on?" Mom said.

"Zoe and her friends decided to steal my car and they messed it up." When Mom didn't look impressed enough, Cooper said, "Police property, by the way." He pointed at me and said, "You're *so* grounded, miss."

Considering the shenanigans we'd just pulled in his car, really, getting grounded was a rock-solid deal. Mom, however, seemed unhappy.

"Not so fast. Mike, may I speak with you one second?"

Cooper threw up his hands and followed Mom into the house.

"Need a ride home?" I said.

"I can call a car." Sloane wiggled her phone at me but then her face fell.

"What? Are you okay?" I said.

"I just realized my parents are on a campaign thing up in Albany," she said.

"You're going to be alone in that massive house tonight?" I said.

"Well, there's staff . . ." she said.

"Invite your friends over," I said.

She nodded, but her vacant stare told me everything I needed to know about the state of her friendships.

"Or . . . you could come in? I could reheat some lentil soup—"

"Okay." She pushed past me and walked to the front door.

Just as Sloane put her hand on the knob, though, the door opened. It took me a second to process that Charlotte and Allie were standing inside my house.

"Wait, did we have plans?" I said.

"Not anymore," Charlotte said. "Hi, Sloane."

"Yes," Sloane said, and walked into the house.

"So, Sloane Bloom is coming to your house now?" Charlotte said.

Allie pointed at Austin's gym bag, which I was carrying into the house. "Is that Sloane's bag? Are you guys going to try on outfits?"

"What? No. And if it were Sloane's bag, why would I be carrying it?" I said.

Austin came to the door. "Oh, hey, that's mine. I was looking for that."

"Austin. I'm so sorry I took so long . . ." I said. "Stuff just came up and then . . . we had to drop off Digby at the hosp—"

"Digby? He was there? I thought you said Sloane needed—" Austin said. "Actually, never mind. Why am I even surprised anymore?"

"Please, Austin, just stay for dinner . . . I can totally explain," I said.

"Actually . . . the three of us were going to get some food," Austin said. "You want to . . . ?"

"But you have a guest," Allie said.

"Um . . . yeah." Charlotte gave me one of her eyeroll-sigh combinations. I couldn't blame her for being hostile. After all the time we spent whining about Sloane, there could be no satisfactory explanation for why she was at my house. "Maybe tomorrow?" I said.

Charlotte shrugged and walked out.

Allie hugged me and said, "Later."

Austin kissed me and said, "Call me later?"

• • •

I poured Sloane some water and reflected on how ironic it was that just days ago, Sloane would've stomped on my fingers had she found me hanging off a cliff and now here I was, making her dinner. I put the soup on the stove to the soundtrack of Mom and Cooper bickering. He followed her from room to room while she unpacked her work bag and settled in. After Mom screamed a particularly creative string of profanities, I apologized to Sloane only to have her look up from her phone and say, "Wi-Fi password?"

Mom and Cooper blew into the kitchen at this point.

"You're throwing the book at Zoe because you're frustrated at work," Mom said. "Not that I want to know what a satisfied cop culture worker looks like."

"'Cop culture worker'? Really? You make being a police officer sound like being part of an evil conspiracy. And it's not throwing the book when I'm not even charging her for what she did," Cooper said. "*That's why* I'm mad. She's forcing me to break laws to protect her from the consequences of her actions."

"Let's move past the fascist police rationalization and talk about why you've been miserable ever since your old partner, Stella, left," Mom said. "Don't tell me you were actually sleeping with your work wife?"

"Why does it boil down to that with you? Stella was my partner," Cooper said. "We're not all your ex-husband, Liza. We don't all cruise the office for tail. Sorry, Zoe, no offense."

"Of course she's offended. And '*grounded*'?" Mom said. "Don't take out your aggression on her."

"Discipline is not aggression, Liza."

I said to Sloane, "I don't want to get sucked into this conversation." I opened two bags of salad, dumped in Craisins, croutons, and double the usual amount of our fanciest salad dressing, and grabbed two forks.

"She doesn't need your discipline, Mike," Mom said. "She *has* a father."

I gave up on the soup. I turned off the burner and brought Sloane up to my room.

"Huh." Sloane walked around my room, picking up my books, checking out my posters. I felt exposed. "You like Bauhaus architecture?" She pointed to a postcard I'd taped to the wall.

"Love it."

"Me too. It sucks because my family lives exclusively in fake American castles." Sloane stuck her tongue out.

"That's Tel Aviv. Apparently, there are, like, thousands of Bauhaus buildings there," I said.

Sloane paced a little more before asking, "So . . . why are you being so nice to me?"

"Excuse me?" I said. "Because I'm a nice person."

Sloane laughed at me. "I mean, you came to lunch to be with Digby, but you didn't have to come with me today. You didn't even know he'd be there."

"First of all, I came today because you stole Cooper's car and as you can see"—I pointed in the direction of Mom and Cooper fighting downstairs—"it's my ass. And second, I turned up to lunch because you cornered me in the bathroom and you really seemed upset. I wanted to help."

"More like you wanted to watch me suffer." Sloane looked at me, defying me to contradict her. "What's with you and Digby, anyway?"

"Nothing," I said. "I'm helping him look for his sister. Besides, I'm with Austin. Digby's with Bill . . ."

"Bill? She's such a try-hard," Sloane said. "You know, it's only a matter of time before you and Digby finally hook up for real."

I tried to keep a blank face. "Whatever, Sloane."

She sat at my desk and pointed at her feet. "Is it okay if I take these off?"

She made an agony/ecstasy groan as she unzipped and peeled off her boots.

"Those are some really stupid boots," I said.

"So stupid." Sloane wiggled her toes. "Want to try them on?"

"Yes, please." I started unlacing my combat boots. I didn't

155

even ask what size hers were. "How much did these cost?"

"Two thousand," Sloane said.

Now, I'd never spend that kind of money on things that go on my feet, but the zipper soundlessly closed over my calves and the leather was as glossy as latex.

I pranced around in front of the mirror, only slightly embarrassed when she said, "Not so stupid now, are they?"

"My brain's like, *capitalism, objectification of women, blah-blah-blah*. But the rest of my body's like *man, look at me in these boots*," I said. "And I can see why you walk so uppity. Comes naturally in these shoes."

"I'll try not to be insulted by that," she said.

"I was praising your posture," I said.

"Sure you were." Sloane pointed at my combat boots. "Can I?" She pulled them on. "These are cool, actually." She did some karate kicks. "It's like, that perfect girl is gone. They're even better than sneakers for keeping you balanced."

"The steel toes act like a weight," I said.

"Trade you? My boots for yours?" she said.

"How distraught *are* you? That's crazy," I said. "My boots were fifty bucks on clearance."

"Mine were clearance too. They *were* four thousand."

"Sloane, you can have those, but I can't take your four-thousand-dollar boots."

"No, seriously, I can't even look at them after today. Swear to God, I thought we were going to die in that car." Sloane pointed at one of my SAT prep books and said, "I have this too. You're taking them next Saturday? I guess everyone is."

She stared, assessing me, before she asked, "Do you think you'll do well?"

I fought my first impulse to say no and then commiserate over how not ready I was. Funnily, I felt like Sloane was the one person who didn't need me to lie to her. "Yeah, actually. I think I am."

"I think I'm going to do well too," Sloane said.

It was weird saying it aloud. We both laughed.

"Wasn't that the most anti-social thing? What we just did?" I said.

"I know, right? You have to be humble . . . end your sentences with your voice going up like this . . . ?" She did an exaggerated uptick. "Because being confident *isn't* nice." She saw me laugh harder and asked, "What's so funny?"

"The idea of you lying to be 'nice' is . . ."

"Is what? I'm nice to my friends," she said.

"Your friends? They're terrified of you. The whole school's terrified of you," I said.

"Whatever. You don't know me and it's unfair for you to decide I'm not nice based on how I treated you last semester when you were making a play for my boyfriend," she said.

"What?" I said.

"You're going to pretend you weren't?" she said.

I didn't.

"Bravo. I totally denied it when Marina asked me the same question," Sloane sat at my desk and played with my lip glosses. "Are you going to Kyle Mesmer's party afterward?"

Kyle Mesmer and his lake house pleasure dome. I didn't go

to the last party and that turned out to be an instant legend that people were *still* talking about months later.

"Honestly? I'd prefer to watch some YouTube and smash my face into a bowl of Tater Tots," I said. "But Austin wants to go."

"How's it going with you and Austin anyway?" she said.

"Good. Good . . ." I said. "He doesn't like Digby."

"Ha. Surprise, surprise," she said.

And then the weight of not telling anyone for months finally broke me. "Digby and I kissed."

Sloane's jaw physically dropped.

"I *know*," I said.

"What does it mean?" she said.

"I don't know. It happened last November. He just kissed me, got on the bus, and he hasn't mentioned it since he got back," I said.

"He didn't text or message you from Texas?"

"Nothing."

"Did you kiss him back?"

"I'm not sure. I think I did. But maybe I didn't. I kinda froze," I said.

"Okay. But then he disappeared and never got in touch with you . . ." she said. "How do you feel now? Do you wish you'd kissed him back or are you relieved that you maybe didn't?"

"I don't know. Maybe the second one? But then, maybe if I *had* kissed him back, he wouldn't have gotten on the bus at all . . ." I came to my senses a little bit. "Please don't tell anyone. No one else knows."

"Austin doesn't know?"

"Of course not," I said. "So . . . not even Henry, okay?"

"Well, obviously, Henry and I are not doing so well," Sloane said.

"Right. Sorry," I said. "But you have to admit . . . what he's trying to do for his team is . . ." I wanted to use the word "noble," but Sloane didn't look like she was in the mood to hear it.

"I can't watch him throw it all away. Things have to line up absolutely perfectly for next season so he gets into a Division I college program," Sloane said. "He's a top prospect and now he's going to blow our entire future—"

"I'm sorry. Did you just say '*our* entire future'? Sloane, you don't really think you and Henry are . . ." I held up four fingers. "Four eva?" I traced a heart shape in the air.

"I don't know why I thought I could have a real conversation with you," Sloane said.

"Oh, come on. You think you and Henry are going to get married?" I said. "That's ridiculous. You're in high school."

"Obviously, not until after college," she said.

"After he gets drafted in the NFL," I said.

"Sure, why not?" she said.

"It's just getting crazier, Sloane."

"What's crazy about my knowing who I belong with?" Sloane said. "Why should I be surprised you don't understand that? You're dating Austin and bickering like wifey with Digby."

"What is *that* supposed to mean?" I said.

"It means you're kidding yourself if you don't think this thing with Digby is a problem," she said.

I had a brief flash of panic. She decoded my grimace.

"Oh, don't worry. I'm not going to tell anyone about 'the kiss.'" She put the words in wiggly air quotes.

"Thanks." I took off Sloane's boots and laid them by her feet. I heard my mother's phone get a message in the other room.

"No, I was serious. Take them," Sloane said.

"I was serious too. I can't take your boots. They're way too much. It'd be taking advantage," I said.

"I'm telling you, I don't want them," she said.

In the next room, Mom's phone got another message.

"I'm saying it'd make *me* feel weird accepting such an expensive gift from you. Like I was just letting you buy my friendship—"

"Excuse me? 'Letting me buy your friendship'? Are you insinuating I buy my friends?" she said.

"What? When did I say that?"

"You don't have to *say* it to say it—"

"Actually, I think I *do* if you're accusing me—"

"Besides, why would I need to buy *you*? I have plenty of friends," Sloane said.

My brain formed a catty response that went something like, "Then why the heck wasn't one of your friends driving you around town spying on your boyfriend?" But before I could deliver my put-down, I heard my mother's phone get a message. And then another one came. I thought that was weird because with me and Cooper both home, there wasn't really anyone else who'd be messaging mom with this back-to-back urgency unless it was a legit emergency.

160

"Excuse me," I said.

More messages came and I followed the pings to the phone in the pocket of the sweater she'd worn that day.

I hesitated for the obligatory three beats before turning on the phone and fully invading Mom's privacy. I hit the home button and saw the screen was filled with messages from my father. They were all variations of "Are you OK?" and "Hey, where are you?"

"What. The. Hell," I said. I punched in Mom's password, but to my surprise, she'd changed it. She'd been using the same four-digit number for everything from her ATM to her gym locker padlock since forever, so her having changed it now was weird.

And then, a new message came in.

It said: "Bora Bora?" The next one said, "Let's do a reunion trip."

I didn't have to call back the number it had been sent from. I rewound and relived the most recent fights between Mom and Cooper and discovered my father's flame bait style of argument embedded in every single one.

Before I could scroll further back into the texts, though, Mom popped into her closet and found me. "Zoe? What are you doing?"

"What are *you* doing, Mom?"

"Imagine the fit you'd throw if I did this to you," Mom said. "I can*not* believe you went through my phone."

"I cannot believe you'd make me go through this crap with you and Dad again."

"Through what? It's nothing," she said. "We're trying to be friends," she said.

"Dad doesn't have friends," I said. "And Bora Bora? Does Mike know about your *friendship*?"

"Don't take that tone with me," Mom said. "Not when you're doing the same thing to Austin, only it's worse because Mike's an adult and Austin is just some poor dumb boy who doesn't have a chance because what you're really attracted to are brilliant sociopaths—"

"Like the brilliant sociopath you're texting with?"

"Twenty years don't go away just because you get divorced."

"Wake up and smell the crap, Mom." Even I was surprised by the finality of the sound of shattering glass when I smashed her phone against the wall. I handed her the completely ruined phone. "Trust me. I just did you a favor."

When I went back to my room, Sloane was putting on her coat.

"You're going?" I said.

"My driver's coming. I'll wait downstairs," she said.

"You can keep my boots, Sloane," I said.

"No, thanks. Fifty dollars, right? I'm sure I can get my own pair of crap boots," she said.

I followed her into the hall. "Hey, Sloane."

Unlike in the movies, she didn't stop walking when I called her back. And then, just to ratchet up the level of drama, my phone rang. "Austin . . . can I call you back?"

My mother walked out of her room, nodded at my phone, and said, "Need me to return that favor?"

Mom followed me into the kitchen. She watched me make a sandwich. Finally, she said, "It isn't what you think."

"Of course it is," I said. "And please don't try to tell me how complicated it is, because—barf."

"Well, Zoe, it isn't as simple as choosing between awesome high school boy number one and awesome high school boy two," Mom said. "Your father and I share a history."

"You realize he's only into you again because now it'd be cheating, right? Cheating on Shereene. With you," I said. "And you'd be cheating too. How does it feel?"

"Why don't you tell me? How does it feel, Zoe?"

"God, Mom. How's that the same thing?"

"What's not the same about it?" she said. "What special ethical pass do *you* carry while you gallivant around town with Digby?"

"He's dating someone else." I hated saying it. "Digby's dating someone else. He doesn't like me that way."

To her credit, Mom snapped out of it. "Oh, Zoe, I'm sorry—"

Mom and I jumped when Cooper walked into the kitchen and said, "Sorry for what?"

Nothing looks guiltier than two people saying "Nothing" and running in opposite directions. Which is what we did.

SIXTEEN

I woke up and started messaging everyone to get my bearings. Henry had been sent home after the ER patched him up. He said he was all right but he couldn't resist sending a selfie of the horrifying bruises on his face. Henry also told me that Digby was still under observation in the hospital because even accidental mishaps with psych meds got a lot of follow-up care. Meanwhile, Austin's responses were short and his phone did that annoying thing of autocorrecting my name to Zero again. Charlotte answered my messages entirely in single emojis. Allie then confirmed Charlotte was still annoyed that I'd blown them off to hang out with Sloane the night before. Thankfully, Allie seemed to be okay with me; she even reassured me that they actually had fun at dinner.

At this point, it occurred to me that I could just stay home from school. I mean, it was Wednesday, the SATs *were* just three days away, and I wondered if my time might be better spent studying at home. Plus, then I wouldn't have to deal with all the drama. And then I recognized the kind of seductive giving in to laziness that had gotten me in truancy trouble my sophomore year at my old school. I propelled myself out of bed and got ready for school.

• • •

I was in the kitchen wrapping up a sandwich when I looked out the window and saw some jerk had tipped over our recycling bins. Pieces of paper were blowing all over the place. Our neighbor Helen Breslauer was staring right at me from her kitchen window when I looked up. When she saw me seeing her, she pointed at me and mouthed, *Yours.*

I mouthed back, *I know, Mrs. Breslauer, I know.*

It took forever, but I finally got it all back into the bins. Through the window, I caught a glimpse of Digby skulking around inside cradling a thick stack of old file folders with the blue River Heights Police Department logo on their covers. Clearly, he'd caused the huge mess I was now cleaning up when he'd stolen them out of our recycling. I then saw him unwrap and start to eat the sandwich I'd just made and take a big pull straight from our milk jug.

None of this would've been particularly weird if he hadn't messaged me just minutes before to say he was still in the hospital, waiting for the attending psychiatrist to sign off on his mandatory psych evaluation.

I messaged him, "Hey, what r u doing?"

I watched him type his response as he headed to the back door, still carrying the milk: "Waiting hosp cafeteria. [Pizza emoji.]"

I messaged back, "Liar."

I was typing my follow-up elaboration on how busted he was when he messaged back, "Gotta go doc's here." Then I watched him turn off his phone, go out the back gate, and down the back alley.

It was equal parts confusing and annoying that he was lying to me. School was starting in twenty minutes. It was time to make a decision. "Dammit."

I snuck out into the alley and hung back far enough so Digby wouldn't spot me behind him. There was one close call when I had to duck behind a trash can but otherwise, I got all the way to the mini-mall bus stop without his catching me. I was hiding in a storefront doorway still formulating a plan when the bus rolled up.

"Now what?" I watched Digby get on and sit near the front. I barely knew what my feet were doing, but I ran to the bus and jumped in through the back doors right as they closed. I sat waiting for the driver to yell at me to pay my fare and it wasn't until the bus had traveled a few blocks that I let myself breathe again. I pulled up my hood and ducked down low.

Stop after stop went by and Digby never once turned around. After a while, I relaxed and noted we were headed south toward the newly constructed business parks. I was relieved he wasn't on his way to Bill's place. I hadn't considered the possibility until the bus was already under way.

I didn't realize I'd been daydreaming when suddenly, I looked up and saw Digby wasn't in his seat anymore. I went up the aisle, checking people's faces, and when I confirmed that Digby was, in fact, gone, I rang the bell, got off the bus, and ran back to the previous stop. We were in an area called Smart Park, which was some River Heights developer's attempt at making the industrial park sound more modern and tech-y than it probably was. I searched the streets near the bus stop but I didn't see him. All around me were groomed lawns, stylishly anonymous glass-and-concrete boxes, and electric vehicle charging stations. But no Digby.

I approached a man in a suit smoking a cigarette in one of the doorways. "Excuse me, have you seen a guy . . . tall, skinny, my age . . . wearing a suit?"

He laughed. "Yeah, sure. Like, seven hundred times today."

And sure enough, the place was full of young working types in suits.

I wandered off and walked about a minute when it dawned on me where Digby was headed. I scrolled back to the e-mail from Barbara and mapped the address of the lawyer's office. It was around the corner from where I was standing. I headed off and was a block away when I heard Digby call out, "Hey, Princeton."

Digby emerged from between two buildings still holding the stack of Cooper's folders he'd fished out of the recycling.

"Pro tip, Princeton: When you're tailing someone, don't stare off into space and daydream," Digby said. "What are you doing here? Are you worried about me?"

"You have an OD drama and then I catch you sneaking around my house while you're lying about where you are . . .

it's all very erratic. Of course I'm worried," I said. "And why are you so chipper?"

"Nothing like spending the night under involuntary psych hold to make you count your blessings," he said.

"What actually happened?" I said.

"I accidentally took too much Lexapro, which caused something called serotonin syndrome . . ." he said. "They gave me cyproheptadine. No biggie." He did a weird rolling thing with his eyes.

"What was that?" I said.

"There's maybe still a little double vision," he said. "Side effect."

"Do you think you should be running around like this?" I said.

"Yeah, sure. Besides, *you're* the one who's shivering." He took off his jacket and put it around me. And then he was standing really close to me and I started to feel like I was forgetting something. Besides my coat, that is.

"We should get you out of this cold," he said. His face was just inches from mine, and he was staring at me. Although instead of feeling exposed like I usually do when Digby stared at me, this time, I just felt like he was letting me see into him too. I didn't want to break the spell, but I was dying to know what was going to happen next.

"Digby . . . ?" I'd started the sentence not knowing how I'd complete it. Thankfully, a text alert sounded.

We both dug for our phones. "Mine," Digby said. He started typing a message. "Let me just tell Bill I got out okay."

"You don't have to ask me for permission," I said.

"I wasn't," he said.

I pointed at the bag of papers he was carrying. "Why do you have Cooper's garbage?"

"I'm going to use it to con my way into the lawyer's office." When I didn't say anything, he said, "You're not going to try to talk me out of it?"

"Would I succeed?" I said.

Digby shook his head and pulled out a walkie-talkie. He looped a blue RHPD lanyard around his neck. I was shocked to see he had official RHPD credentials.

"Why do you have that?" I said.

"They needed interns. I went in on Sunday after I talked to Cooper," he said. "One last thing. Smoothies."

Digby used our time in line at the juice place to explain to me his plan to pretend to deliver packages and somehow cause a diversion that would get him time alone in the office.

"Wow. That plan sounds majorly half-assed," I said.

"The best ones always do . . . if you go in with the whole thing planned out and with dialogue and stuff, you're just gonna trip yourself up when it doesn't go exactly the way you planned. And it *never* goes exactly the way you plan." When I still looked dubious, he said, "Just go with it, Princeton."

By the time we got to the lawyer's office, my hand was numb from the strain of balancing my stack of envelopes and my smoothie and I was as stressed about keeping all the stuff from falling as I was about getting away with the scam we were about to perpetrate.

The office door didn't have anything like a nameplate announcing its occupants, merely a magnetic key pad, a camera lens above it, and a sign that said PLEASE RING BUZZER. When Digby did, a voice said, "Yes?"

"Courier for J. Book?" Digby said.

There was a gasp, the sound of frantic scurrying, and a buzz as the door opened.

The room we stepped into was aggressively nondescript and bare: just a desk, two chairs, and a bookshelf. Except for the computer, printer, paper, and scattered office supplies, there was hardly any indication that actual work took place. A door off to the side hinted at an inner office where the boss might sit.

The assistant who'd buzzed us in was rummaging around and throwing documents into envelopes and then piling them into a delivery crate. "Is it Thursday already?" she said. "I don't have all the stuff ready for you to pick up. Can you wait while I print the rest? Wait. Where's Dex? Has he been fired?"

Digby held up his police ID. "Um . . . it's Wednesday and there's no Dex where I work."

The assistant sighed and relaxed. "The police? What's all this?"

Digby shrugged. "I just deliver the stuff," he said. "Can you sign for this? Or do we need to wait for your boss? Is he coming?"

"Oh, he doesn't . . ." she said. "I can sign for it."

Digby took a step toward her, tripped, and dumped his

smoothie all over her front. When she finally stopped screaming and cursing, she said, "Okay. Out. Please wait in the hall
while I run to the ladies' to get cleaned up."

"Seriously?" Digby said.

"Yeah, seriously," the assistant said. "Sorry. I can't leave
anyone alone in here."

"Okay," Digby said.

The assistant pulled her handbag off a hook by the door,
took a key card off her desk, and put it in the pocket of her
blazer. "I'll only be a second."

Digby and I went out into the hall ahead of her but just as
the door shut behind us, Digby abruptly turned around and
bumped into my hand so *my* smoothie spilled over the assistant.

"Holy crap, what is the matter with the two of you?" she
said.

"I'm so sorry. I was just going to ask where I could buy
another smoothie," Digby said. He dropped the envelopes and
started wiping her jacket with the napkin he'd had wrapped
around his cup. I saw it, but the assistant never even felt Digby
slide the key card out of her pocket.

When he started focusing on her chest, she slapped away his
hand and said, "Okay, thank you. That's enough." She trotted
down the hall toward the bathroom.

As soon as she went around the corner, Digby used her key
card to open the door. "We don't have much time," Digby said.

"What are we looking for?" I opened the door to the inner
office to reveal that it was an empty room.

"Wow. This is the weirdest lawyer's office I've ever seen. There should be files everywhere. Where's the work?"

Digby inserted a USB key into the assistant's computer and started copying. "Check it out." He pointed at the folders on the screen. "Look at the names on this. EverFries, Corner Bay Corp, Gilder Bay. And look at the amounts attached to these accounts."

The figures on the pages Digby scrolled through were at least in the tens of millions.

"These are kind of big companies . . . do you think one of these has something to do with Sally's kidnapping?" I said.

"I bet you all of these companies are actually just one big corrupt basket of snakes belonging to the same guy," Digby said. "I don't know if they have anything to do with Sally." He unplugged the USB drive and held it up. "Let's find out."

The copying done, Digby started closing out the folders he'd opened and restoring the desktop to its original state. But then he changed his mind and started reopening stuff.

"What are you doing? She's going to be back any minute," I said. "She's going to know."

"I'm counting on it. I want to see what she does next," he said. "Call my number." I did and he picked up. After he made sure our connection was good, he cracked the window and laid his phone on the outside ledge just beyond the glass pane.

We left the office door wide open and ran out the back door of the building. We put the call on speaker and listened to the assistant come back in, panic when she realized what had happened, and then pick up the phone and make a call.

She was obviously nervous, because she misdialed twice and slapped the desk before finally getting it right the third time. Her voice shook when the other party picked up. "Mr. Book? There's a problem. People broke in and . . . some kids pretending to be messengers . . . n-nothing . . . physically. But I think they opened my files. They left documents about the Irving property open on the screen." She was silent a long while. "You want the place cleaned up? Cleaned up or . . . ?" We heard her opening drawers. "I see. Yes, all right. This afternoon. I'll call them right now."

She hung up and dialed again. This time, she was more composed and all she said was, "For 152 Irving. Same day service. The works." And then she hung up.

A few minutes of normal office sounds later, we disconnected.

"That's Bullet Time's place," I said. "Wait. She's not even calling the police to report us breaking into her computer?"

Digby retrieved his phone from the windowsill and we dumped our armfuls of recycling on our way to the bus stop.

"We need a Batmobile," he said.

To my surprise, he flagged down the bus headed downtown. "We're going right now?" I said.

"You heard them. They're cleaning it up," he said.

"What does that mean?" I said.

"Means we better hurry," he said.

SEVENTEEN

We went back to 152 Irving—former crack house, possible former kidnapper's den, now home to Mary and Al, possible moonshiners with definite violent tendencies, who, this time, were definitely home.

Digby began to talk fast, running through the different ways we could break into the place. In the middle of his tirade, my phone rang with a message from Austin asking me to save him a place at lunch. I started to write a response, when Digby stopped his rambling to say, "Somewhere else you need to be?"

"Look, I think there's an easy way to do this," I said.

"Like what?" he said.

I knew he'd try to stop me, so I just headed toward the front door. For a change, it was Digby's turn to stop me. "What are you doing, Princeton?"

"You're overthinking it, Digby," I said. "Not everything calls for a dumb-ass stunt. I bet we just need to ask."

"Princeton, this might be our last chance to get access to

this place. And this place might be my last connection to my sister," he said.

That kind of shook me up. "Digby," I said.

"Whoa." Too real. He shook his head and said, "Or it could be *nothing* because anything that was ever there is long gone. Are you sure you know what you're doing?"

I nodded. "I mean . . . I think so."

He said, "Then okay."

I walked toward the front door, took out a five-dollar bill, and rang the bell. Mary answered the door. She didn't recognize me at first but when she did, her face turned to stone and she said, "Go away. That was one time. I ain't giving you more money."

"Please. We don't want any money. In fact, here." I held out the five-dollar bill. "I'd like to pay you back." And then I held up a twenty-dollar bill. "With interest."

Mary opened the door a crack, but when she went for the money, I moved my hands back out of her reach.

"But," I said.

"What?" Mary said.

"When I was last in there, I lost my mom's brooch," I said.

"I ain't found nothing," she said. Mary reached for the bills again, but I jerked them away again.

"Can *we* look?" I said.

"Yeah, right. I'm not letting you junkies back in here," she said. "Keep your money." She tried to slam the door shut on us, but luckily, I'd gotten the steel toe of my boot through the threshold, so the door bounced open.

"Fine. Then what say I call the police and have a talk about that little DIY drinks machine in your living room?" I said. I heard Digby's breath catch.

Mary moved aside and reached for the money as we walked in, but once more, I jerked it away and said, "I'll give it to you on our way out."

"Don't take nothing," Mary said.

I surveyed the heaps of junk and said, "I'll try to control myself."

• • •

"You look on that side and I'll look over here," Digby said. "And, Princeton, start near the corners."

"What?" I said. "Why the corners?"

"Because when people are afraid they usually"—Digby mimed curling up with balled fists in front of his face—"in the corner."

It was hard to imagine what tricks Digby's brain played on itself for him to be able to imagine that kind of stuff. I realized right then that Digby would either find Sally or go completely insane trying.

We walked the perimeter of the room, but it was soon obvious that even if there had been anything to see, it had been scrubbed by the cycles of deposit and erosion of Mary and Al's stuff. Digby pointed at a door leading to the back and asked Mary, "Can we?"

"I thought you said you were looking for something you dropped. It ain't in there . . ." Mary said. "No one's gone in there all seven years I've been here. I don't even have the key."

I smacked down the twenty-five dollars I'd been baiting her with on a nearby table and said, "And you can have fifty more after we finish taking a look."

Digby picked the lock and opened the door. The room was filled with piles of junk and we needed both hands to clear a path in front of us.

"Well, I suppose the good news is that we have more of a chance to find something here because clearly . . ." I pushed over a newspaper tower. "No one's cleaned up in years."

We split up and restarted our search. I knew neither what I was looking for nor what I was looking at. It was just junk. Furniture broken beyond salvage. Piles of bundled paper once headed for recycling that decayed on the spot instead. I tried not to think too deeply about the weird crunching noises my boots made as I walked across to the wall. I fanned my phone's light across the wall, wondering what qualified as noteworthy in a landscape as weird as this. And then I saw them.

Brightly colored scribblings hovering just above the baseboard where the walls met at the corner. Against the grimy palette of misery that colored the room, the oranges, reds, and pinks of the drawings qualified as noteworthy.

"Digby," I said. "Over here."

He scrambled over and shone the light on the spot I pointed out. He was silent.

"In the corner. Where you said it would be." I helped him clear the garbage in front of the drawings so he could take a closer look. "Is it her?"

Digby stared. "I don't know." He took photos of the drawings of blobby circles with squiggly lines trailing them. There were triangles floating around among them. Digby scratched at one of the images, studying the stuff that collected under his nail. "Crayon."

He shone his light on the other side of the corner where there were more drawings. These, though, were ominous: each one was of two black circles, one smaller circle set inside a larger circle, with crosses in the middle. "All the drawings look similar, but these are"—he pointed at the black circles and crosses—"closer to the baseboards, like she didn't want anyone to see them."

"She was only four," I said.

"She wasn't a normal kid," Digby said.

"So you *do* think it's her," I said.

"I don't know what to think." Digby shook his head. "Of course I want to believe, but—" He suddenly reared up and sniffed. "You smell that?"

I sniffed. "No . . ." And then I smelled it. "Someone's smoking?"

Digby and I navigated back through the junk piles to the hall, where, scarily, the smell of smoke got stronger.

"Fire?" I said.

Digby didn't answer, but when we got to the end of the hall, he touched the doorknob with the back of his hand, so clearly, he suspected there was a fire. When Digby pushed the door open, we were hit with a blast of air so hot, it blew us back onto our heels.

In the main room, a solid wall of fire was blocking us from the front door.

"There's another door on this side." Digby almost couldn't get the words out for all his coughing.

"Digby! Look!" I pointed at Mary, prone on the floor not far from where we were standing. He and I stumbled to her. By the time we'd dragged her over to the side door, we were half dead from the exertion. We peeled back the junk in front of the door and started crashing against it to get it open. I weakened with every hit. I felt like I was drowning, and my throat burned more every time I inhaled.

Behind us, one of the bottles of moonshine exploded. The alcohol caught fire and started spreading toward us. I was suddenly very aware we were standing in what was, essentially, a warehouse of kindling.

Then, just when I was about to pass out, I heard the distinct bursts of a fire extinguisher. A woman with a bandanna tied across her face was moving toward us, spraying the fire as she came. The extinguisher died and she chucked it and signaled for us to get away from the door. Digby was still pounding away at the lock, so I had to physically push him aside. Once we were clear, our rescuer drew a gun, blew apart the lock with two shots, and kicked the door open.

We stumbled out. I sucked down some air but panicked again when I still couldn't catch my breath. By this time, our rescuer had removed the bandanna to reveal that it was, in fact, Cooper's old partner, Detective Stella Holloway, who'd run into the fire and saved us.

Holloway had carried Mary out of the building and after setting her down on the ground, took a bottle of water from her coat pocket and tossed it to us. "Wash out your mouth. It'll help. Deep breaths, kids." And then, alarmingly, she didn't holster her gun and instead, she crept back around the building to the front, looking like she was expecting trouble.

Finally, we heard the fire engines' sirens and Holloway came back, holstering her gun. She had paramedics with her.

"That was close," Digby said.

I managed to whisper "Yeah" before I passed out.

EIGHTEEN

I was on a bed in the ER wearing an oxygen mask when I came to. I looked over and saw Digby on the bed next to me, arguing with a nurse that he didn't need his mask anymore. My head felt helium-filled, and everything was blurred at the edges.

Officer Stella Holloway came in the room and said, "Well, there I am when you two walk right into the middle of my stakeout followed by a pair of double-wide gangster types who start lighting the place on fire. Now, given our history, I guess I shouldn't be surprised anymore, but I should still ask . . ." She sat down next to me. "What the hell were you two doing?"

I was afraid to ask. "Is Mary all right?"

"She's been admitted, but she's okay," Holloway said. "I'm still going to book her for felony manufacturing, though."

"Zoe?" My mother walked into the room with our doctor. Her worry was instantly replaced by anger when she saw Holloway leaning over me on the bed.

Mom and Holloway traded stiff hellos and eyed each other

while the doctor discharged us and explained how our mild smoke inhalation was going to play out over the next few days.

"Can I talk to Zoe and Digby?" Holloway said.

"Are they under arrest?" Mom said.

Holloway looked surprised. "No, of course not. As far as I can tell, they're victims—"

"I don't understand. I thought you aren't working for the police anymore," Mom said.

"I'm a detective for the New York County District Attorney's office now," Holloway said. "And I really need to ask them—"

"Well, clearly they're in no shape," Mom said. "Maybe you can ask *Mike* later."

I thought my mother's hostility was weird, but Holloway's resulting embarrassment at the mention of Mike's name seemed a confirmation of some longer story I hadn't yet been told. In the next bed, Digby mouthed "uh-oh," replaced the oxygen mask over his face, and sank back into his pillow.

Mom barely acknowledged either Digby or me on the ride home. It was tense, but the awkwardness of Mom seething next to me was blown out of the water by the sight of my dad exploding out of our front door. I guess Mom didn't know he was coming either, because she moaned and said, "Oh, God . . ."

"Oh, man." I got out of the car and, as usual, felt both guilty and defensive the second my eyes met my father's. "Dad? What are you doing here?"

Digby said, "Hey, Dick, long time no see—"

"Shut up and piss off." Dad pointed at Digby. "You don't live here anymore. Go pack your things." Dad pointed at me. "You. Inside."

"Okay, okay . . . maybe we should all just calm down," Mom said.

"You can't throw him out," I said. "Where will he go?"

"I'm sure there are shelters downtown." Dad took a couple of hundred-dollar bills from his wallet and held them in Digby's face.

Digby looked past the money and said, "Zoe, you okay here?"

"That's rich coming from you. That's the second time you've put her in the hospital." Dad waved the bills even closer to Digby's face. "Take this and stay away from her." When Digby wouldn't take the bills, Dad threw them at him. Neither broke off from staring at the other as the bills flitted down and stuck to the driveway.

"This is ridiculous," I said.

Digby wasn't going to budge, so to end the standoff, Mom said, "Well, if someone's going to hit someone, then let it happen now because I'm getting hungry." She waited a long beat and said, "That's what I thought." She walked into the house and we all eventually followed her in.

"I'll go pack," Digby said, and went upstairs.

I was about to sit down in the living room, when my father said, "Sit down," so I instead went into the kitchen and put bread in the toaster. He followed me in, rubbing his eyes to dramatize how tired I made him.

183

Dad said, "It is three days before the SATs and here you are again, sabotaging your future—"

"First of all, we rescued a woman today. If we hadn't been there, she would've died in that fire—"

"What were you doing there in the first place? And are you skipping school again?" he said.

"The school called this morning," Mom said.

"I am seriously concerned about your lackadaisical approach to your future," Dad said.

I said, "You have no idea how much I've studied—"

"You haven't been studying," Dad said. "Your mother said you've been out every day."

I knew I was majorly selling myself out, but I said, "I've finished all the practice tests I bought and I've done about a hundred online ones. I've been preparing for months. I'm ready."

Dad snorted. "Ready? I doubt you're Ivy League ready."

That slap in the face was an excellent reminder of why you should never negotiate with terrorists. I said, "Why are you here, anyway? Couldn't you have yelled at me over the phone?"

"Glad you asked," Dad said, and walked out of the room.

As soon as we were alone, I asked Mom, "You asked him to come?"

"I just mentioned that you'd been out a lot these days. I *never* invited him to come," Mom said. "I'm sorry."

"Where's Mike?" I said.

"At the gym. I hope your dad's gone before Mike gets back," Mom said.

"Mom, why are you whispering? This is *your* house," I said.

Dad came into the room with a cotton laundry bag.

"What's that?" I said.

"This"—Dad tipped the bag and wads of bound bills dumped out—"is two hundred and seventy-five thousand dollars. It's what four years at Princeton looks like. Actually, this is what it cost a few years ago. It'll probably be over three hundred by the time you go, but I didn't want to be dramatic."

I noticed that in his effort to not be dramatic, my father had fattened up his statement pile by using bundles of twenties instead of hundred-dollar bills. I guess I wasn't awed enough, because he gave me the breakdown.

"Forty-two thousand tuition, eighteen thousand room and meals, college fees, student health, books, allowance, travel . . ." Dad sat next to me. "You know, Zoe, I didn't want to unnerve you on the eve of the most important exams you will face until the LSATs—"

"Well, thanks, Dad, that's not unnerving at all," I said.

Dad said, "Listen. You're young. It's hard to think about the future because the present is so fun." He struck a pose and rolled his eyes. "Lalalala . . . life is but a dream—"

I said, "What are you talking about? I think about the future all the time—"

"But you need to wake up, Zoe."

"I am awake."

"Wake up!" Dad said.

I said, "Yes, I keep telling you—"

"Wake up!" Then he clapped really loudly right in my face. "Because this is your *life*."

"No, it isn't."

"Excuse me?"

"It isn't my life. Princeton was your life. The LSATs were your life. You don't know anything about my life," I said.

"You mean catting around with boys?" Dad said. "*That's* what your life is?"

"Isn't it better I get it out of my system now than have some affair at work that blows up my marriage later?" I said.

Dad looked at Mom and said, "You let her talk to you like this?"

"She isn't wrong, Richard," Mom said.

"What are you talking about, Liza? Were you or were you not just texting me that you were worried . . ." Dad put on a high mocking voice and fluttered his hands. "Oooh, Richard, Zoe hasn't come home yet and she won't answer my texts. Oooh, Richard, now she's with that criminal kid again and I haven't seen her pick up a book all week long."

"Is that supposed to be Mom?" I said.

"Or is that limp-wristed feeble act an insult aimed at *all* women?" Mom said.

Dad said, "Oh, for God's sake, don't turn this into another one of your feminist rants . . ."

The fight was on. My work done, I took my toast and coffee and went into the living room just as Cooper walked in the front door.

"Who's your mother yelling at in there?" Cooper said.

"My father. You should probably just . . . go upstairs," I said.

"But I need to eat something," Cooper said.

I gave him my toast and coffee and we walked up the stairs together.

"So, Stella called me," Cooper said. "Is Digby still here?"

"He's packing up. My dad kicked him out," I said.

"We'll see about that," Cooper said. He knocked on the guest room door.

"Hey, Officer Cooper," Digby said. "I can see you already know."

"Can you please tell me how you've managed to insert yourself in Stella's investigation?" Cooper said.

"Do you know a lawyer named Jonathan Book?" Digby said. "His office is in the south-side business park?"

Out of habit, Cooper retrieved his notebook and wrote down the name. "Uh . . . no, I don't think I know him."

"I need help looking him up in the system," Digby said.

I eased past Cooper into Digby's room. "Whoa," I said. I suppose I'd expected to be bowled over by a huge mess, but the stacked and folded clothes and toiletries in little Ziploc bags were even more of a shock.

Cooper saw my expression and said, "It's the neat ones you really need to watch . . . they're organized, so they're harder to catch." To Digby, Cooper said, "Of course you know I'd be violating his rights if I started investigating him without cause. Who is he, anyway?"

"He's on the board of a real estate corporation that owns and manages a bunch of places in town . . ." Digby said. "One of them might be the building where my sister was held after she was kidnapped."

"What?" Cooper was shocked. "You're sure?"

"Well . . . I think. Maybe," Digby said. "Definitely maybe."

"Even if it were the place . . . it isn't a crime to have felonious tenants, Digby," Cooper said. "But. I *will* ask Stella. Maybe she turned up something on him while she was working her case. Illegal manufacturing and distribution of alcohol . . . but I guess you know that." Cooper flipped his notebook shut. "Good enough?"

Digby nodded. "Good enough." He held out his hand for Cooper to shake. "You know my number."

Cooper said, "Want me to make a stink? You don't have to go."

"Nah. I'm ready to go." Digby held up an empty bag of Cheez Doodles. "Besides, this house is officially out of food."

I walked Digby downstairs to the front door.

"I'm really sorry, Digby."

"It's okay, Princeton. I'm sorry that your dad is the person he is. On the upside, this'll probably make things easier between you and Austin," Digby said.

Austin. I hadn't answered any of his messages all day.

I went back upstairs after Digby left and found Cooper hanging around outside my bedroom door. He pointed in the direction of my parents' yelling in the living room. I was glad to hear that unlike her past arguments with my dad, my mother was putting up a fight. "What are they fighting about?"

"They're worried I'm not ready for my SATs on Saturday because I've been goofing off with Digby this last week," I said.

"Well? Are you ready?" Cooper said.

"Yeah. I mean, can I guarantee I'll do well?" I shrugged. "But I'm ready to take it."

Cooper looked at me hard and then nodded. "Okay."

"Ha. Just like that," I said.

"Sure. But then again, I haven't spent seventeen years of my life worrying about you, so I can afford to be cool," Cooper said. "So, uh . . . did you know your dad was coming?"

I shook my head.

"You're flying down to see him next weekend, so it's weird he's here, isn't it?" Cooper said.

I shrugged again.

"You said they're worried about you? So they're talking? How much are they talking?"

I didn't say anything. I remembered Digby once explained to me what dry snitching was. I wondered if I'd done just that with my silence.

A heartbeat later, Cooper said, "Sorry . . . I'm sorry. That was not appropriate." He fled the scene in shame.

I was still hungry, so I went back down to heat up some food. Mom and Dad's fight about me had blossomed into a retrial of my parents' past crimes against each other. I was at the sink, washing dishes and thinking about how, perversely, all the yelling made me nostalgic, when Digby's face suddenly popped up outside the window in front of me.

I opened the window and threw the sponge at him. "You scared the crap out of me. Did you forget something?"

"I need a favor," he said. "Come with me?"

"What?" I pointed in the direction of the shouting. "I don't think I'm even done getting in trouble for the last thing I did wrong."

"Please," he said. "I'm going home and I haven't spoken to my mother in years. I'm nervous. Help?"

"How can *I* help?" I said. But the look on his face told me this was one of the rare instances when Digby wasn't being even a little bit sarcastic. "Okay." I shut the window and pointed toward the back.

On the way to the stairs, I ducked into the living room and said to my parents, "I'm going to bed." And, as was always the case, they were too busy fighting over my welfare to actually pay attention to me. Even when I said I was going to bed at five p.m.

I went into my room, locked the door, climbed out onto the tree branch by my window, and shimmied down. I was creeping toward Digby when Mom looked out the window and caught sight of me. We both froze. After a second, though, Mom maneuvered herself so that I'd be obscured from my father's view as I ran across.

"Too bad your mother can't seem to stay away from your dad," Digby said. "He's such bad news and yet she keeps coming back for more."

"Yeah," I said. "What's her problem, right?"

And we jogged to the bus stop.

NINETEEN

I realized it wouldn't be a normal homecoming when he had us sneak back to his house via the back door and he signaled me to tiptoe when I went up the stairs. I said, "I don't know why when you said you were going home, I assumed you meant through the front door."

Digby led me to the room at the end of the second-floor hall, shut the door, and turned on the light. After my eyes adjusted, I found myself standing in what must have been Sally's room. Dust covered everything and it looked like it had been left untouched for years. The window's sash, I noticed, was patchy with black fingerprint powder.

He ran his fingers along the spines of the books on Sally's shelf before pulling off the blanket on his sister's bed to reveal the bedding underneath.

"I thought I'd made up the memory," he said.

I didn't need to check the duvet's pattern against the photo on Digby's phone to know the balloons and circus tents on

191

Sally's old sheets looked just like the crayon scribblings we'd found on the warehouse wall downtown.

"God. Then that *was* her writing on that wall," I said. "But not the other ones. The black circles with X's."

"Wait. I just remembered . . ." Digby walked down the hall into what must have been his childhood room. It was neat, which would've been a surprise had I not seen the way he kept the guest room. What was interesting, though, was that instead of normal boy stuff like pictures of robots or superheroes, Digby's walls had things like a periodic table and charts summarizing the reigns of English kings and the Egyptian pharaohs tacked up. I felt like I was getting a glimpse into how his evil genius developed.

He got out his knife and tore off part of the wallpaper beside his bed. There were more triangles and circles in various kinds of ink on it. "She started drawing on walls the second she could hold a pen . . ."

"That's why I put up wallpaper." We both jumped at the sound of Digby's mom's voice behind us. I hadn't even heard the door open. "Because it was easier to wash the ink off wallpaper. But it backfired because then she thought I could wash the ink off all the walls in the house."

I'd never seen Digby's mom up close before. I realized for the first time how much Digby looked like her. They had the same puppy dog eyes and the long gangly body. Steady and sober, she looked like an entirely different person from the one I'd seen last fall swigging champagne from a bottle and lighting an impromptu bonfire on her lawn.

"Philip? What are you doing here? You found something?" Digby's mom said.

Digby said, "Maybe? I might have seen Sally's drawings on a wall in a building downtown."

His mother looked stunned. And then she said, "I need to call him." To the empty space where she'd been standing, Digby said, "Also, I'm fine, Mom. Glad you asked. Haven't seen you in years . . ."

I sat down on the bed. He plopped down next to me and we both lay back.

"My God, this day just keeps going," I said.

"Hey . . . girl in my bed," he said. "Eleven-year-old me just high-fived present me."

"Really? You can still joke?" I said.

"Who's joking? How many times do I need to remind you how the mind of a seventeen-year-old guy works?" Digby said. "We are always good to go."

"Wait. Did your mother say, 'I need to call him'?" I said. "Who's 'him'?" When Digby didn't seem to want to get out of bed, I said, "Don't you think we should go find out?"

"Yeah. I just need a second. It's . . . I haven't spoken to my mother in years . . ."

I wanted to comfort him but I'd seen him like this before. He needed to retreat into himself, so I lay next to him, silent.

"Okay," he said. "Let's go."

We walked into the kitchen just as Digby's mother finished her phone conversation and hung up.

"Mom, we need to talk about Sally," Digby said.

To me, Digby's mom said, "I'm Val. It's nice to meet you, Zoe." She shook my hand. Then she went over to Digby. Her hand hesitated in midair before she reached out to stroke his arm. "Look at my guy . . . too proud to ask how I knew who you are."

Digby looked away when she hugged him. "I think I know what happened to Sally after they took her," he said.

Val stayed in the hug and said, "Yes, honey, I do too."

Digby pulled away and stared at her hard. And then he walked out of the kitchen.

Val turned to me and said, "Would you like some milk and cookies . . . or maybe pretzels? Actually, it's time to bring out the big guns. Go on in. I'll make Hot Pockets. I bought some when I heard Philip was back in town."

"You knew he was back?" I said. "How?"

"Go ahead. I'll bring them in," she said.

I went out to the living room.

"You know when you're a kid and the grown-ups would spell out the words so you wouldn't know you were going to the D-O-C-T-O-R?" he said. "I just realized the last nine years of my life have been like that."

"Are you okay?" I said.

"I just feel like an idiot for ever thinking I knew what was going on," he said.

I walked around the room, pretending to look at pictures and books while Digby stewed.

Val came in with Hot Pockets and little cartons of chocolate milk. I was relieved to see Digby wasn't too upset to eat. He

194

took a huge bite and of course, burned his tongue. As I handed him the chocolate milk I'd opened in anticipation of exactly this, Val patted my hand. "I'm glad Philip has a girlfriend looking out for him."

"Nope. Zoe has a boyfriend," Digby said. "Do you know a man named Book?"

"You know, it'd be better if we waited. The negotiator who was helping us back then is coming over." Val peeked out the window. "He'll be here any minute."

"Negotiator? Like, a *kidnap* negotiator?" Digby said. "So all these years you've known it was a kidnap for money? Then what are we waiting for? Let's call the FBI."

"It isn't that simple," Val said.

"Is Sally dead?" Digby said.

"They never gave us any proof she died," Val said.

"But there's no proof she's alive either?" When Val was quiet, Digby said, "So, that means she's dead. Grow up, Mom."

Even for Digby, that was too crappy a thing to say. "Dude, come on," I said.

"Probably dead and at the bottom of a lake somewhere," Digby said. Now he was just being cruel. "How much did they want?"

Val sat down, staring at her hands and crying.

"Shut up." I threw the half-empty milk carton at him. "What's the matter with you?"

Digby took his time wiping the milk from his face. When he was done, he said, "Thank you for that, Princeton. I think that's as close as I'll ever get to being possessed."

"Don't kid yourself. You're also like that when you're hangry," I said. "Why do you think I carry granola bars everywhere?"

The back door opened. Digby peered around the corner and said, "Oh, thank God. I at least called that one . . ."

And then Fisher walked into the room. Without having changed anything at all since I last saw him at the store, the Fisher standing in front of me was a completely different man. He had a slightly apologetic smile, but there was a hardness to his face I'd never seen before.

"Fisher?" I said.

"Who are you, really?" Digby said.

"Your parents hired me," Fisher said.

"Then why have I never seen you before?" Digby said.

"Your parents couldn't let the police or FBI know they were negotiating independently for your sister's return," Fisher said. "I worked behind the scenes."

"What? Why? The FBI has negotiators," Digby said. "Couldn't *they* do the negotiating?"

"Philip, nine years ago, I was part of a research group subcontracted to the government. Your father and I decided not to tell you kids anything about my classified research until Sally was old enough to consistently tell our cover story correctly," Val said. "When Sally was taken, we got a ransom demand telling me to turn over material on one of our top secret projects."

"But you couldn't just turn over classified government research," Digby said.

"A friend in Washington put me in touch with Fisher and he coached us through our double agenda . . . we pretended to cooperate with the authorities while hiding the fact that we were negotiating for Sally . . . that's why we didn't tell the police or the FBI about the ransom demand at all," Val said.

"And what happened when you didn't give them what they wanted . . . ?" Digby said.

"No, honey . . . you don't understand. We did give it to them. Well, we tried to," Val said. "I made copies of my work—"

"Mom." I'd never seen the expression on Digby's face before. He looked more frightened than he had even at gunpoint. "That's . . ."

"Treason. Yes. I know." Val nodded. "And your father tried to stop me. He wanted to tell the FBI. Things weren't the same between us after I did that."

"But what? They double-crossed you?" Digby said. "Why didn't we get Sally back?"

"Well, the problem was, I couldn't get to all of my research that night we broke in, and when I tried again, my credentials had been revoked. Perses put me on administrative leave," Val said. "They claimed they were doing it for me . . . for my health, they said. I think they suspected I was trying to steal information, but since they couldn't prove anything . . ."

"But what were you actually working on?" Digby said.

"Just . . . theoretical stuff. A goof of mine, really," Val said. "We were playing with using nanotechnology to substitute for chemical interventions in biological organisms. Deliver drugs with more precision, for example—"

"Or biological weapons," Digby said.

"We never intended that," Val said. "It was just a grant proposal I never expected to go anywhere. I mean, I was riffing on a physics joke Richard Feynman made . . . FUN. Feynman's *Unbuildable* Nanorobotics. Except somehow people heard and started talking—and, I mean, it was mostly to laugh and say it was doomed to fail," Val said. "Scientists are bitchy creatures."

"Wait, sorry . . . nanotechnology and chemistry. Isn't that Felix's dad's job?" I said.

"Yes, they gave it to Timothy Fong after they put me on leave. He's good, but . . ." Val shrugged in a way that made it clear what she meant. She laughed. "I told you. Scientists are bitchy creatures."

"Did you tell the kidnappers you couldn't get the whole ransom together?" Digby said.

"I turned over the research I *did* have with some . . . bridging material to make the whole thing more cohesive," Val said.

"You made stuff up," Digby said. "Sally was counting on you and you gave them garbage?"

"It was my idea. Two weeks had gone by. Your parents were starting to crack," Fisher said. "I made a judgment call."

"You probably got her killed," Digby said.

"We don't know she's dead, Digby," Fisher said. "There's never been any proof—"

"What, you still drawing a retainer, buddy? Stop it. She's dead. You got her killed," Digby said. "And if I'd known what you had my mother do, I would never have bothered coming back here looking for Sally."

It occurred to me that the disappointment and anger in Digby's voice was the first hint he'd ever dropped that he'd been hoping to find his sister alive even after nine years.

"But I feel her, honey. I still feel her. Even though it looks bleak . . ." Val said. "I choose to listen to my feelings."

"Well, *I* choose to grow up. Which is a choice I made a long time ago when you and Dad checked out on me." To Fisher, Digby said, "So. Sally's dead. Now, what can you tell me about the people who took her?"

Val walked out. She wasn't crying anymore, but it was obvious she was going to the next room to do exactly that.

"Before we get into it . . ." Fisher turned to me. "I owe you an apology, Zoe. I'm sorry I lied to you."

"Why me, even?" I said.

"When Digby left town last year, he asked for copies of his sister's police files and the request Detective Holloway filed triggered an alert I put in place nine years ago," Fisher said. "I figured, I'm retired, this case has always bothered me . . . I came here and asked around. I found out who you were and I knew he'd seek you out when he came back. I got a job as a manager so I could keep in contact." Fisher put his hand on my shoulder. "I'm very sorry. I want you to know that even though I had an objective, my friendship with you was real."

"How much?" Digby said. "How much did my parents pay you?"

"I didn't keep any of the money," Fisher said. He knew where Digby was going with it, though, and said, "They ran into financial trouble because they both lost their jobs with Perses. And after the media was done with them, they also both lost their security clearances, so they had problems getting even civilian work."

I could tell that Digby hadn't known any of this. I could also tell that he hated being caught off-guard in front of Fisher. "Tell me what you know about Sally."

Fisher took out some thick files from his bag. "Here's what I've got. Ever heard of the de Groot family?" When Digby indicated he hadn't, Fisher said, "The public knows very little about them, but they have a piece of everything: petroleum, pharma, defense, agriculture, food processing, telecom, logistics, insurance . . . it's easier to name industries where we wouldn't find their money."

"How can a family that rich stay anonymous?" Digby said.

"They use their influence to stay invisible. Google the Mars family—it's the same thing. They have people working to keep them out of sight. No photos, no interviews, just a lot of insane rumors," Fisher said.

"Like?" Digby said.

"They're a New York Old Dutch family. They've been here since pre-Colonial times and they've been rich since the 1500s too. And they say even now, the de Groots raise their kids speaking Dutch. And there's more urban legend-y stuff like the cousins intermarry. Or, how since the fifties, they've been cryogenically preserving their dead," Fisher said. "Just weird stuff."

"And you think they took Sally because—?" Digby said.

"For a while before Sally was taken, representatives of the de Groot family were hounding your mother, asking her to come work for them. They promised her the kind of funding and support not even the government could give . . ." Fisher said. "They were so aggressive. Of course, we don't definitely know it's them, but . . . there was something about how persistent they were and then they suddenly backed off."

"There's a lawyer here in town. Jonathan Book. He runs a holding company—a series of them, actually—that owns and manages the building where I think Sally was held after she disappeared. We found these drawings there." Digby showed him the photographs. "They look like her drawings upstairs."

"Where's this?" Fisher said. "Let's go."

"It burned down," I said. "With us in it."

Digby passed him a photo of Book that he'd found online. "This is from at least ten years ago when he was a partner at his New York firm, which is exactly when you might've come across him. Ring any bells?"

"Jonathan Book? Book . . ." Fisher said. "Not the face, but the name might be familiar. Help me look. Maybe on a letter somewhere . . . they wrote to offer Val a job at one point?"

Fisher and Digby dove into the files. There was a huge crash in the kitchen, but Digby and Fisher didn't even look up. They didn't miss me when I left to go into the kitchen, where I found Val on the ground, crying and picking up shards of broken dishware. When I walked in, she said, "I always imagined they were watching . . . and I thought if they maybe saw I'd given them everything I had and there was nothing left, they'd just let Sally come back," she said. "I destroyed my career . . . my family . . . my son . . . destroyed my mind, really . . . But when I heard Philip was back, I just felt hopeful again. For the first time in years, I felt hopeful. I'm not even drinking anymore . . ."

Val's hand was cut and bleeding, so I led her to the sink.

"Don't *you* think I'll get her back?" Val said.

"I think . . ." She didn't want to hear me say anything besides yes, but on top of everything she was going through, I also didn't think she needed me lying to her. "Digby is trying very hard and he's really good at things like this."

"He trusts you. I can tell." Val smiled. "And Fisher says he thinks you two might be . . ."

"No, no . . . we're just friends," I said. "And trust me . . . that's exhausting enough."

Val sighed. "I can guess it isn't easy being Philip's friend." I didn't say anything, so she went on. "The thing is, when Sally disappeared, I think everybody forgot Philip was just a little boy himself. Especially his dad . . . for days after Sally disappeared, Joel tortured him." Her entire demeanor changed as she mimicked her husband yelling at Digby. "'What did you see, Philip? How did you not hear anything when you were in the next room, Philip? Remember *something*, Philip. *Try*, Philip. Try *harder*.' And I was so devastated about Sally, I didn't protect Philip . . ."

Val's hand finally stopped bleeding and I helped her dry off.

"Thank you, Zoe," Val said. She'd stopped crying. "Thank you for taking care of him."

"Um. I should . . ." I pointed at the living room and ran off.

• • •

Fisher and Digby were still hunting through the stack of papers. I watched them for a while until the mess got to me. I started picking up the pieces of paper they'd dropped.

"I could swear I saw that name somewhere," Fisher said. "Maybe in one of these newspaper clippings?"

"Nah. Then it would have shown up on Google," Digby said.

I was organizing the stray papers into a discard pile when I found an IPO brochure for one of the de Groots' companies that offered Digby's mother a job. Out of habit, I turned to the last page. And there I saw it. "Digby," I said. When he started instead to talk to Fisher, I put the brochure right in his face. "Look. Look who the lawyers were on this de Groot deal."

Digby read out, "'Legal Matters: The validity of the shares of common stock offered hereby will be passed upon for us by Arkin, Walham, and *Book* LLP, New York, New York.'" Digby got on his phone to check that the law firm's Book was our guy.

"I used to read the back pages of these things because I loved seeing my father's name on big stock offerings," I said.

"It's the same guy," Digby said. "Jonathan Garfield Book. Partner Emeritus."

Fisher flopped back onto the couch. "Oh, thank God . . . I felt like I was going crazy," he said.

"I hate to be the party-pooper, but the de Groots seem to

have lots of fingers in lots of pies . . . I mean, wouldn't we find a link between them and basically every big law firm there is?" I said.

"Yeah, but how many partners of big law firms end up in River Heights owning a company that manages a building with my sister's writing on its walls?" Digby said. "This is all the proof *I* need."

"The narrative works for me," Fisher said.

"But will it work for the police?" I said.

"The police?" Digby said. "Who's going to the police? You heard my mother. She committed treason."

"Then now what?" I said.

"Yeah, now what?" Fisher said.

"Now I need to think," Digby said. "I want to make these guys pay."

"Well . . . let me know what you come up with. This is as far as I got nine years ago," Fisher said. "And I've been stuck ever since."

"Why *are* you here? How is my mother paying you?" Digby said.

"Sally Digby is the one and only victim I never found. I'm done working the job, but Sally . . ." Fisher said, "she's stayed with me."

Digby nodded. "Yeah."

TWENTY

When I left Digby's house, he was running through potential next moves with Fisher. To be honest, I didn't think he'd make it through the night there and I'd gone to bed half expecting to be woken up by him, coming in my window, asking to stay in the guest bedroom. He was either better adjusted or deeper in denial than I'd thought, though, because, according to his text, he slept in his old bed and woke up feeling good.

I, on the other hand, was a wreck. The ER doctor had warned us that the effects of smoke inhalation were often worse the day after, and boy, was she ever right. I still felt fine when I left Digby's place. And then my throat started to feel raw when I crawled into bed. By the time I woke up the next morning, my head was throbbing and my throat was so sore, I could barely swallow. I hadn't been to school all week, but Mom could see I was legitimately in no shape to go in, and after she called school to get my absence excused, she left me to sleep.

Later that afternoon, I got a text from Austin that he wanted to meet me in my backyard. He was lurking by the garbage cans when I got outside.

"I didn't want to bother you in case . . . you know . . ." Austin said. "I don't want you to get yelled at again."

"Oh, my dad? He's not here. In fact, no one's home. You could've just come to the front door," I said. "You're welcome to come in. But you should know . . . I'm still all messed up."

"No, I know . . ." Austin said. "It's okay. I just came to give you this . . ." He handed me a gallon jug of milk.

"Milk?" I said.

"You said your sinuses were dry, so I asked around . . . one of the trainers said maybe you needed help making mucus," Austin said. "Milk helps with that."

"Austin. That's so sweet." I hugged him and stayed in the hug for a long time, seriously questioning some of the choices I'd made in the last few days.

"Zoe . . . I wanted to talk to you about something—"

"I know, I know. I've been a crazy person this past week. I'm so sorry. Just let me get through this test and I promise I'll be a totally different person," I said. "Back to normal."

"You mean I won't see you until then?" he said.

"No, I mean, I'm coming to school tomorrow, but I don't think I can really be a human being until after I take the test," I said. "Plus, my dad is taking me to dinner tomorrow and that's a whole nother kind of stress."

"He's still in town?" Austin said.

"I think he wants to physically make sure I get to my test before he leaves," I said.

"Yikes," Austin said. "Okay. It can wait . . ."

I closed my eyes for our kiss and when I opened them, I was shocked to see Digby standing directly behind Austin.

I said, "Digby."

Austin said, *"Austin."*

Digby said, "Zoe."

"Digby," Austin said. "Why am I even surprised?"

"Who knows, man. The mind is a mysterious labyrinth," Digby said.

Austin turned his back to Digby. "What's he doing here? Allie said your dad kicked him out."

"He did," I said. "Digby? What's up?"

Digby pointed at the gym bag he was carrying.

"I was just at Henry's place."

It took me a second to work out that it was the bag of steroids from our failed fake drug deal with Silk and Papa John.

"Listen, can I come in? I'm pretty sure I'm being followed." Digby didn't wait for an answer and pushed past us.

"Did he just say he's being followed?" Austin said.

Austin and I went into the house, where Digby was lowering the shades in the front room.

"What's going on?" I said.

"Come here. Look." Digby pressed up against the wall beside the window, parted the blinds, and pointed at a black SUV parked across the street.

"This again?" I said. "Are you sure that isn't the Dans' car?"

"No, these guys have been on me since I left my mom's house," Digby said.

"Why would someone be following you?" Austin said.

Digby gave me a look that was, essentially, a plea not to talk about his family's situation in front of Austin.

"Sorry, Austin, can Digby and I just . . ." I guided Digby into the hallway outside the front room.

"I mean, it could be about the drugs." I pointed at the gym bag.

"That actually would make sense, because someone broke into Henry's house last night and beat him up," Digby said. "But then again, I've had this bag with me all day and they haven't made a move to get it back."

"Is Henry okay?" I said.

"Well, they tore him up again, but it could've been a lot worse. Thank God his sister got home when she did. She beat the tar out of one of them," Digby said.

"Henry got beaten up? Is that his bag? Did you say drugs?" Austin said. When Digby and I traded looks instead of answering him, he said, "I'm sick of this. How long am I supposed to be cool with you and him acting like you have some big secret I don't get to be part of? You know what? Fine. Whatever." Austin walked toward the front door but at a slower than normal pace because he fully expected me to call him back.

And of course he was right to be mad. I wouldn't have been nearly as patient with him if he'd acted the way I'd been acting.

"Austin, wait. That bag is full of steroids. Henry . . . found it. And he wants us to get it to the police without busting the guys on the team who are juicing," I said.

I was just congratulating myself on doing a good job at sketching out the situation when Austin said, "I *knew* there was no way he was naturally recovering from his injuries so fast. Who else is doing them? He's selling?"

"Wait wait wait, no. Henry isn't using them *or* selling them—of course not." I grabbed Austin's arm. "And you have to swear you won't tell anyone, Austin, seriously."

"Okay, okay, I swear," Austin said. "Ow. That hurts."

Digby turned around and ran upstairs.

"Oh, come on. What are you doing?" I dropped Austin's arm and followed Digby. I found him digging through my closet.

"Excuse me? Can I help you with something?" I said.

The pile of stuff he'd thrown out of my closet was growing. He found a bright green duffel bag Mom had gotten as a free gift for a magazine subscription. Digby dumped the contents of Silk's gym bag onto my bed and started repacking it into the green bag. When he was done, he slid the bag of steroids under my mattress.

"Um . . . what are you doing?" I said. "You're not leaving that here. What if they come here next?"

"This is a cop's house. They wouldn't be that stupid," Digby said. "It's really the safest place for it."

"So, you don't think the guys in the truck outside are here for the steroids? You think they're Book's people following you because you broke into that office," I said. "But, really, you don't even know for sure if they *are* following you."

"I can prove it." And then he gave me that look.

"Oh, no. I know that face. What? You have a dumb-ass stunt in mind," I said. "I can't. I have company." I pointed downstairs.

"Oh, but he gets to participate in this one," Digby said. "In fact, we *need* Austin for this next play to work."

"Need Austin for what play to work?" Austin joined us in my room.

Instead of explaining, Digby started to strip off his clothes.

"Um . . . Zoe?" Austin said.

• • •

We were ready to go a half an hour later. Austin and Digby had switched clothes. We'd stuffed old newspapers into Silkstrom's gym bag.

As he and Digby swapped car keys, Austin recapped the plan. "So I'm going to get in Digby's mom's car, drive to the store, then make sure they see I'm not Digby. They'll think they lost your tail, and then you two can follow without them suspecting. Got it," Austin said.

"You and Digby can switch keys tomorrow at school," I said.

"I guess that's your way of telling me we're not hanging out tonight?" Austin kissed me on the cheek. "That's okay, babe. You know, I think I see how this could be fun."

Seeing Austin in Digby's clothes was a shock. I'd expected him to be bursting out of it like Henry had when he'd borrowed Digby's jacket but somehow, Digby's suit fit Austin. And it looked great.

"Is it just me or do I look *sharp* in this suit?" Austin said.

"Looks sharp on everybody, man," Digby said.

"And I didn't think it would be this comfortable," Austin said.

Digby, meanwhile, looked comical in Austin's off-hours jock uniform. The sweatpants, the letterman jacket, the baseball cap . . .

Digby slipped his feet into Austin's running shoes. "Echhh . . . they're warm," he said. "God, I hate this stupid plan."

"It's *your* plan," I said.

"Will it work?" Austin said. "Or will they, like, attack me when they realize I duped them?"

"Oh, it'll work. The only question I have is, will I get athlete's foot?" Digby said.

Austin slung the decoy bag over his shoulder. "All right. Let's do this." And then he clapped like he was breaking from a huddle.

"Austin, you know you don't have to . . ." I said. "But thank you."

"No, I want to," Austin said.

"Just be careful, please." I said. I kissed Austin. I didn't care that Digby was rolling his eyes at me and I kissed Austin a second time before letting him go.

Austin jogged to Digby's mother's car. I noticed that he even changed the way he ran to imitate Digby's loping stride.

We watched Austin drive off and my heart lurched when the black SUV drove off behind him seconds later.

"You know, sometimes, I hate it when I'm right," Digby

said. "But interestingly, I mind it a lot less now that those guys think Austin is me."

"Let's go," I said.

Austin followed Digby's instructions perfectly and got out of the car at the supermarket parking lot. He turned and looked around so the people in the SUV could get a good look at his face. Clearly, it came as a surprise to them that it hadn't been Digby in the car, because the SUV actually parked for a while, probably so its driver could regroup. After the SUV set off again, Digby was careful to keep a good distance as we followed in Austin's mother's car.

"By the way, it was super-devious the way you got Austin to do this by calling it a 'play' and making it sound all football-y," I said.

"Tapped into his lizard brain, you mean?" Digby said.

"Yeah. Makes me wonder . . . how do you tap into mine to get me to do things?" I said.

"Oh, come on, Princeton. I don't do that to you," he said. "You're too evolved."

He exhaled and shook his head.

"What?" I said.

"I guess maybe I'm nervous?" Digby said. "I haven't really worked out a plan, exactly. In my mind, it'd always been a question of figuring out who did it and then telling the police."

"Well, but, I mean, like you said, we're just following to see where we end up," I said. "You don't have to have the whole thing worked out."

• • •

We eventually turned onto the interstate and went on what turned out to be a long ride before the SUV signaled to exit.

"I should've guessed," Digby said.

The SUV was headed for Bird's Hill, the same place as Sloane's family's summer home. We turned onto the road that wound upward. Digby stooped over the wheel, peering through the windshield at something farther uphill.

"What's that?" he said.

All I saw ahead were huge old-growth trees and a spectacularly steep rocky slope all the way down toward the river. "Trees? What? I don't see anything."

Digby held me by the chin and turned my face. "Look."

"But—"

"Look with your eyes, Princeton."

I was about to protest that I still didn't see anything when the hilltop glinted in an unearthly way. "What . . ."

"It's a huge mirror." Digby pointed. "Watch that bird."

A big black crow swooped past a patch of hilltop and was abruptly doubled. Its reflection indicated that the mirrored façade stretched at least a hundred yards across.

We watched the SUV disappear through a discreet gate set into a huge stone wall. "When people work this hard not to be seen . . ." Digby drove a little ways past, parked on the side of the road, and killed the engine. ". . . I really want to look."

Digby got out of the car. I opened my door but didn't commit to following him.

"Digby, we're going to get busted for trespassing."

Digby threw the car keys for me to catch. "Say you got lost," he said.

"Why don't *you* say you got lost?" I threw the keys back to him.

"They'd believe it more if you were driving." Digby threw the keys to me again.

This time, I threw the keys *at* him. Hard.

"Hey," he said.

"That was sexist," I said.

"*I'm* not sexist. I'm saying *they* are." He shook off the hand he'd used to catch the keys and said, "Now help me punish those sexist pigs with some trespassing."

We hiked past the gate and went along the stone wall. Soon we were in the trees, where the ground was a combination of mud, slippery rocks, and gnarly roots.

"Aha," Digby said.

"What 'aha'?" I didn't see any vulnerabilities.

"They cut all the lower branches by the wall." He pointed at a nearby tree. "But they missed this one."

The branch he was talking about wasn't much more than a nub. "That thing's not going to take your weight," I said.

"Oh, come on, Princeton . . . what's happened to you?" He shimmied up the tree and straddled the branch.

"Well?" I said.

Digby put his finger to his lips, pointed at the scene over the wall, and held up two fingers. I assumed he meant there were two people on the other side who'd hear me. He took out his phone and wiggled it at me so I'd put it on vibrate. Then he texted: "Need some big rocks."

I found one and used both arms to throw it up to him. I overestimated the distance it had to travel, though, and if Digby hadn't ducked, I would've taken his head off with it. He reemerged from ducking down low on the branch, angry. I grimaced and pantomimed my apology.

He texted: "holy cow P put some smaller ones in ur pocket n get up here."

I'd never climbed a tree before, but I went. One foot up, one hand up, and repeat until I was easing myself onto the branch behind Digby. Only then did I notice how high up we were.

The compound beyond the wall was enormous. It was a cluster of big buildings covering the entire hilltop. Some were old and ivy-covered while others were starkly modern. The compound had obviously grown over a long time. The mirrored building facing the public road was closest to us and judging by the many black vehicles parked outside it, it was some kind of garage.

"This is huge," I said.

"It has a helipad." Digby pointed at the back of the property.

"What is this place?" I said, even though I suspected we already knew.

There were three identical black SUVs and a dark blue sedan parked side by side. Two men in coveralls removed one of the SUVs' wheels and walked into the garage.

"Hand me those rocks." When I gave him the two rocks I'd brought with me, he said, "Two? That's it? How good do you think my aim is? Oh, I forgot. You've been dating a jock."

Digby hurled the rock over the wall toward one SUV that

had an opened door. I cringed, anticipating the crash of breaking glass. Instead, the rock thunked off the windshield without
breaking it.

"Look how thick that is." Digby pointed at the cross-section
of the SUV's opened door. "All that is armor and the glass is
obviously bulletproof . . . they probably all are." He threw the
second rock at the sedan, expecting the same ineffectual thunk
he got from the first rock. This time, though, the sedan's windshield blew up into a cobweb of broken glass.

"Ooops."

I heard the mechanics shouting and without discussion,
Digby and I swung off the branch and partially climbed and
partially slid down the tree. We hit the ground running.

TWENTY-ONE

For a brief second, as we rounded the tree line, I thought we were going to get away. But then I saw two men in matching buzz cuts and suits standing near Austin's mom's car, all business and unspoken threats. Their differing heights were the only feature I could use to distinguish one from the other.

The taller one said, "Would you two come with us, please?"

"Hey, guys. We were goofing around and we seem to have broken a window. Sorry about that," Digby said. "Kids these days, amiright?" He kept walking to the car. "I'd be happy to get my mom to mail you a check."

Taller Guy stepped in front of the driver's-side door.

"The boss said he wants to talk about your sister," Shorter Guy said.

"Is this an invitation or a demand?" Digby said.

I took out my phone and after a quick round of calculations, chose to send an in-case-we-go-missing message to Sloane. True, we still hadn't made up from the last fight we'd had at my house, but she was part of our unholy alliance and I knew that if things went wrong, she'd mobilize for Digby and me without needing a ton of explanations. Plus, her house was just down the hill. "I've let our friend know we're here," I said.

"The boss just wants a chat," Taller Guy said. "He even ordered you food."

When Digby and I didn't move, Shorter Guy said, "You can keep your phones. Honestly, it's okay."

Digby and I followed them on foot through the gate and up the long driveway to the main house. As we walked, Digby said, "Should I have left you behind so you could call the cops if I didn't come back?"

"I wasn't going to let you go alone. You aren't even thinking straight," I said.

"Not thinking straight?" Digby said. "Says who?"

"If you were, you would *never* have let me come with you and you certainly wouldn't have thrown that second rock," I said.

Digby tapped Taller Guy on the shoulder. "So, *are* we being kidnapped?" When he didn't get an answer, Digby said, "Do we get to see a de Groot in the flesh?"

"It'll be just a few more minutes," Taller Guy said.

"Yeah, no spoilers. The boss likes to manage his appearances," Shorter Guy said.

"With a build-up like this, I'm going to be disappointed if he doesn't come out high-kicking in sequins and feathers," Digby said.

Shorter Guy laughed, but Taller Guy looked at him hard

until he stopped. Shorter Guy cleared his throat and said, "Anyway. It'll be just a few more minutes."

They ushered us through the predictably grand main house done in what Sloane had called fake American castle style. We passed room upon stuffy room, including one with a dining table long enough to seat everyone I knew.

Taller Guy led us into a renovated hallway entirely unlike the rest of the stone-and-woodwork mansion. The glossy white annex beyond was lit to convey cleanliness and hygiene. It smelled like disinfectant and there were no dust-gathering edges or corners anywhere. Even the lights were sunk smooth into the wall.

"Like a hospital spaceship. I love it," Digby said.

We all went through into a sitting area with multiple doors leading off it.

One of the doors slid open. "Come in, Mr. Digby." The voice that wheezed out was faded at the edges but it was obvious that it had spent most of its life bossing people around.

The room we entered was crowded with medical equipment and nursing staff. Everyone was in white, including the frail old man lying on a mechanized bed while a muscled orderly rubbed one of his withered legs. I tried not to stare at the pool of wrinkled skin gathered around his knees.

"I was going to come out, you know. It's just that your visit caught me by surprise," the old man said. "I needed a little extra time getting pretty."

"Which one are you? Hans or Johann de Groot?" Digby said.

"Ah. So you think you know things about my family . . ." de Groot said. "Well, that isn't impossible to find out. Even with all the money we spend on staying invisible. You'll have to work harder to dazzle me." He tapped his chest. "I am Johann."

"Johann fought in the Pacific and injured his leg taking a bridge outside Manila." Digby pointed at de Groot's legs. "You don't even have a scar."

It surprised me that Digby had known that and hadn't told me. But when I saw the slightly sad look he always got when he was concentrating, I understood. Digby was here to fight this duel one-on-one.

"You asked in order to see if I would lie. Now you know I'm a liar. So," de Groot said. "Was that it? Or is there more to this parlor trick?"

"As the younger brother, *Hans,* you only inherited the family fortune when Johann died in a freak climbing accident. He was the smart, good-looking one. You were the runt. Small but cunning . . . who wants *that,* right? But under you, your family went from run-of-the-mill old-money rich to being so rich the *New York Times* wrote a profile which you then got disappeared—how did you do that, by the way?" Digby said. "And from the way you loved saying, 'I am Johann'"— Digby tapped his chest just like de Groot did—"I wouldn't be shocked if you pushed him off that mountain yourself."

De Groot winced and closed his eyes. "My own mother said exactly that at my brother's funeral. I remember how painful it was to hear." His orderlies dressed him in a housecoat and lowered him into his motorized wheelchair.

Meanwhile, Digby took a tour of de Groot's room, reading labels on the vast collection of prescription bottles and medical equipment littered all around.

"My lawyer said you visited his office yesterday," de Groot said.

"Did he also tell you he burned down a warehouse while we were in it?" Digby said.

De Groot smiled. "He often withholds details he thinks I'd find upsetting. But I'm very glad you are all right. You and your girl Friday are by far the most interesting characters I have come across in this backwater Erewhon. You accomplished more last year than law enforcement here has in an age." De Groot powered up his wheelchair and headed to the door. "I assume you're hungry." And then he motored away.

We walked through the network of glassed-in walkways to the rhythmic hiss of the oxygen tank strapped to de Groot's chair. It was a long way and if he intended to show us how vast his wealth was, it worked.

After a while, I started to smell the food he'd promised. De Groot led us into a glassed-in conservatory where staff was organizing trays of food on a large buffet table. They finished up and by the time the three of us had arranged ourselves around the table, we were alone.

"I knew your mother, Philip, in ways you do not. Hers is a great mind that ran circles around everyone else's. When I met her, she was working on something she knew would change . . . well, everything. And because she realized how important it all was, she and her team gave up the paths scientific ambition normally takes and worked solely on that problem. No professorships, no publishing, no fawning from bitterly envious fellow scientists. It takes a rare moral courage to do that," he said. "Which is why when they threatened to cut off her funding, I offered to fully fund her myself. No strings attached. But before anything could be decided, your sister was . . . well, misfortune struck."

"You're talking about her nanorobotics lab," Digby said.

"Yes . . ." De Groot said. "What has she told you? How much do you know?"

"Why don't you tell me what *you* know first," Digby said.

"Oh, I see. So in other words, you know nothing." De Groot visibly unclenched and laughed. "That was an inferior bluff. You must do better if you want to play liar's poker for real stakes."

"Why did you want her research?" Digby said. "For what? What else could you possibly need at this point?"

"You mean, because I am old, what more could I need with worldly things? You're right. I personally don't need anything," de Groot said. "But I am just one link in a long chain. Your American individualism might have problems grasping that."

"*My* American individualism?" Digby said. "*You're* American."

"Oh, we are quite a bit older than America. Our ancestors were here long before there was an America, and there will be de Groots here long after," de Groot said.

"Long after what?" Digby looked delighted. "You must have the inside track. Have you already started negotiations with our future alien overlords?"

De Groot laughed again. It was pretty obvious he'd already started checking out of the conversation.

"I don't get you. You're doing this for future de Groots?" Digby said. "To leave them more money?"

"Better than money," de Groot said.

"What?" Digby said. "More power?"

"Better than power," de Groot said. "You are not ready to have this conversation."

Digby stared at him hard and then he pushed away from the table. De Groot laughed harder when Digby took a big drink of water and helped me put my jacket back on.

"Come now, we both know you aren't leaving," de Groot said. "What did I tell you about bluffing?"

Digby nudged me. I wasn't ready for it, though, and as I tripped forward, my foot caught and I smashed my leg against the oxygen contraption attached to de Groot's wheelchair. A frightening hiss emanated from a hose I'd detached. De Groot flailed, but he couldn't turn far enough around to reach the back of the chair. I tried, but I couldn't work out how to replace the hose. His oxygen was no longer connected.

Digby got in de Groot's face. "I don't know why you need to see me beg, but get this: I won't do it." Digby took the hose from me. "Whatever happened to my sister . . . I'll find out and I won't need you to tell me. It's just a matter of time and unlike you, I have plenty of time. Now tell me . . ." By now de Groot was gasping. "Am I bluffing?"

After a scary long pause, Digby plugged the hose back in

and de Groot started breathing again. Slowly, his lips regained their color.

I didn't notice he'd been reaching for the armrest of his wheelchair until Digby grabbed de Groot's arm. "Or, how about this?" Digby paused. "You tell me what I want to know and I'll get you the rest of her research."

And then Digby reached under the armrest and pressed the silent alarm button de Groot had been going for. An orderly ran into the room and began fussing over de Groot's oxygen tank.

"Call me when you're ready to have *that* conversation," Digby said.

We exited through the French windows and went into the garden. When I started to speed-walk, Digby pulled me back and slowed me down. "Don't run," he said.

That was actually kind of a relief, since the leg I'd bashed on de Groot's chair had started to throb. We passed the house and made our way to the guardhouse at the gate. As we approached, the security guard stepped out and stood in our path with a phone to his ear, nodding to whatever instructions he was getting from the other end.

Digby didn't break stride. He took out his own phone and dialed. When we got within earshot, Digby turned on the speakerphone so the security guard could hear the voice on the other line say, "911. What's your emergency?"

The security guard muttered into his phone.

"Hello," Digby said into the phone.

"Yes? 911. What's your emergency?"

The security guard finally budged. He went into his hut and opened the gate for us.

By the time we got to the car, I was limping. We climbed in and Digby floored it out of there.

"Did I really just put hands on a ninety-year-old geezer?" Digby said.

"I believe you did, yeah," I said. "I also think you promised to get him your mother's research. Can you do that?"

"Of course not. That's crazy," he said.

By this time, my leg was really hurting. I rolled back my leggings and found I was cut and bleeding. It took me a moment to get over the fright of seeing my bloody and bruised leg, but then finally, I registered the peculiar shape of my injury.

"Digby. Look at the mark I got when I fell over his chair," I said.

Digby almost swerved off the road when he saw my leg. The mark was the shape of the strange drawing we'd found on the warehouse wall of the double circle with a cross in the middle.

"Then he was there. He went to see Sally for himself. She saw his wheelchair and copied the mark." Digby gripped the wheel. "I should have killed him."

TWENTY-TWO

"Feeling better, I see." Mom was waiting in the kitchen for me when I got back, looking mighty pissed. "So, I made a special trip after work to Costco to get you a nebulizer because I was so worried about your lungs, but I come home and you're what?"

"Sorry, Mom," I said. "Austin came by—"

Mom made a rude buzzing sound. "Liar. I saw. It was Digby dropping you off in Austin's car. Fakeout fail."

"If you let me finish. I'll tell you that Austin came over and then all three of us went to the store . . ." I said.

"You have the ex and the new guy hanging out now?" Mom said. "Wow. You have to teach me how to do that. Your father refuses to come to dinner with Mike and me."

"Why would you want that even?" I said.

"Because they're in my life and I don't want the different parts of my life to be in conflict," Mom said.

"But Dad *isn't* in your life. He's in *my* life," I said. "And he hasn't said anything to me, but I'm pretty sure it bothers

226

Cooper that you and Dad are back up in each other's business again."

"Like I said before, nothing's going on with Richard and me," Mom said.

"Yes, I absolutely know that now," I said. Mom looked surprised. "When I was sneaking back into my room last night—"

"Excuse me?" Mom said.

"I overheard Dad in the backyard calling his housekeeper and asking if Shereene is still mad." When my mother looked confused, I said, "Don't you see, Mom? He's only here because Shereene kicked him out. Or to make her jealous. Either way, he's not here to be 'in your life' like you think."

Mom suddenly got really busy emptying the dishwasher.

"I don't even understand why you're upset by this. It's not like you want Dad back, is it?" Her silence freaked me out. "You don't, do you?"

"No, of course not," she said. "Look. Mike wakes up every morning a hundred percent sure he's doing the right thing. And, I mean, after eighteen years of watching your dad using his big, genius brain working for the Dark Side . . . Mike was so refreshing and simple. But sometimes . . . I need a little complication."

Mom poured herself some coffee and said, "At this point in the conversation, I should check if you understand what I'm talking about, but I know for a fact you do."

"Ha-ha." I poured coffee for myself too and started to leave the kitchen.

"Anyway, no more sick days," Mom said. "I don't want you to fall behind too much."

• • •

"You are *so* behind. You missed a couple of days of school and it's like . . ." Allie threw up her hands at lunch the next day. "Spring fever plus spring-cleaning equals hookups and breakups. It's total chaos."

While I ate my lunch, I zoned out while Allie rattled off a list of what she considered the week's highlights, so I didn't immediately notice when Digby walked into the cafeteria. People at school had heard he was back, but hardly anyone had seen him. The room hushed and Digby milked it, doing a series of twirls and curtsies for the people staring at him, before joining Henry at a nearby table.

Charlotte came over to my table, then said "Hey" in a tight voice and sat down. Allie said "Hey" back to her in the same tight voice and then the two of them made painfully frosty chit-chat with each other. Clearly, something was going on between Allie and Charlotte.

Over at Digby's table, Henry's face was a mess, the partially healed bruises from his first beating layered with the brand-new ones.

I was just crafting my excuse to get up and talk to Henry when Charlotte elbowed me really hard in the ribs and said, "Right, Zoe?"

"I'm sorry, what? I missed that," I said.

"You've been missing a lot lately," Charlotte said.

"You're still coming to the party, though, right?" Allie said.

"You're not bailing on the party, are you?" Austin dropped his backpack and sat at the table with us. I noticed Charlotte looked annoyed at his arrival.

"No, of course I'm coming," I said. "It's huge. Everyone's talking about it already."

"Meh," Charlotte said.

"You okay?" I said.

"I'm not feeling the party vibe these days," Charlotte said. She glared at Allie.

"You're always like this. Just wait until you get there," Allie said. "We need this party. We *deserve* this party."

"I don't know. People go to these parties and then go do really shystie stuff like hook up with someone else's boyfriend and say, 'Oh, I was drinking . . . I didn't even know what I was doing . . .'" Charlotte said. "I hope this isn't that kind of party. Know what I mean, Allie?"

"What is up with you two?"

"Oh, nothing," Charlotte said.

I was glad that for once, I wasn't the one in trouble.

"Hey, there's Digby," Austin said. "You know what? I'm not saying I like the kid, but yesterday was kind of . . . exciting, I guess?" He took out car keys from his backpack. "I should switch back my car keys with him."

"Was there a key party we didn't know about?" Allie said.

"Ha-ha. No. We literally had to switch cars last night," Austin said.

"Can you imagine, though? I mean, you'd end up with Bill," Charlotte said. "She's all over social media with how she and Digby are together."

"Yeah, but look how he's looking at Zoe right now." Allie pointed at Digby. "He is *so* sprung. I bet if you whistled, he'd come running over."

"Allie, what are you trying to make happen?" Charlotte said.

Austin laughed and said, "Yeah, Allie, what the hell?"

Felix arrived at Digby's table and sat down.

"Now *that* is a really random collection of people," Allie said. "Although, I guess they're the ones no one else will hang out with?" She counted them off. "Felix is like, super-young. What, did he skip, like, four grades or something? Even the nerds think he's kinda weird. And everyone's still mad at Henry for what he did to Dominic. And Digby . . . well."

"*I* hang out with Digby," I said. "And Felix skipped *three* grades. Also, I hang out with Felix and Henry too."

"Well, it's not like you go anywhere you're *seen*," Charlotte said.

I don't know if I succeeded in keeping the irritation off my face as I stood up and took the keys from Austin. "I'll switch the keys."

Austin grabbed my arm as I turned to leave and said, "Let's not wait until the party to talk, okay? Maybe after the SATs tomorrow we could go get coffee?"

I nodded just to get out of there. When I got to Digby's table, I said, "Henry, God, your face looks like raw steak. Are you okay? Did you see who it was?"

"Yeah, I'm fine," Henry said. "But I didn't see who they were. They had masks on. My sister Athena walked in and got one guy real good, though. I'm pretty sure his nose will be messed up. She got her finger in a nostril and just pulled. The place looked like someone had gotten shot, there was so much blood everywhere."

"Damn," I said.

"But we have a problem. My sister heard the one guy yelling at me to give back their stuff. So I told her what was going on and she says she's going to call the police if I don't take care of it," Henry said.

Sloane came over. "This is getting out of hand. On top of the black eye and cracked ribs from last time, Henry now has a new black eye, a chipped cheekbone, a separated rib, *and* he's going to have to cut bangs in for life to cover that scar." She pointed at Henry's forehead and then poked Digby. "You need to get those drugs back to Silkstrom before those people finally kill him."

"Okay, Your Highness, we're working on it," Digby said.

And then Sloane said to me, "I got your message. Was that a joke? You were in the de Groot house?"

"Not a joke. We were in there all right," I said. "Wait, so you know about the de Groot house? Have you been?"

"They invite the neighbors to a garden party once a year, but they themselves never show up," Sloane said.

"Weird," I said. "By the way, now that you're finally talking to me again . . . I think Henry should talk to a lawyer right away. He won't want to, but—"

"I don't need a lawyer," Henry said.

Sloane and I exchanged looks. Nothing more needed to be said. "I'll ask my dad," Sloane said.

"I still have the recording of Silk beating up Henry," Felix said. "I'll make copies so we can turn in the originals."

"But that recording makes it sound like *we're* there to buy stuff," I said.

"We were undercover," Felix said.

"The cops won't believe that," I said. "Maybe I should talk to Cooper."

"Or, we could go with my plan." Digby had that look again.

"I vote no on Digby's plan," I said.

"I second," Sloane said.

"We could put the bag in Papa John's locker and call the cops on him. Cut ourselves out completely," Digby said. "He'll definitely make a deal and tell them who he's working for . . ."

After a beat, Sloane said, "That's actually not bad."

"We're all going to be here tomorrow morning for the SATs. Let's do it then," Digby said. "Meet up an hour before the test?"

"Because tomorrow isn't stressful enough already," I said.

"How many times do I need to tell you? Chill about the SATs already," Digby said. "You'll be fine."

"Besides, the distraction might actually help us relax," Felix said.

"What do you know about academic stress?" I said.

"Test taking is a specific skill set. Sitting in a room, coloring in circles? That's not where I shine," Felix said.

"We're putting it in his school locker, right?" Henry said. "Because if we put it in his football locker, they might open up the lockers of everyone else on the team. A lot of guys who aren't selling might get busted."

"Using isn't allowed either, Henry," Sloane said.

"Sorry, man. If we're going to do this, then I think we need to get them all out," Digby said. "All the guys selling and all the guys using."

Henry looked utterly miserable.

"You guys know they put cameras in the hallway outside the locker rooms, right?" Felix said. When Digby groaned, Felix said, "But I have the keys to the coaches' offices. That's where they keep the hard drives. I could wipe the footage."

"Don't just erase the film. It'll look bogus. You need to create a loop so it's just empty hallway the whole time," Digby said.

"That *is* better," Felix said.

"Sounds like a plan," Digby said.

"Sounds like a criminal conspiracy," I said. It didn't help that when I looked up, I saw everyone in the room was watching us.

• • •

That night, I rescheduled dinner with my father and brought a dinner tray up to my room. I was at my desk, about to start eating, when out of the corner of my eye, I spotted a dark figure. I thought my heart was going to explode.

But it was just Digby, lying face-up on my bed. I threw my fork at him. "Dammit. You scared me."

"So I said to myself . . ." Digby sighed. "Self, there's no way Princeton was ignoring us at lunch, is there? I mean, she came over, but only after everyone else got there . . ."

"Is it a problem that you and your 'self' are two completely different entities that have conversations with each other?" I said.

Digby said, "Because maybe she doesn't appreciate our she-nanigans anymore—"

I said, "I wasn't ignoring you—"

"Except she didn't call them shenanigans. What did she call them?" Digby waited. When I didn't supply the word, he said, "'Dumb-ass stunts.'" He took my spaghetti off the tray, shoveled in a huge mouthful, and then immediately spat it back out. "Aaargh . . . that is frickin' hot."

"Look at it. It's *steaming*," I said. "Do you still need some-one to blow on your food?"

He drank my milk. "You know, Bill's mom is a nutritionist and she says cooking food too hot kills all the nutrients."

"You met her mom?" I don't think I fully succeeded in keep-ing from my face how annoyed that made me. He dipped a fork-load of spaghetti in what was left of my milk and crammed it in his mouth. "So." I changed the subject. "What *would* you do if de Groot did call you?"

"I don't know," Digby said.

"You told him you could get the rest of your mom's work . . ." I said. "Did you mean that?"

"You know that saying about your ego writing checks your body can't cash?"

234

He paused. "I mean, I always thought the end of the road would be when I figured out who took Sally and why. I know all that now, but I still have no idea what really happened to her. All of a sudden I need to know things I didn't think were important to me before, like whether she died alone and where her body is buried."

"You really believe your sister's gone?" I said.

"All this time, I held out hope that she was being kept in a basement room or being raised by some deranged woman with baby fever. But now . . ." Digby balled up the napkin and over-handed it into the garbage.

"Your poor mom said she could feel Sally's still alive," I said. "It's really sad."

"She feels whatever she needs to feel. But a fact's a fact. Sally's gone," Digby said. "All that's left now is filling in the details . . ."

"And what about de Groot? Are you going to tell the police?" I said.

"There's no point. Even if it were an open-and-shut case, with his money and influence, the only people who'd end up in jail would be my parents and Fisher," Digby said.

"Couldn't you get a lawyer to argue for mitigation?" I said. "Explain why they did it . . . the kidnapping . . ."

"First, my mother stole classified government property and at least some of what they gave de Groot was real. Second, my parents can't use intent as a defense. Espionage Act," Digby said. "Even legit whistleblowers automatically go to prison. I need to know what actually happened to my sister, but I'm not sure getting the closure is worth my mom getting life in prison."

"Why do you think de Groot's guys were following us around?"

"Probably the same reason Fisher was. He noticed I've been looking into things. Plus, he didn't get what he wanted nine years ago," Digby said. "And I bet he's hoping the game isn't really over yet."

"But it is over?" I said.

"Well, now we play *my* game," he said. "In which I figure out how to nail de Groot without getting my parents thrown into federal prison."

I noticed that Digby had slipped his hand under my mattress and was digging around. "What are you doing?" I opened my drawer and took out my diary. "You're looking for this?" I flipped through the pages to show him they were empty. "Nothing to see."

"What's this? A decoy diary? Might the student have bested the master?" he said.

"Nope. That's it. I've been too busy to write," I said.

"You were too busy to document your own teenage dream coming true? Come on. After all that wishing and praying, what? No happy daily recap?" he said.

"Like I said, I've been busy. I study, I work, Austin and I . . . we do stuff. Go out—"

"How's it been going, being a normal? I remember you were all twisted up about this when you first got to River Heights," Digby said. "Well?"

"It's great," I said.

"What do you do? Besides put in streaks . . . talk about celebrities? Who's a virgin?" he said.

"Look, I'm not, like, insane just because I enjoy other people's company," I said.

Digby said, "Yeah, but these are the little rubber people we used to mock—"

"Right. We used to. When you were here. But you left." I tried not to sound like I was sulking. I wasn't succeeding.

"I didn't leave you. I had to go," Digby said. "I'm not like your father."

"Seriously, don't do that. This is not me having a Daddy hissy fit at your expense. I'm pissed off that you're mocking me, because you have no right to," I said. "You left. I moved on."

"Okay, fine. I'm not here to attack your way of life or anything," Digby said.

"Why *did* you come here? What do you need?" I said. "Don't you have a date with Bill tonight?"

"Relax. I just wanted to give you this . . ." Digby said.

He handed me the locket in which he'd hidden the SD cards. He'd put our selfies back in the slots.

"I didn't even realize you'd stolen it back again," I said. After I'd gotten it back from him on Sunday, I'd stashed the locket in my jewelry box in the back of my closet. "Nothing weird inside? No tracking chips or miniature explosive that'll blow my head off?"

Digby took the locket back from me. I was surprised by

his embarrassed expression. "You don't have to wear it. I just thought—"

I snatched it back from him. "No. Sorry, I do want it. Thank you." I put it around my neck. "God. So sensitive suddenly."

"Exam day tomorrow. Early night tonight?" he said.

"Yeah, I'm exhausted. I just hope I'm not too wound up to fall asleep." When Digby started to laugh, I said, "You know, I don't have a football scholarship or a multi-million-dollar inheritance waiting for me. I'm not a prodigy like Felix and unlike you, I don't have genius-level BS Factor to carry me through life," I said. "This test matters to me." It infuriated me that he was scrolling through his phone. "You know, you could at least pretend to be sorry that you're completely ignoring me."

Digby held up his phone so I could read the screen. "These are *my* SAT study notes. I sometimes trip up on basic factoring. It's really frustrating. I care too, Princeton. I joke about it so I don't end up caring too much," Digby said. "So, I should leave you, then?"

I shrugged. Certainly, I needed to rest. But I also wondered if I just didn't know how to ask him to stay.

He typed on his phone and said, "I guess Bill's down to hang."

Nope nope nope. Now I wanted him to go. He needed to go right that moment. "Bye-bye, then, see you."

"Okay, wow . . . take it easy," Digby said. He returned the now-empty spaghetti plate and the milk glass to my tray and propped open my window. "Just like old times, right, Princeton?"

He climbed onto the tree branch outside my window. "But it ain't old times, is it?"

The whole time he'd been back, we'd both known something was broken, but this moment was the first time we were both willing to admit it. And I wanted to lay the blame where it belonged.

"You never called, Digby. You just left," I said. "You never called."

But whatever relief I got from finally unloading on him lasted exactly as long as it took for me to speak those words, because Digby said, "The phone rings on both ends, Zoe. You never called me either."

And then he left.

TWENTY-THREE

"The phone rings on both ends," he'd said.

That pithy little tidbit kept me up half the night. At first, I was angry. How dare he, I thought. He's the one who suddenly tried to change the track of our relationship and *he* should take the responsibility for it. But then I started to wonder if I was maybe being passive in that awful way girls are when they wait around hoping people will guess how they feel and give them what they want. And then I saw the time and started to worry I'd be tired during the SATs, which, naturally, kept me up even longer.

• • •

I woke up the next morning thinking about Wonder Woman.

During a mild comic book fascination I once went through, I'd started reading Wonder Woman thinking, you know, strong woman, doesn't need men, et cetera, et cetera. Unlike Batman, who was also billionaire playboy d-bag Bruce Wayne, or Superman, a.k.a. clumsy nincompoop Clark Kent in his off-time,

Wonder Woman was Diana Prince: a competent and successful military intelligence officer. Wonder Woman kicked butt at both her day job *and* her side job.

And it was in that same way that, after spending the last couple of days running around town double-crossing drug dealers and helping Digby shake down geriatric billionaires, I now had to go ace my SATs.

I packed my flash cards, my little red notebook, and my wallet, keys, and phone into the big green gym bag of drugs. I turned down Mom's offer of a ride and took the bus instead because even though she tried to hide it, I could feel her anxiety for me oozing out of her.

I went into school and headed toward the main gym, where they'd be administering the test. I saw the school resource officer, Harlan Musgrave, who disliked me almost as much as he hated Digby. I tried not to take it as an ill omen that he was obviously going to be one of our exam proctors.

"Hey, Princeton."

I'd been so focused, I'd blown straight past Digby and Henry in the hall.

"Wow. Look at that determination," Digby said.

Henry nodded at the green gym bag. "Sorry about making you hold this, Zoe."

"Is it weird that you didn't ask Sloane to take care of it?" I said.

"Yeah," Henry said. "Things are complicated with us right now. She's really mad."

"Well, you need to talk to her," I said. Henry took the bag

from me. "Oh, wait." I unzipped the bag and retrieved my own things.

"Are you going to tell her?" Digby said.

"Tell me what?" I said.

"Coach Fogle called Henry at home this morning. He might not be starting QB this fall," Digby said. "Austin's got a shot now."

"What? Did he give you a reason?" I said.

"He just said he might want to make some personal changes and try someone with a better ground game," Henry said.

"Henry . . . I'm so sorry. Are you okay?" I said.

"Yeah, I'm surprised how okay I am, actually," he said. But, really, he did not look okay. He was in the kind of autopilot people engage when they don't want to add to their humiliation with an honest reaction. "I'm okay."

"Austin didn't tell you?" Digby said.

"No . . . he didn't mention it when we messaged last night," I said. "Maybe he doesn't know?"

"Oh, look. Here he comes. You can ask him," Digby said.

I waved at Austin coming down the hall, but he just waved back at me and abruptly went around the corner.

"Oh, he knows," Digby said.

Sloane came up to us just in time to see it. "That was weird," she said. She hugged Henry and said, "Are you better?"

"What was weird?" Bill walked up and jammed herself right against Digby. "Hello, chaps." She was wearing a brown beret that I found unbelievably annoying. "I'm collecting people's sexy sip faces." For some reason, she was talking in a fakety-fake-fake British accent. "Taking selfies relaxes people."

"So, really, you're doing a public service," I said.

"What's a sip face?" Henry said.

Of course Bill demonstrated. Wide eyes, sucked-in cheeks, shoulders raised, lips puckered, looking more satisfied than a Frappuccino could ever make anyone feel. Bill held out her phone to Henry and said, "What about it, Petropoulos?"

I wanted to knock the beret off her head.

"It's not really a good time, Bill. Maybe later," Henry said.

"You guys nervous?" Bill said. "Just take it again in the fall." As she was walking away, she said to Digby over her shoulder, "Come get me for the party tonight?"

"The hat? The phony accent?" I said. "What?"

"She's just trying stuff out," Digby said.

"That doesn't bother you?" I said. "One time, I said 'coinkydink' and you lost your mind. But she's walking around talking like fake Madonna and you're not going to say anything?"

Digby cocked his eyebrow at me. "Don't let this get in your head, Princeton." When Felix came up, Digby said, "You brought the office keys?"

"Yup," Felix said.

"So, Sloane," Henry said, "Digby, Felix, and I can take care of it from here—"

"I'm coming," Sloane said. "Who else is going to keep you from checking and cleaning out every guy's locker just to be sure your teammates don't get caught with drugs. I dare you to say you weren't going to." When Henry couldn't, Sloane said, "That's what I thought."

Meanwhile, I didn't want to point out what no one had said, which is that technically, they didn't need me to go with them. Felix would fix the CCTV, Digby would pick open Papa John's locker, and Sloane would watch Henry so he wouldn't do anything heroic while he planted the bag. I was glad, then, when Digby released me by saying, "See you after the test, Princeton?"

Yes, I felt a twinge of guilt watching the four of them hustle away with the gym bag. And yes, I felt another twinge of guilt when I tucked myself into a science prep room so I could eat my cherry Danish and do my flash cards one more time without getting sucked into polite conversation with the other students as they arrived. But it was all worth it because in the silence, I was able to sink back into my test-taking Zen state.

I was so relaxed that it was a full two minutes of looking directly at Coach Fogle talking to someone before I realized he was, in fact, talking to Austin. Austin gestured with his hands, seemingly describing an object about three feet wide and a foot tall. I watched Coach Fogle leave Austin and cross the field toward the back entrance to our school's athletic department's subterranean offices. There was something very off about his grim-faced, purposeful stomp toward the building.

And then I noticed his bandaged nose and I remembered Henry had said his sister had gotten her finger in one of the attacker's nostrils and just pulled.

I called Digby's phone but got the "subscriber is not available" message three times, so I decided to go get him. I barely bothered getting my stuff together before I exploded out of the room and ran down the stairs to the offices and lockers in the basement. On the way, I tried to work out the following problem: Where would two people meet if they are three hundred yards apart heading toward each other, one at the speed of a dead run, the other at a speed of an angry walk. From this, I realized two things. First, I had actually found a rare instance in which algebra was useful in real life. And, second, I couldn't figure out the answer, so I should probably brace myself for a not-so-great score on the math portion of the SATs. Instead, I just ran.

I got downstairs and was dancing around in the hallway, trying to figure out which way to go, when Digby's head popped out from one of the offices.

"Princeton? What's the matter with you?" he said.

I pushed him back into the office and shut the door behind us. "Get inside quick. Coach Fogle's coming," I said.

"You ran all the way down here to tell me that?" Digby said.

I said, "Yes, because—"

"Awww. Princeton was worried? I would have just told him—"

I could tell he wasn't going to stop making fun of me anytime soon, so I pinched his nose hard and said, "Coach Fogle's nose is all messed up."

"What?" Digby said.

"I just saw him with a big bandage across his nose," I said. "Doesn't that mean he attacked Henry?"

"That makes so much sense. He's supplying steroids to his championship team," Digby said.

"Wait. I think he might know the stuff is here," I said. "Maybe."

"What? How?" Digby said.

"Because Austin knows you gave me the bag of stuff at my house and then I turned up with a huge bag today," I said. "And I just saw Austin talking to Coach Fogle before the coach started walking toward the athletic offices. He made this gesture." I copied the way Austin had moved his hands while he was talking to the coach. "Wouldn't you say that's about the size of the gym bag?"

"You think Austin told him?" Digby said. "You really think he'd do that?"

Of course I didn't want to think he'd do that, and I silently cursed Digby for the doubt I now felt. Until Digby had shown up last Friday, I never even would have had to ask myself a question like this. But now I was asking. And I thought about how strange Austin looked when he avoided me earlier that morning. And how much he used to talk about wanting to be the QB . . . And then I started to think that maybe he'd told Coach Fogle about the bag last night to mess with Henry. But why would he have told the coach about seeing us with the bag in school?

I heard Coach Fogle's wheezy cough in the hallway. I grabbed Digby and squeezed the two of us into the supply closet and shut the door.

"So you *do* think he told him," Digby whispered.

"I think he told the coach about the drugs last night to get Henry in trouble and I think he told the coach about seeing the bag here today because he's afraid we'll get rid of it," I said. I tried to hold back tears of disappointment. "Why are all men scumbags?"

Digby laughed but was sympathetic. "Oh, Princeton. Don't cry. There are still good guys . . ."

I don't know what got into me at that point, but before I knew it, I'd grabbed his collar and pulled him closer.

"Hey," Digby whispered. "Princeton, wait."

"What?" I said. "Why?"

"Because number one, you haven't told him yet but mentally, you've just broken up with your first serious boyfriend. You're whacked out on feelings and you should probably cut your hair or get a tattoo instead. Number two . . ." My stomach did that up-down thing when Digby reached for my chin, wiped off some jelly that had dripped out of my Danish, and licked it off his thumb. "I'm not in my right mind when you're standing this close."

We stopped our whispering when the door to the office opened and someone, presumably Coach Fogle, walked in. He rummaged around for a while before he retrieved what sounded like a big bunch of keys. And then he left the office. Digby and I waited a few seconds before we stumbled out of the closet.

"We should focus, but I should just say it," I said. "Old Digby would've totally kissed me."

"See? And that proves there are still some good guys left in the world," he said.

"What has happened to my life that you're one of the good guys now?" I said.

Then the door opened. "A good guy who's stealing from me," Coach Fogle said. "I need my bag back."

TWENTY-FOUR

"Heeey, Coach Fogle . . ." Digby started to vamp. "We were just looking for the bathroom and I thought it was around here somewhere . . ." Digby tucked me in behind him and started edging us toward the door.

When the coach made a sudden leap to his desk, Digby and I bolted. Just as I got to the hallway, I turned and saw the coach get a shiny silver gun out from his drawer.

Digby and I ran down to the enormous locker room. Sloane and Henry were in the special area at the back wall sectioned off for the football team's lockers. We found them transferring the drugs from my green gym bag back into the black one they'd originally come in.

"Hey, guys, he's coming and he's got a gun," Digby said.

"Who's coming?" Henry said.

"Coach Fogle," Digby said. "Henry, his nose is messed up."

Henry cursed and he and Digby got to work jamming the door handles shut with upended benches. Sloane and I, meanwhile, finished repacking the gym bag and putting it into Papa John's locker.

"It was Coach Fogle?" Sloane said. "How did you not realize it was him?"

"I got jumped. It all happened so fast. Plus, why would I even think it was him? He never tried to give me any . . ." And then Henry remembered. "Or maybe it's just because I never went for any of those weird treatments the other guys would get from Chris."

Once the benches were holding the doors, Digby turned off the lights and led us with his phone toward the emergency exit. As we got closer to it, though, Henry said, "Coach keeps that exit locked. People kept coming in and stealing stuff."

By this time, Coach Fogle had started bashing against the door. And then we heard the benches squeal against the floor as Coach started to move them out of place. They weren't going to keep him out for very long.

"End run?" Henry pointed at another door. "Can you unlock this one? The training room's back door opens into the hallway."

We heard Coach Fogle's footsteps entering the locker room and the lights came back on. The idea came to Digby and me at the same time and we both pointed to the top of the lockers on the far side of the room. Digby gave me a boost and I crawled onto a locker as Henry did the same for Sloane. I reached down to help Digby climb up but instead of hiding with the rest of us, he stayed behind and began to pick open the lock on the training room door.

Across the room, Coach Fogle had started searching the closets and bigger lockers. From my vantage point, I could see that he'd worked himself up to the point where he'd made himself physically unwell. He was drenched in sweat and was moving erratically. He ran his palm across his eyes every few steps he took. He found the green gym bag, but when he saw his drugs weren't in it, he got even angrier and thrashed the empty bag around.

Henry slid off from atop the locker, found a hockey stick, and positioned himself behind Digby, ready to defend him when Coach Fogle came around the corner for them. It was agony watching Coach Fogle edge closer to us, and when he crossed a line I'd imagined on the locker room floor, I decided I had to do something. I took my calculator out of my pocket and threw it back toward the door where the coach started from. Thankfully, Fogle fell for it and ran back to investigate.

Finally, Digby got the door open. Sloane and I slid off the lockers as quietly as we could and went through the door into the training room.

So apparently, this is what a successful high school football team's training room has: a long row of stationary bikes, multiple sets of free weights, massage tables, and a physiotherapy torture machine. The crowning glory of this temple to high school athleticism, though, was the faux log cabin sauna that dominated a corner of the room.

This is the same school, by the way, that can't afford a full-time librarian.

Digby tried the door to the hallway, but that too was locked. He got to work on opening it. As I had been for the past few minutes, I checked for a signal so I could call the police.

Henry whispered, "There's never a signal down here."

And then we heard Fogle coming closer. There wasn't enough time for Digby to pick yet another lock, so, with the sound of Fogle's heavy breathing coming even closer, we all climbed into the sauna, pulled the door shut, and waited.

Fogle turned on the lights and shuffled around the room. Then, finally, just when we were looking at each other, starting to hope he'd gone away, Fogle's face popped up in the glass pane in the door. We heard him take out his keys, turn the lock shut, and snap off the key in the barrel. He held up the broken key to the glass pane to make sure we knew we were screwed.

"Coach Fogle . . . *Coach*." Henry pushed his way to the front. "Coach Fogle, please. What are you doing?"

Digby stepped up to the glass pane and said, "Do you understand what you're doing? If you hurt us, your prison sentence goes from months to years—"

"I won't last a month in prison . . ." Coach Fogle said. "I can't go to prison. My whole life is this team . . ."

Fogle wandered away from the door. He was still talking and cursing, though, and we could hear him barking away unintelligibly while he worked at whatever insane thing he was up to.

"He isn't going to cook us in here, is he?" I said.

"It takes my sauna half an hour to even warm up enough to

make me sweat," Sloane said. "We'll be out of here before that happens, right?"

Digby was already at work on the lock, but his tool couldn't penetrate the keyhole with the key broken into the other side. And then we heard the sound of clanging pipes.

Digby had Henry help him move the stove from the wall and said, "He isn't trying to cook us. He killed the pilot light and turned on the gas." Digby took my scarf and stuffed it in the pipe. By now I could smell the gas. "He's going to suffocate us."

Henry went to the door and hammered at the glass pane with the hockey stick he'd brought in with him. The small hole he created helped a little, but the smell of gas was becoming overpowering fast. By this time, Sloane and I were coughing hard. More unsettling than my struggle to breathe, though, was the spacey, faraway sensation I got. For a split second, the reason I was scared in the first place slipped my mind and then when I remembered, I didn't much care.

"Get down on the floor," Digby said before pushing me down and lying next to me. He took out his phone.

"No signal," I said.

"I'm not making a call," he said.

He took the battery out of his phone and I think I actually passed out for a little bit while he disassembled it.

"Stay awake, Princeton." He touched my cheek. "You'll want to see this."

"See what?" I said.

"Stuff's about to go boom," he said.

"Won't we blow up?" I said.

"Not if the gas is under nine percent of the air in here . . ." Digby said. "Or did they say six percent?"

"Did *who* say six percent?" I said.

"Or was that a dream?" Digby said.

"*What?*" I said.

Digby worked the stripped-down battery into the space between the door and the jamb right by the lock. "People might say . . . explosion in a roomful of gas . . . bad idea . . ." He paused for a coughing fit. And then he eased off one of his shoes. "But I'd say . . ." He hammered at the battery with his shoe. "Could things get worse?"

And, finally, whatever he'd hoped would connect in the battery did. There was a small but brilliant flash of hot white in the doorjamb that left the lock visibly damaged. The gas that had piped into the sauna ignited and a sheet of fire rose up the wall and crawled across the ceiling. I would've screamed if I'd had the breath to do it.

Digby and Henry kicked at the door, not really able to give it their all as they cowered from the flames. The door was rattling, but it wouldn't completely open. Digby and Henry started faltering but then, suddenly, the door flew open.

Standing in the doorway was Felix, holding the dumbbell he'd used to bash open the lock.

I got out of the burning sauna, pulling Sloane along with me. Felix disappeared around the back of the sauna and turned off the gas and then we all staggered back out through the locker room and into the hallway.

"Oh, my God, Felix," I said. "We would've died—"

"You guys . . . I killed Coach Fogle," Felix said.

"What?" I said. "How?"

"Good," Sloane said. "He just tried to kill us."

"Where is he?" Digby said. "Because if he isn't actually dead . . . he has a gun."

"That was a real gun?" Felix said. He led us around the corner, where right at the base of the stairs, Coach Fogle was lying on his back next to the gun and my empty green gym bag.

"Well, Felix, you always did say you wanted to see a real dead body," I said.

"I just didn't think I'd DIY one with a jumpscare," Felix said.

"What happened?" I said.

"So I suspended the feed on the cameras and I was waiting for you guys to finish so I could turn them back on, but you were taking forever and they're about to shut the doors to the test center, so I decided to come check on you, and when I turned the corner, Coach Fogle was right there. I guess I startled him and then there was a loud bang, which I guess I know now was an actual gun and not a starter pistol," Felix said. "He grabbed his chest and walked away. And then, BAM, he just dropped dead."

"But did you check, Felix?" When Felix hesitated, Digby said, "So, we're not actually sure he *is* dead."

Felix shook his head.

Digby kicked away the gun and then nudged Coach Fogle with his foot. "Although I don't really feel like mouth-to-mouthing this dude."

"Come on, Digby." Henry pushed past us, dropped down, and started chest compressions on Coach Fogle.

After a while, Felix checked Coach Fogle's neck. "Ooh, there's a pulse."

"Okay, that'll do, Captain America." Digby patted Henry on the shoulder.

"We better get up there and call 911," I said.

"What are you talking about?" Digby pulled the fire alarm and as the klaxons rang out, he said, "This might be the first time I've pulled one of these for a legit fire."

They'd evacuated the whole building and everyone who'd been in school to take the test was standing outside watching the first responders working. Most of the kids were goofing around, relieved about getting out of taking the test that day. I overheard Kyle Mesmer complain that his party wouldn't be as good that night because people wouldn't be partying to celebrate the SATs being over.

The crowd gasped when Coach Fogle was wheeled into the ambulance and even though he was still unconscious, I was relieved to see he was breathing on his own.

"Digby, what do we do?" Henry asked.

"Well, the bag's still in Papa John's locker," Digby said.

"How are we going to get the bag to the police without having to explain how we know it got there?" Henry said.

"I think I got it." Digby pointed at Harlan Musgrave, our school resource officer, standing across the parking lot from us. "I'm going to go get Musgrave to help us."

"Musgrave?" What I meant was, Do you mean Musgrave,

the guy whose career you destroyed nine years ago, who you got fired from the police force for bungling the search for your sister? "Less than five months ago, he practically assaulted you in the cafeteria. He *hates* you. He's going to use this to put *you* in jail."

"Oh, come on . . . bygones," Digby said. "I'm going to talk to him."

"I'm coming," Henry said.

"Then I'm coming," Sloane said.

"Nobody's coming," Digby said. "I'm the only one here with nothing to lose. Just wait."

"Yeah, *right*. I'm coming," I said. "He knows my mom is with a cop. He won't screw with me."

"Yes," Digby said. "Princeton can come."

Musgrave watched our approach and by the time we got to him, he was already halfway to enraged.

"You two did this to get out of taking the test?" Musgrave said.

"How bad do you want to get back to your old gig?" Digby said.

"I should write you two up. You *stink* of smoke. You obviously started that fire," Musgrave said.

"See? It's ace instincts like that that make me think you're wasted around here," Digby said.

Musgrave told us where to go and what to do with ourselves when we got there.

"Come on, Digby, let's go back to my place and give this information to my mom's boyfriend," I said. "He's a real police officer."

"What information?" Musgrave said.

"I mean, I'm sure you know a lot of this stuff already, but I noticed you watching Coach Fogle the other day, so you probably know he's been supplying steroids to some kids on the football team?" To Musgrave's confused expression, Digby said, "Yeah, that's what I thought. You have the personality of week-old garbage, but your mind's like a steel trap—nothing's getting past you. Especially if it's happening right under your nose."

"Uh . . . yeah, yeah . . . what's your information . . . ?" Musgrave said.

"We saw him putting something in one of the football players' lockers," Digby said.

"You didn't see which one?" Musgrave said.

"Seriously? You want us to do the paperwork too?" Digby said. "Check them all, Musgrave."

• • •

About half an hour later, we were standing around outside the school with the thinning crowd of kids still waiting for their rides when Musgrave pranced out the school's main entrance carrying the gym bag. Full of cheer and self-importance, he joked around with the cops.

"Do you ever wish you could get credit for some of this stuff?" Felix said. "I mean, we didn't even get our names in the paper for what we did last year."

"We have a lot of lawyers to thank for that," Sloane said. "Trust me, Felix, if people found out, it wouldn't be credit we'd be getting. It'd be blame."

We watched Musgrave climb into a waiting squad car cradling his golden ticket back into the big time.

"It's better no one knows what we did," Digby said.

"Coach Fogle knows," Henry said. "And Papa John, and Silkstrom . . ."

"Their lawyers aren't going to let them talk," Digby said. "It won't help their case to admit all the things they've done to us."

I noticed Sloane hugging Henry while Henry stared at the crowd of law enforcement at the school's entrance.

"Henry, are you okay?" I said.

"Well . . ." Henry said. "I think I just got my coach arrested. Pretty sure our entire football program's going to be under investigation . . . and that's going to get us suspended for at least the next couple of seasons because . . ." Henry laughed in a borderline hysterical way. ". . . there was drug use. I mean, there was a *lot* of drug use."

"Henry, they used drugs. There are consequences," Sloane said.

"But what about all the guys who didn't do steroids but still won't be able to play next year? I can think of at least three juniors who'll probably miss out on a scholarship because of this," Henry said. "You know what? We should've just let the whole thing burn. If we had let that locker room burn down, we wouldn't be having this problem—"

"Excuse me?"

We turned to see Principal Granger standing right behind us.

"Did you say 'we should've just let the whole thing burn'?"

"Oh . . ." Sloane laughed. "He's just very upset, what with Coach Fogle having a heart attack . . ."

"And he meant 'we' like, 'we the selfish people of River Heights High School football' because we worked the coach to death and we should just burn this place down for almost taking that sweet, sweet Coach Fogle from us," Digby said.

Principal Granger looked unconvinced.

"He's upset. It's just crazy talk," Digby said. "You don't say crazy stuff when you're upset?"

Luckily, a police officer called for Principal Granger just then, but from the look on his face as he walked away, it was clear Principal Granger still thought something was up with us.

"Okay, I know you're upset, but you have to *cool it*, Henry," Digby said.

Sloane's car drove up and she said to Henry, "Come on, let's go to my house."

But Henry waved her off and started walking away. "No, I need to clear my head. I'm going home. I'll see you later." And then he turned around and started jogging.

Sloane gave us an almost forlorn look and raised her hands like, Now what?

"Just give him time," Digby said. "He'll be all right."

Sloane got into her car as Felix's mom arrived to pick him up. As he was about to walk away, Felix said, "Hey, you guys are still going to the party tonight, right? To celebrate?"

"Celebrate what? They're just going to reschedule the test," I said.

"Celebrate *life,* Zoe. We're *alive.*" And then he climbed into his car.

"I know he's right, but I'm just not feeling it," I said. "Do you think Henry's going to be okay?"

"Coach Fogle ran Henry's whole life for three years. Told him what to eat, how much to sleep . . . it's like Henry killed his father today," Digby said.

A little way off in the parking lot, Austin and a bunch of his football bros were climbing into their cars.

"Ugh. I guess I should go to this party tonight. I told Austin I would," I said. "But I feel like bailing now."

Digby sighed. "Isn't it nice to get back to dealing with regular old teenage drama?"

"It's horrible," I said. "I need a nap."

TWENTY-FIVE

Later that day, I was awakened from a deep sleep by some idiot leaning on the doorbell. As I resurfaced from the bliss of feeling nothing, the afternoon's craziness started coming back to me bit by bit and with it, a whole raft of physical pain. Everything I owned was hurting and I just could not get myself off the couch.

But the doorbell was still ringing. I staggered to my feet and answered the door.

"Sloane? What are you doing here?" I said.

"Is that what you're wearing?" Sloane said. She, of course, was looking chic in a tight all-black leather outfit.

"My sweats? What else am I supposed to wear to take a nap?" I said.

"Oh . . . I thought that's what you were wearing to the party," she said.

"You thought I'd turn up to a party dressed like a hobo?"

I looked down at my clothes. "Well . . . that was a horrifying glimpse into what you really think of me."

"So you *are* going to the party?" she said.

"I didn't say that," I said. "I don't feel like going now."

"What? But you have to go," she said.

"Have to?" I said.

"Seriously? This is your moment," she said, pushing past me and into the hall.

"My moment?" I said. "Moment to do what?"

"Come on. Are you kidding? Dumping Austin at Kyle Mesmer's party will make you a legend," she said. "That'll keep those wannabes Charlotte and Allie talking for a while."

I rubbed my eyes. "I'm done for today. I can't take the excitement."

"Oh, come on, you love it," Sloane said. "Why else would you keep hanging out with that drama king Digby if you didn't?"

"I'm not coming to the party, Sloane. You can't make me. I'm exhausted. My father will be here any minute to take me to dinner . . ." I said. "Plus I have nothing to wear."

"Is that the problem?" Sloane said. And then to my alarm, she unzipped her pants and started peeling them off.

"My God, have you gone full crazy? Get upstairs. Cooper will be back any minute." I stepped aside and waved her upstairs.

"This is your makeover moment," she said, and then took off running up my stairs.

"Ugh . . . I hate you so much," I said.

. . .

By the time I got to my room, Sloane had already taken off her boots and leather pants and was wearing my coat as a dressing gown.

I didn't even have the words. "Sloane. What?"

"Put these on," she said. "Just try them on, okay?"

I picked up her pants. They were made of the softest leather I'd ever touched. "What are you up to?"

. . .

After about half an hour and five fights with Sloane, we stepped back from the mirror and checked the results.

"I must still be traumatized from the fire, because I really like this outfit. Especially your boots," Sloane said. Having given me her clothes, she'd picked out a hoodie and leggings outfit for herself from my closet. She looked upsettingly good in my clothes. "*You* look great, by the way."

"Yeah, if I suck in my stomach all night and don't sit or eat or drink," I said. "Or breathe."

"But look at you. You could bounce quarters off your butt in those pants," she said. "How do you feel?"

"Um . . . terrified? Everything's tight and jacked up about two inches higher." I wasn't joking. The reflection in the mirror was a me/not me chimera who creeped me out. "I can't do this. It's too weird." I unsnapped the fly, but I couldn't get the waistband past my hips.

"Stop. You'll ruin them," she said. "You need me to pull them off from the bottom."

264

I lay down on the bed but instead of helping me with the pants, she slid a high-heeled boot onto my foot.

"These are the zillion-dollar ones you wore that other time, right?" I said. "God, they are . . ." And then I stood up and saw my reflection. *"Wow."*

"I don't want to hear how you couldn't possibly and it's too expensive and blah blah blah," Sloane said. "You're dumping Austin tonight. He'll try to break you down." She zipped up the boot. "You need to win."

"And these boots will help me win?" I said.

The pants were so tight, they made me stand ramrod straight and tall, and in these boots, tall was *tall*.

"Don't *you* think they will?" Sloane said.

"Dammit," I said. Because of course she was right. "Although, I don't even know for sure if Austin and I are breaking up tonight."

Sloane showed me a picture of Austin on her phone. He was surrounded by tons of people—mostly girls—behind a table full of drinks in red cups.

"I turned off my phone for my nap," I said. Sure enough, there were a thousand notifications when I turned it back on. "He's pre-gaming at Lexi Ford's." I kept swiping. There really were so many pictures. "It's almost like he wants me to look."

Which is what I did for a while, until finally Sloane said, "Okay, enough. Don't start obsessing over his page now . . . it's so unhealthy."

"*You* told me to look at this crap," I said. "Besides, aren't you being hypocritical? You used to have your little blond mafia follow Henry around town."

"Like I said, I recognize this," Sloane said.

"What happened with that, anyway?" I said. "And don't look at me like you don't know what I'm talking about and I'm the one being crazy. You and your friends were a tight little coven. Everywhere that Sloane-y went. And now . . ."

"What?" Sloane said.

"Well, I mean, you're *here*. With me . . ." I said.

"Whatever . . ." Sloane said.

"Fine. But there are a million rumors already, and if people see us turn up at the party together . . ." I said.

"I just needed a break from them," she said. "Besides, so what if I cause a little conversation?"

I took that non-answer at face value and just went about redoing my makeup.

"Okay, okay, I'll tell you . . . So, I was at an event over Christmas. I saw my mother with her friends. She calls them friends, anyway. But all they do is stress each other out. They sit there comparing the most meaningless things in their lives," Sloane said. "And I got to thinking that *my* friends stress me out."

"Well, what the hell are you doing here? You and I stress each other out. People are just stressful, that's all," I said.

"I don't think you're stressful. You annoy me," Sloane said. "But that's a real feeling, at least. I don't know what I feel when I'm with my friends. I just know I'm exhausted after I hang out with them."

"You have this weird way of insulting people even when you're saying something nice," I said. "Or is it just me?"

"What was insulting about that?" Sloane said.

"You just said I annoyed you," I said.

"But I also said it was a real feeling. Which is a good thing," she said.

"Okay, are you seriously going to make me explain the concept of a complisult to you?" I said.

"Ha-ha," Sloane said. "Anyway. Can I wear these clothes to the party tonight? I've always wanted to try dressing like you. It'll be great to finally be able to eat without having to worry about getting sauce on myself."

"Again. Complisult," I said.

From downstairs, I heard my father yell, "Zoe? I'm here. How did the test go? And why is the front door open?" He started climbing the stairs to my room. "I made a reservation . . ."

"I told you. I'm supposed to be going to dinner with my father tonight," I said. I did not feel like doing that. My eyes wandered over to my window. "Unless we . . ."

"I'm not climbing out the window," Sloane said.

"Well, then, I can't go to the party," I said. "This is already my rain check and there's no way he'll let me reschedule him a second time."

"Just let me do the talking," she said.

Dad did his usual no-knock-door-blows-open entrances, saw Sloane in my room, and said, "Who's this? You're not canceling on me, Zoe."

Sloane put out her hand and said, "Sloane Bloom. Nice to meet you." As my father shook her hand, she said, "I know you have dinner plans, but I was hoping to steal Zoe. My father's having a campaign event tonight."

"Campaign event?" Dad said.

"Daddy's running for the United States Congress and he wanted Zoe and me there for the edgy youth vote . . . you know how it is," Sloane said.

"Oh, well, of course, of course," Dad said.

"I would've comped you, but Zoe didn't tell me you were in town," Sloane said. "It's a thousand dollars a plate and it's sold out."

"No, of course I wouldn't presume . . ." Dad said.

"You don't mind if she takes a rain check?" Sloane said.

Of course he didn't mind. I'd never seen my father submit to someone else's will and I didn't really believe we'd gotten away with it until we were driving off.

"Sloane. Really?" She had me sitting in the car with my legs sticking straight out in front of me.

"You can't bend your knees in that," she said. "Leather's a one-way ticket. Once it sags, it's over."

"Ugh." Digby was right. The stuff rich people own owns them right back.

TWENTY-SIX

Which brings me back to where I started my story. Specifically, riding in Sloane Bloom's fancy SUV to *the* party of the year wearing her impossibly nice clothes. As recently as nine days ago, this all would have added up to a triumphant teen dream of a night for me. But Digby is back in town and nine days with him is an eternity. Now I'm on my way to blowing up my life and, as is typical on Planet Digby, it is the only move that makes sense.

• • •

When we get to the party, Sloane's driver jumps out and runs around the car to open the door for us. A few kids from school immediately run up and photograph themselves against the limo. One guy pushes it too far, though, when he opens the door and tries to climb in. The driver yells at him and pulls off down the road to park.

"They do this every single day. How many limo selfies do

they need?" Sloane says. "Good luck with Austin. I'm going to look for Henry."

"Maybe I'll come find you later."

I feel the disgusted/impressed combo that I've now come to expect from my encounters with the River Heights rich when I behold the façade of Kyle Mesmer's lake house. A smaller stone structure wedded to a glass extension that's so much larger and taller than the original structure, it looks like it's eating the old house whole. A full-on circular drive with a huge mini swimming pool fountain at the top of it.

And it's by that mini swimming pool fountain that I find Allie and Charlotte. When I approach them, it becomes clear they are annoyed that I've been AWOL all day.

"Hey," I say.

Charlotte pantomimes shock. She turns around and looks over her shoulder like, Who is she talking to? "So is this, like, a drive-by, or are you going to actually hang out with us now?"

"I'm sorry, you guys, it's been so crazy," I say. "And, honestly, I didn't even know I was coming until an hour ago."

"Austin said you told him you were coming," Charlotte said.

"Well . . . actually, Austin and I . . ." I had no clue how to finish that sentence.

Allie jumps up and hugs me. "Oh, my God, Zoe . . . are you two breaking up?"

"I think I should talk to him before I say . . ."

I see them trade meaningful glances that they pretend to hide but actually want me to see.

"What?" I say.

"Nothing. Allie is being annoying." Charlotte is talking through gritted teeth. The look she and Allie share confirms what I started to feel at lunch yesterday: Their relationship has an entire dimension that not only doesn't include me but that involves discussing me and making up policies about what to conceal from me.

"But seriously . . . what are those boots?" Allie says. "Let me see how high the heel is."

"Well . . . it's high." I lift my foot to show her. She and Charlotte gasp when they see the telltale red sole.

Allie grabs me and turns me around. "And are you kidding with those pants?" she says.

"What?" I say.

"My chills are multiplyin'," Allie says.

"Sloane lent them to me," I say. "And the boots."

Allie pulls me to sit with them and offers me her Solo cup of something toxic-smelling. "Tell."

"Wait, is she here?" Charlotte says. "I didn't think she was coming."

"I mean, Henry is out as QB and she's like . . ." Allie made a YIKES face. "The prom queen is dead and you inherited her closet. Can we have your rejects?"

"Anyway, have you guys seen Austin?" I say.

"In the house. Come on," Allie says.

As I follow her and Charlotte, I start thinking the party might not live up to all the rager hype that had preceded it. I can't say what it is exactly. Maybe Kyle's right. Maybe people do need to have had the stress of taking the SATs to really let loose.

Turnout isn't the problem. And yet . . . something seems off. I can't put my finger on it, but I watch a boy do a three-point toss with a beer can into a bin and think that maybe proper waste disposal means there isn't enough chaos for it to be a rager.

Then again, it's also a possibility that hanging out with Digby has given me a heightened appetite for chaos.

Allie, Charlotte, and I take the wraparound porch to the back of the house. From outside, I look into the living room window and see that things aren't going much better inside. A whole line of girls on the couch are surfing their phones. Tellingly, they aren't taking party selfies.

"I know, right . . . lame party," Allie says. "Like, literally *no one* is having fun. Lexi's pregamer was better, actually."

"I'm not worried." Kyle Mesmer is bouncing around to convey the energy he knows his party doesn't have. "The seniors haven't gotten here yet."

"Sorry, Kyle. Just saying," Allie says.

"No, no, I'm really not freaking out. It'll pick up. I'm not worried," Kyle says. "Every party's like this until that moment. You know . . . the *moment*. This happened at my last party. It was dead but then Angela Davison was standing too close to the heater and her hair caught fire. Everyone went nuts and after that, nothing was the same." He takes a gulp of his drink and breaks out into a whistling, barking cough.

Allie takes a cautious sip from his cup and her right eye closes involuntarily in pain. "What is that?"

"Justin made it," Kyle says. "I think he's calling it Murder Suicide."

I take his cup and sniff. "God. It's making my eyes water," I say.

Allie takes the cup. "But it's not supposed to go in your eyes." She takes a huge drink as someone farther down from us leans over the porch railing and splashes some people below.

"Aha . . . watch someone get puked on. That's number three." I tense at the sound of Bill's voice. She comes up from behind and hands me a card on which number three literally says: "Someone gets puked on by someone else."

"What is this?" I say.

Kyle catches on and gets excited. "Awesome. A party dare scavenger hunt."

I read out numbers thirteen and sixteen. "'Make someone falsely believe their crush is into them'? 'Ruin someone's hair in a way only a hairdresser could fix'?"

Bill rolls her eyes at my outrage. "Gol-ly gee, Zoe, relax. It's just a joke."

"Your sense of humor is pretty toxic," I say.

"Uh-huh, honey," Bill said.

Charlotte says, "You're just pissed because you'll probably be number five tonight."

We all look down and read "Find a power couple breaking up."

"You and Austin are breaking up?" Bill says.

"She hasn't even told him yet," Allie says.

"Allie," I say.

"Oh, I'm so drunk, you guys, I didn't know what I was saying," Allie says.

"I better get her to a bathroom before her own breath makes her puke again," Charlotte says. They leave.

Kyle looks at the time on his phone and says, "Oops. Excuse me, ladies. Something I've got to do." He raises his cup, says, "To the moment." He chugs his drink before leaving me alone with Bill.

"Zoe, I'm sorry," Bill says. "Are you bummed?"

I don't feel like having a conversation with her about this. Thankfully, a loud commotion summons everybody to the front yard. We all stream to the sound of sirens and unintelligible yelling. I catch a glimpse of Austin and his friends running alongside the house from the backyard.

At this point, the lights suddenly die. There are gasps, some nervous laughs, and some people start to howl. I push my way to the front of the porch, where I see the source of the commotion: a pair of policemen carrying a portable searchlight. Their guns are drawn and they're yelling. One of them shouts, "In the house. In the house. Lock the doors. Right now, right now."

Instead of complying, the crowd raises their phones to film.

Kyle shouts, "What can we do for you, officers?"

The cop's searchlight beam sweeps the tree line at the property's edge. On the third or so arc the light makes, we catch a glimpse of something unnaturally orange.

"Whoa. Go back," First Cop says.

The beam tracks back and finds two dudes in orange clothes a hundred yards from us. They freeze and in the second they are motionless, we collectively realize that they are, in fact, dressed in orange prison jumpsuits.

"Freeze," First Cop says.

But they don't freeze. The last thing we see before Second Cop drops the searchlight is the two escaped convicts charging right for us. The crowd in the yard screams and scatters. There's panic on the porch when the stream of people running into the house is cut off by someone inside slamming the door shut.

My eyes adjust to the dark and I see the figure in the orange jumpsuit running at me. Before I know what I'm doing, I pick up an abandoned bottle of beer and throw it. The bottle shatters on his head. Agonized swearing follows.

Kyle shouts above the general chaos. "Hey, people, it's a *joke*. Stop throwing crap, it's a joke."

The lights come back on. Kyle and the cops see to the guy I'd hit. His head is bleeding from his cut forehead.

"Ohhh . . . that's Paul Mason," Bill says.

"Who is?" I say.

"The convict you hit with the bottle," Bill says. "He was a senior here last year."

People trace back the bottle's trajectory to me. A weird hush follows. Suddenly, from within the middle of the ring of concerned friends, Paul Mason jumps to his feet and screeches, "Goddamn! That was awesome."

Cheering breaks out. Chanting starts up and ripples out until the entire place is shouting, "Mason! Mason! Mason!"

Bill says to me, "Turns out, you can't cause brain damage when there's no brain . . ." and then joins in on the *Mason Mason Mason* chant.

I have a vague memory of some TV show about a murder victim who died of a head injury after being hit in the head many hours before. I wonder if I should worry. I take heart, though, when the crowd picks up Mason and passes him around over their heads. Chances look good he'll injure his head at least once more tonight.

TWENTY-SEVEN

"That's my girl! That's my girl!" Austin dances over to me. I cannot help noticing how insanely handsome he is. All he is wearing is a black evening jacket with tails he's probably taken from one of the closets. He's shirtless underneath and every hour he's ever spent in the gym is recorded on his Hershey's bar abs. I let him nibble on my neck for a second because I don't want to make another scene.

"Let's go somewhere, okay?" I keep my tone light and I even find the right muscles to smile. But I soon realize he isn't in any shape to decode subtle hints about my mood. "Wait. You're drunk? Already?"

"Nah. Just a little happy . . ." Austin says. "Happy you're here now. *Finally*."

"Oh . . . that's great, Austin. I'm glad to see you too." I am too exhausted to put much genuine emotion behind that, but he is too excited to notice.

"Yo, Shaeffer! What's *up,* my bruvva." Kyle Mesmer high-fives Austin. "Hey again, Zoe."

"'Sup, Mesmer," Austin says.

"Hey, I heard Coach is in the hospital," Kyle says. "What does that mean?"

"I heard he's going to be all right," Austin says.

And then he's going to prison, I thought.

And then ensues a roll-call of people who'd heard about something awesome that Austin did earlier involving a keg and a Frisbee and want to congratulate him. After a few minutes, my face hurts from all the obligatory smiling. At one point, I feel like I've sprained my cheeks, because while I am already smiling and chatting with one of Austin's teammates, another cluster of people arrive and I smile even more widely to reassure them that yes, in fact, I am very excited to see them too. This, by the way, is one of the earliest lessons I learned when Austin and I started dating: It is vital to act intensely happy to see people. In fact, it's kind of important to maintain a minimum excitement level all the time or they'll say I'm "off." If I failed to consistently match their level of enthusiasm, they would call me "boring" or, worse, "artsy" or, even worse than that, "emo." Certainly, all the times Digby and I have sat in silence watching *Twin Peaks* would be unthinkable with this crowd.

But, after a while, I realize that, since I am about to break up with Austin, I don't have to care if these people think I'm not cheerful enough. I let my smile drop. As Austin and Kyle continue to talk, I look around and notice the crowd's energy is dialed up higher. The whole scene feels . . . different.

278

"This party suddenly got insane," I say.

Austin says, "*Dude,* yeah. It got hectic up in here."

Kyle points at me and whoops. "What did I say? What did I say? The *moment.*"

There's a loud crash inside the house and Kyle's face momentarily freezes before he starts the crowd in a triumphant new chant of "Bust it up! Bust it up!"

The swarm of people isn't moving out of our way, so Austin sweeps me off my feet and with me cradled in his arms, he gets people to step out of our way and we're able to get off the porch.

Once in the open, I say, "Okay, I can walk now."

"That's all right, Princess, I don't want your pretty shoes getting muddy," Austin says. "Those are staying on later, by the way."

I climb off him and we cross to the pool house. I remember the promise Sloane forced me to make about giving her feedback on the outfit and I construct the wording on the first line of my report to her: Know your terrain. A power stomp across my bathroom floor does not translate to a fierce walk across Kyle Mesmer's muddy lawn.

The moment we are inside, Austin grabs my waist, pulls me in, and mashes his lips onto mine.

I say, "Stop stop stop, Austin. I have to . . ." But he won't get off me, so I softly knee him in the groin and pretend it was an accident.

Through his moans, Austin says, "God, what? That really hurt."

"Did you tell Coach Fogle about the gym bag?" I say.

I have to give it to Austin. His face barely twitches before he says, "What are you talking about, babe?"

"I'm talking about your almost getting us killed just because you wanted a shot at Henry's spot on the team this fall," I say.

"That's ridiculous," he says. "Is this Digby's idea? Is he getting you all paranoid and crazy?"

"Don't turn this into a Digby thing," I say.

"Are you kidding? That kid's been trying to break us up since he got into town," Austin says.

It's true, of course, and admitting that to myself sparks a moment of weakness in me during which Austin leans in, all beautiful white teeth and soft floppy hair. He pulls me in by the waist. When I don't immediately respond to him, though, his smile drops and he lets me go.

"Actually, I'm not done talking about this," I say. "*Did* you tell Coach we had the bag in school? Because I saw you talking to him today."

"I really don't know what you're talking about," Austin says. "Okay, look, alls that happened was . . . Coach talked to me about maybe taking over as QB next season. That's all he said."

"I don't believe you. I don't *trust* you." I want to slap the smirk off his weasel face. "What are we even doing together?"

"That's a great question," Austin says. "And I've been trying to ask you that all week long. I tried on Thursday afternoon, but you and Digby made me drive to the grocery store in Digby's clothes for some reason. I still don't know why those guys were following you, by the way—which, if you were really my girlfriend, is kind of a weird thing not to tell me."

And then it dawns on me. "Are you implying that you've been trying to break up with *me*?"

Right then, the door to the pool house slides open and Charlotte and Allie stumble in.

"So sorry," Allie says. "Oh. Wait. Are you breaking up with her right now?"

Austin and I both say "Yes" at the same time.

"Wait. Did you just say 'breaking up with *her*'?" I say. "You knew?"

Charlotte says, "Okay, Allie. You're on," and leaves the three of us.

Thank goodness it all gels into place quickly so that even before Allie gets all the way across the room to stand with Austin, I know what they were going to say.

Allie actually has the audacity to look sorry as she takes Austin by the hand. "Zoe, we—"

"Never mind," I say. I'm surprised and pleased by how not upset I feel as I walk out.

• • •

I go back into the party and find Charlotte sulking in the kitchen.

"Did you know?" I say.

"Hey. Don't you yell at me," Charlotte says. "I told her it was shady. Maybe, though, none of this would've happened if you weren't so busy having your little adventures with Digby."

"Are you blaming me?" I say. "Besides, Digby's only been

281

back for a week. How long have Allie and Austin been to-gether?"

"Okay, she's shady, but she isn't a snake. They weren't 'together' together . . . but they will be now," Charlotte says. "Anyway. What did you expect? You've been dating almost four months now and it's not like he's getting any from you."

"Excuse me?" I say.

"I'm just saying," Charlotte says. "You probably shouldn't expect too much from Austin."

"Well, now I don't expect *anything* from him," I say. "I hope he and Allie are happy together. They *so* belong together."

I go to the wet bar in the kitchen and hands shaking, I pour myself a soda. All I want to do is go home and crawl back into bed.

Bill saunters up, smoking very self-consciously, and says, "So, from the look on your face, I am guessing you've found out about Allie and Austin?"

"You knew?" I say.

"Yeah," Bill says.

"So people know?" I say.

"No, no . . . sorry. I didn't mean that," Bill says. "I saw them talking earlier tonight and I figured . . ."

I wonder where Digby is, but given the topic of the talk I want to have with him, I don't think it'd be cool of me to ask Bill where he is.

"Thing is, high school dating is like musical chairs," she says. "Whoever gets up is going to want to sit down somewhere. Oh, hey, if you see Digby, tell him I found a guy with some X and I got one for him."

"X? Like . . . ecstasy?" I say.

"Yeah, dance a little trance, throw some shapes," she says. "I want to do a whole '90s thing this spring."

"Is it safe for him to take X with his other meds?" I say.

"Are you kidding? I was actually thinking he might not even feel it, the stuff he's on is so strong," she says.

None of what she just said involves any kind of rational reasoning.

"Anyway, I feel like he's been avoiding me all night," she says. "You wouldn't know anything about *that*, right?"

I try to look innocent. I don't think it works, though, because as she leaves, she says, "Well . . . keep it classy." And then she drops her cigarette in my soda.

I chuck my soda in the trash and head toward the back of the house to find Felix in a scrum of players on the girls' soccer team he manages. He builds a row of short shot glass pyramids with an overturned shot glass at the apex of each one and then expertly pours tequila over the butt end of the upended shot glass so that the glasses below all fill at the same rate.

"Wow, Felix, how are you doing that?" one of the soccer players says.

"It's easy, actually, it's all about creating laminar flow . . ." Felix says. But he senses his audience isn't into that and he pulls up short. Instead, he yells, "Tequila!" And they all drink their shots and fling their glasses into the fireplace across the room. Felix then reaches into a brown box of new shot glasses that he starts to stack into another row of squat little pyramids.

I approach them and say, "Um, hi . . . can I just borrow Felix for a second?"

There's a round of disappointed moans when Felix gets up.

"Hey, you're okay?" I say.

Felix says, "Yeah, I finally found something they enjoy more than tormenting me."

"So you're going to let yourself get alcohol poisoning just so they don't attack you?" I say.

"Nope. I let all of it run down my chin. My shirt's practically flammable at this point," Felix says. "Feel."

"It's okay. I can imagine," I say. "Look, if something goes wrong, come find me, all right?"

"Yeah, sure . . . but what could go wrong? It's a party," Felix says.

The soccer team cheers him upon his return and I pour myself another soda before I push off again on my search for Digby.

TWENTY-EIGHT

On the second-floor landing, I find a series of doors lining a hallway dead-ending at a door that's larger and much grander than the others. It is quieter here and there's a sprinkling of couples pushed up against the walls, talking and making out. I can't help being *that* nerd: I take a cigarette out of the hand of one guy who's so deep into his make-out partner's face, he doesn't realize he's about to set her hair on fire. I drop it into my soda. Another drink bites the dust.

The rooms are full of people, but Digby is not in any of them. In one of the more crowded guest bedrooms, I find Henry sitting in an armchair, getting a little too cozy with a sophomore girl I recognize from the yearbook committee. Daisy? Pansy?

"Heeeeey . . . it's my friend, Zoe! *Zoe!* Come and talk awhile," Henry says.

"I thought you didn't drink." I point at the red cup in his hand.

"I don't, but I do tonight. Because *tonight* we're going to have fun." Henry tries to take another sip from his cup but I get it away from him before he can. "What? Boring!" The girl boos me and Henry says, "Maisie thinks you're boring too."

Maisie grabs the cup from me and hands it back to Henry.

"Okay, Maisie, if you think you're ready to take on Sloane Bloom, then be my guest," I say. I tap on my phone's screen and make sure she hears it send. "She'll be glad to see you're keeping her seat warm."

"Sloane! Maisie was just asking me about Sloane, actually," Henry says. "I haven't even seen her tonight. Is she at the party yet?"

"Oh, yeah. She was my ride up here." To Maisie, I say, "You should probably go find your friends now."

She doesn't want to but Maisie gets up, sneers at me, and says, "I like those boots. Are those even yours?"

"No, in fact, they're Sloane's." I point at the door. "And you can tell her how much you like them yourself, because here she comes now."

Maisie takes a few quick steps before she realizes I'm messing with her. She leaves anyway, cursing me out as she goes.

"Oh, no, ladies . . . why are my lovely ladies fighting?" Henry says. "Why did you make Maisie go away?"

"Really? Her?" I say. "I can't believe I'm saying this, but she's quite a step down from Sloane."

"What? That was nothing," Henry says. "We were just talking."

"I don't think *Maisie* thought it was nothing." When Henry

286

rolls his eyes at me, I say, "I just don't want you to do anything you'll regret later."

"Then where were you when I was torching the school earlier?" Henry says.

After I check that no one nearby is listening to us, I lower my voice and say, "Henry, you need to stop saying that kind of stuff, okay? Someone's going to hear you and if you think your life is bad now—"

"Oh, it would get worse? Worse than no football?" Henry says. "You don't get it, Zoe. *Football.* I was all set." Henry drinks deeply.

I take the cup away from him. "You've probably had enough, Henry—"

"I was going to go to Florida State, earn the starting QB spot, throw at least three thousand yards—"

"You could still go to Florida," I say.

"What?" he says.

"Just because you aren't playing football, it doesn't mean you can't go to school in Florida," I say.

"What? No, you don't understand. It's not about Florida. I don't like the humidity," he says.

I say, "Then go somewhere else—"

"No, that's the point. There *is* nowhere else. I needed football to pay for college. Now what? What do I even tell my family?" he says. "I mean, how would you tell your parents if you didn't get into the school they wanted you to go to?"

Thoughts of a skinny envelope and my father's angry face flash before my eyes.

"Now imagine telling them you didn't get in *anywhere* and you weren't going to college *at all*," Henry says.

It's a sobering thought, all right. I give him back his red cup. "But take it easy on that, because I'm seriously telling Sloane you're up here this time." I message her on my phone.

"Didn't you already before?" he says.

"Nah. That time I put up a post about these boots," I say. "If I leave you, can I trust you to stay out of trouble until Sloane gets here?"

"Where are *you* going?" Henry says.

I say, "I need to find Digby. I'll see you later—"

Henry grabs my arm. "Hey. Do me a favor?"

"Sure," I say.

"Don't hurt him," Henry says.

"Who? Digby? How could I even—"

"You could. So please don't. You're with Austin now. Stay in your lane," Henry says.

I want to object, but Sloane comes in the door just then. As I pass her, she says, "Is he okay?"

"Nope," I say. "Not okay at all." I push off and leave them to it.

I get to the last door at the end of the hall and find it locked. I twist and yank at the doorknob and then finally knock. "Umm . . . Digby isn't in there, is he?" I say. I immediately feel like a nerd and right then, I decide I should just go home before I humiliate myself any more at this party. But then the locked door opens and I'm pulled into the room.

"You made it, Princeton," Digby says.

"Why are you lurking in here?" I say.

"Hungry?" Digby points to a desk where he's set up a little buffet of chips, guac, salsa, and a sushi plate. "I caught the caterers when they were setting up," he says.

"Do you mind if I . . . ?" I point at the bed. The relief I feel when I sit down is immediately complicated by worry about making saggy knees in my leather pants. I lie down, unbutton my fly, and breathe deeply for the first time in hours.

"Well, Princeton, your seduction game is interesting," he says.

"Sorry, these are Sloane's pants and there are a lot of rules to follow when you wear leather," I say.

"Where's Austin?" Digby says.

I say, "How am I supposed to know?"

"Uh-oh. Do we have a number five?" Digby says. He sits down next to me.

"What?" And then I see that he has one of Bill's annoying party bingo cards.

"She's the worst," I say. "No, wait. I take it back. Austin is the worst. And by the way, I lied before when I said it was a good luck ritual. Austin really does still confuse his left and right when he's under pressure, so he labels his hands with marker."

"So you did break up with him tonight?" Digby says. When I nod, he says, "Should I be sorry?"

"*I'm* not," I say. "He wouldn't admit it, but he totally told the coach about the drugs. But the main reason I'm so annoyed is that he and Allie are together now. They *claim* nothing happened before we broke up, but you know . . ."

289

"Wow. You are having *all* the sticky drama tonight," Digby says.

I point at the huge stash of food in the room. "Why are you sitting in a locked room? Looks like you have your own sticky drama," I say. "You know, Bill thinks you're avoiding her." When Digby rolls his eyes, I say, "What? That fake accent finally got to you?"

"I went to the bathroom at her place and when I got back, meds were missing from my jacket," he says. "The fun ones."

"Let me guess . . . she helped you look for the bottle for a while and then she found them in a place that you know—*you know*—you were never at." When he nods, I say, "Oh, I am very familiar with this move. This is how she got your number from my phone and started texting you behind my back last fall. And by the way, now she says she has some X she wants to take with you."

"She's exhausting. Like, her on top of everything else that's going on is just . . ." Digby says. "I can't anymore."

"It's been crazy since you got back, all right," I say.

"Hey, Princeton, do you think I'm sexist for assuming my father was the one doing all the important work?" He looks crushed by the idea.

"Digby, your mom worked on a top secret project and lied to you about being an assistant. Were you supposed to investigate her when you were seven years old?" I reach over and pat his arm.

He squeezes my hand to thank me for comforting me, but

after a couple of seconds, I realize that we are still holding hands. He starts pulling away, so I squeeze his hand a tiny bit to let him know I don't want to stop. Digby leans over me slightly but hangs back enough to give himself plausible deniability.

"Wait. I have to ask," I say. "Why *didn't* you call me when you were away?"

Digby tilts his head back and sighs. "Really?"

"Yes," I say. "It's been bothering me for months."

"Fine. You really want to know why I didn't call?" I nod and Digby says, "Because you didn't kiss me back at the bus station and I just assumed I'd made a mistake and . . . I was embarrassed. And then Henry tells me you're with Austin . . . what would *you* think?"

"Okay," I say. I notice how nervous he looks. "I will take that answer. But to be fair, you just suddenly took off. I wouldn't have had a chance to kiss you back even if I wanted to."

"And did you?" Digby said. "Did you want to kiss me back?"

I pull him closer and nod.

Every thrill of every rule we've broken together, every electric jolt I've ever gotten when he peeled back my defenses and exposed the real me, everything that's good and true about being Digby's friend . . . I feel all that when he buries his face in my hair and breathes in; when I turn and find his lips and kiss him. The first few seconds are intense. The roughness of his stubble against my cheek makes his soft lips even more of a surprise.

291

I am pushing off his jacket when Digby suddenly stops. He looks worried.

"What?" I say.

"Bill," Digby says, kissing my cheek.

"What about Bill?" I say, kissing him back.

"Technically, Bill and I are dating, so . . . I shouldn't . . . with you . . . until I talk to her," he says. "Dammit, Princeton. I'm sorry."

"What? First of all, don't act like you pity me because I can't have you," I say.

"I wasn't—"

"And second, you and Bill were serious already?" I say. "You've gone on one date."

"Or four—"

"When did you have the time to do that?" I say.

Digby gets up, walks into the en suite bathroom, and splashes his face with water. "Okay. Let's do this." He towels off. "Let's find her and tell her."

I remember her line about my staying "classy." "I'm not coming with you. I'm pretty sure she just warned me off you downstairs," I say. "You can do it alone."

"What if she cries?" Digby says.

"Unbelievable," I say. "So what if she does cry?"

"I can't make a girl cry," he says.

"You know before, you were worried about being sexist? Well, *now* you're being sexist," I say. But he looks so worried, I give in. "Fine. Let's go."

"Thanks, Princeton."

• • •

"Remember how this afternoon, you asked if I wasn't glad to be back to just dealing with teenage drama?" I say. "Well, I'm not. I'm really, really not. I'd rather deal with murderers and arsonists. All day."

We wander back out into the party and are in the kitchen when booing breaks out in the living room. Digby turns to me and says, "Sounds like this party just got more interesting."

Every head is turned toward Musgrave standing in the corner. Digby catches Musgrave's eye and when Musgrave points at first Digby and then me, it becomes clear that he has come here looking for us. Digby signals for Musgrave to come outside the house to talk. While Musgrave picks his way through the crowd to the door, Digby and I climb out of the living room window onto the porch and then onto the turf beside the house.

"What do you think he wants?" I say.

Digby shrugs and says, "I don't know, but if I know Musgrave at all, he's here because he's managed to screw up what little he had to do today." When Musgrave finally lumbers his way to us, Digby says, "Hey, Harlan. What's up?"

"What's up? *What's up?* You messed me up is what's up," Musgrave says and then, weirdly, points at me.

"Excuse me? Uh . . . and how did I do *that*?" I say.

"Uh . . . by leaving your little red notebook in the bag of evidence you had me turn in is how you did that," Musgrave says.

"Notebook? Princeton?" Digby says.

I rewind the day in my mind and find the memory of putting

the red notebook into the bag but then, when I try to conjure the image of taking it back out when I unpacked my test-taking stuff earlier that morning in school . . . nothing. "Damn it," I say. "I was so stressed about taking the test, I didn't even remember that I'd brought it."

Digby asks Musgrave, "Okay, so . . . did you get it out?"

"Get it out? Get it out? Did *I* get it out?" The veins in Musgrave's neck are throbbing. "No. I did *not* tamper with police evidence. And by the way, I thought you said you saw Fogle put it in the locker. Does this mean you planted it yourselves?"

"Po-tay-to, po-tah-to. Fogle is selling. John Pappas—the kid they call Papa John—will flip and testify against him. That's all you need to know," Digby says. "Where's the bag now?"

"In the evidence locker. Where else would it be?" Musgrave says.

"They logged the notebook already?" Digby says.

"Well, they logged the bag and the stuff inside, but no one's processed what's actually in there," Musgrave says. "Except the drugs. Those have already been sent to the lab."

The three of us watch a shiny black sedan cruise up and park just short of the house's circular driveway. A door opens and a man in a suit steps out and dials his phone. A second later, Digby's phone rings.

"What the hell?" Musgrave says.

Digby picks up, doesn't say a word, and he and the man in the suit hang up at the same time.

"Princeton?" he says.

"Yeah," I say. "I'm coming with you."

We walk away with Musgrave yelling out his demands for an explanation at us. Neither of us even needs to ask what's going on. We get in the car with the man in the suit and he drives us up the road, where we see an enormous black high-top custom van parked with the engine running. There are two SUVs in front and behind it.

I can see Digby is trying to put on his game face. We get out and walk to the van.

The door slides open to reveal de Groot ensconced in a plush throne at the center of the customized passenger compartment. As always, he is hooked up to his oxygen. We are ushered in and the door is closed again. In the silence that follows, the sound of his wheezy respirations are thunderous.

De Groot raises his arms and says, "I am ready to have that conversation."

"I'm listening," Digby says.

One of de Groot's anonymous security guys hands Digby a large brown envelope. From the way it crinkles, I guess that it contains something made of fabric. Digby takes the envelope but just puts it on his lap and stares at it.

After a long minute, I touch his arm and say his name.

He nods and I take the envelope and tear it open to find a small hot-pink T-shirt. A Dora the Explorer T-shirt. I remember Digby had said his sister was in the grips of a Dora the Explorer obsession when she'd been taken. "This is Sally's."

"I can tell you what happened to her," de Groot says. "All you need to do is get me the research."

"This . . ." Digby struggles to get himself back in control. "This could be any kid's T-shirt."

I search the fabric for a clue. I flip over the tag and find "Sally D." written on it in now-faded marker ink. There is an ominous bloodstain near the neck. I am still digesting all this when suddenly, Digby explodes beside me. He lunges for de Groot.

De Groot doesn't twitch, much less duck. He doesn't have to. Two of his security guys have Digby pinned to the seat before he gets within touching distance of de Groot. I never even see a gun come out, but as soon as Digby is fully subdued, I hear the metallic clicks of at least two guns de-cocking.

"I need to get out of here. Let me out. Let me out," Digby says. He's grabbing at the latch and pounding on the door, but he isn't able to open the van door himself, so I reach over and open it for us. I've never seen him this way—not even when we thought we might die—and I am terrified.

We climb down and Digby fast-walks back toward the house. When we get to the perimeter of the party, I reach for him and pull him toward me.

Digby wraps his arms around me and whispers, "Princeton, I can't do this."

"Digby, I think you have to at least try," I say. "You need to know the truth about what happened to Sally. It needs to be over."

He stands still, thinking. Finally he says, "You're right. It needs to be over."

Then, not caring whether or not we're seen, Digby kisses me.

This kiss isn't the tender stuff of walks on the beach or shared plates of spaghetti. This feels apocalyptic. He clings to me long after our lips part. And I suppose it's natural that Digby is apprehensive. I've often wondered whether he knows who he will be once he comes out the other side and no longer has Sally's disappearance to tell him how to feel and what to do.

"Zoe, this time, it might be *real*," he says.

"The explosion, the fire, getting gassed," I say. "Wouldn't you call those real?"

"Do you really want to do this?" he says.

"I do," I say.

We run back to the road and flag down the convoy of cars. Digby bangs on the van's window. When it slides open, Digby says, "Yes. I'll do it."

"You will get me the rest of your mother's research? All of it?" de Groot says.

Digby nods.

"How?" de Groot says.

"That's proprietary," Digby says. When de Groot looks unsold, Digby drops his smile and says, "I'm going to break into Perses and steal it."

"That facility has an enormously complex security system," de Groot says. "How will you do it?"

"It's going to be an inside job."

A long beat passes while de Groot and Digby stare each other down. De Groot smiles and extends his hand for Digby to shake but Digby ignores it and walks away.

• • •

On our way back to the party, I feel that electric jolt pass through me again. This time, I recognize that there is so much more to it than the thrill of breaking rules and whatever attraction I have to Digby. It's knowing that what we are about to do matters.

Here we go again.

Acknowledgments

When in the acknowledgements of my last book, I thanked Kathy Dawson for giving me an education in writing YA, I hadn't meant for it to sound like some kind of graduation day speech. The gods must've gotten angry at my hubris, though, because they set out to show me exactly how little I know about writing. Thank you, Kathy, for being so patient and thank you so much for finding the book I was trying to write. Thank you so much, Claire Evans, for sharing your sports expertise and for all your help getting this book out. Thank you also, Regina Castillo, for your sharp eyes. I also want to thank Anna, Venessa, Marisa, Rachel, Carmela, and so many more awesome Penguin Random House family members . . . you really know how to take care of your authors!

Thank you, David Dunton, for knowing exactly how to 'agent' me when not even I knew what the heck my problem was. Nikki Van De Car, you are awesome and you know what the heck my problem is. Thank you so much for your notes and comments.

Thank you also to my family—Mom, Dad, and Steve—for coddling me during some pretty dark days. Never once did they make me feel bad that I wasn't keeping it together very well. People ask where the laughs in the books come from and the answer is: these frickin' guys.

Luke and Stella get an extra big thank you for dragging me across the finish line. No one would believe me if I listed all the things they did to keep me alive and working. I'm so lucky to have their awesome minds helping me.

And, finally, a big shout out to my kid who is young but already has more chill than I ever will. Hey, Henry: manual, manual, automatic!

About the Author

Stephanie Tromly was born in Manila, grew up in Hong Kong, graduated from the University of Pennsylvania, and worked as a screenwriter in Los Angeles. She is the author of *Trouble Is a Friend of Mine* and *Trouble Makes a Comeback*. Stephanie lives in Winnipeg with her husband and son.

Follow Stephanie on 🐦 @StephanieTromly